Escape from

HEATH HALLS

BEARERS OF LIGHT: BOOK TWO

Published by Moonlight Publications, Salt Lake City

Cover design by Novak Illustrations
Interior design by NovelNinjutsu.com

WHAT HAPPENED BEFORE

Bearers of Light, Book 1: Dark Mage

Dark Mage is a fantasy set in a world similar to Victoria's England. Three gifted young people – Malin (18), endowed with earth speak; his cousin, Karis (17), a light weaver; and Myrrha (16), a magically gifted mistress of sound – are drawn together in the town of Godsel to fight against a dark mage.

Malin is accompanied by a young, white wolf, Rilse, with whom he can communicate directly mind to mind. Rilse can shape-shift into a nightmare creature, one that is huge and black, called a gytrash. At his father's request, Malin must move to town from the old tower fortress where he has been assisting with the training of Godsel's young men in case the war finds its way south to them. His father, Lord Lindsey, the area's regent, has requested Malin's help against the kidnapping forays of southern riders. New to town, Malin will have to learn the ways and complex manners of society. However, he will have help. He will live with Basil, a scholar and society expert, and his wolf companion will come with him.

Karis, Malin's cousin, can use light to sense information, create images, or enter the Spirit Walks to far-see. He comes south to Godsel to flee a dark mage, who has shadowed him since his 8th birthday, and whose power seems to have grown immensely. He has almost assimilated Karis on at least one occasion. Karis' hope is that in Godsel he will be safe from the black wizard, and that he will distract the mage from Lon back in Heath Halls. However, his personal, private hope is that he will be called to pass magically through the fire gates to another world, where he will find the city of light and be forever out of the reach of the dark mage.

Myrrha, stranded by a flooding river in a primitive society at a young age, with a mother who no longer is really conscious of her surroundings, has to make her own way. She poses as a young minstrel (male), and survives many hardships through her music, including a witch hunt. Her dreams draw her south to Godsel and to the scholar Basil. North of Godsel, in Mythro, she meets Karis' twin, Lon, and feels an important connection to him. But she does not know he is a twin. Then she meets Karis, she mistakes him for Lon, though her heart can't accept what her eyes see.

On the eve of Malin's sister's coming out party that is held aboard ship in Godsel harbor, the mage makes an all-out effort to capture Karis in order to assimilate his mind and take over his physical body. Myrrha, Malin and Rilse combine forces to try to defeat the mage's attack.

HEATH HALLS

Awakening in the middle of the night to a psychic cry for help from his twin, Karis persuades a reluctant Malin to accompany him on a three week journey to Mythro. It is the middle of the night in December, with a snowstorm on the way and the cousins are not prepared. Furthermore, Karis is unwilling to wait until they are. He is convinced terrible things will happen to his family, who are now prisoners in their own house, if he and Malin do not leave immediately. They may already be too late.

So they go, accompanied by an enthusiastic Rilse, Malin's white wolf companion, who is sure he will meet up with other wolves in the colder north. Malin and Karis are also sure they will meet up with other wolves — human wolves — though what faces the enemy will wear and whose colors is unknown. If they are successful at freeing the royal prisoners, they will make the return trip south to Godsel in inclement weather, with an ill king, the queen, a small child and a fully mounted pursuit behind them. The odds are not in their favor. Will their combined resources and gifts be sufficient to get them to safety?

Malin and Karis continued their journey back into the passage, around the curve, and up the narrow stairs to the second floor, where the sick king lay, slowly wasting away. They moved in silence now. They could not risk being heard by the guards on the other side of the wall.

When they finally stood by the king's bedside, Karis found he was not prepared for what he saw. Even in the shadowed chamber, the king's face seemed thin and fragile, his form lost in the huge bed. The three weeks of "care" had done their work.

Karis reached out his hand and touched his father's face. It was damp and cold. He drew back the blankets, wrapped one around his father and lifted him up and into Malin's arms, amazed at the lightness of what had been a strong, solid man.

Malin answered Karis' questioning glance and nodded. "Yes, I can carry him," he mouthed.

"Take him to Rast."

Karis half-closed his eyes and tilted his head. Malin knew he was light-reading, listening with the light to the placement of the guards. Then he spoke. "Now. The guards are gone on rounds. Careful of the library."

Malin hoped he remembered which room was the library. He shifted Karis' father, making sure the king was solid in his grasp. A thump in the walls would not be helpful at this point. "And you?" he asked Karis.

Karis' grin shot out as he whispered, "Lon and King Arnon will be gone. Someone must fill their beds." Karis fairly pushed Malin into the passageway. Then he turned back to the bed and Malin, watching, saw him sag against it a moment, his face tense and pale, his body taut.

Then Karis straightened and sounds came from him – strange sounds, half chanted. His body seemed to grow, reaching upward. Around it gathered a half light, half haze. The substance grew, swelled to man-size, and moved to a horizontal position on the bed, a figure half of light and half of mist that shimmered between being and nothing.

A moment it was thus, then King Arnon lay upon the bed. Karis swayed, then stumbled. His hands reach out to catch himself, reached out through the figure that lay there to the solid bed beneath. Anyone watching would have seen a white-faced young man up to his elbows in a king. His hands could not be seen.

In Mithrond's bed, the impostor Fardon stopped thrashing about. He sat up suddenly, rigid in the big bed. Sweat trickled down the back of his neck; his face flushed then went cold.

Escape from HEATH HALLS

BEARERS OF LIGHT: BOOK TWO

JOLAYNE CALL

MOONLIGHT PUBLICATIONS

"Your story keeps me reading and reading." – *Judy*

"It was so fun to read. The events in the story are so easy to visualize with the detailed description; I felt I was there. I was especially pleased to have the story revolve around a loving and loyal family, with each family member risking it all to help each other. What a fun, fanciful story to cuddle up with in your favorite chair!" – *Sharon*

"Enchanting and mystical – a tale woven together with magic and mystery. Each character has a personal story that captures the reader, leaving them wanting more. The sensory imagery is vibrant. I became one with the characters and surroundings. I did not want the narrative to end and, luckily, it doesn't. Book three? Hope it comes out soon. A great read for anyone who enjoys fantasy – adolescents and adults alike." – *Dawn*

"Fabulous book! The characters are so engrossing and real. The book invites you in and keeps you in. The story is one that keeps you wanting more. The characters are warm, funny and believable. Truly a delight to read. I'm looking forward to the next book, and the one after that, and the one after that..." – *Tara*

"Just when it was getting good, you had to go and pull the rug out from under! When can we expect the next installment? A very good read. I was especially caught up in the actual escape from Heath Halls and the frantic journey to safety. Compelling." – *Gerri*

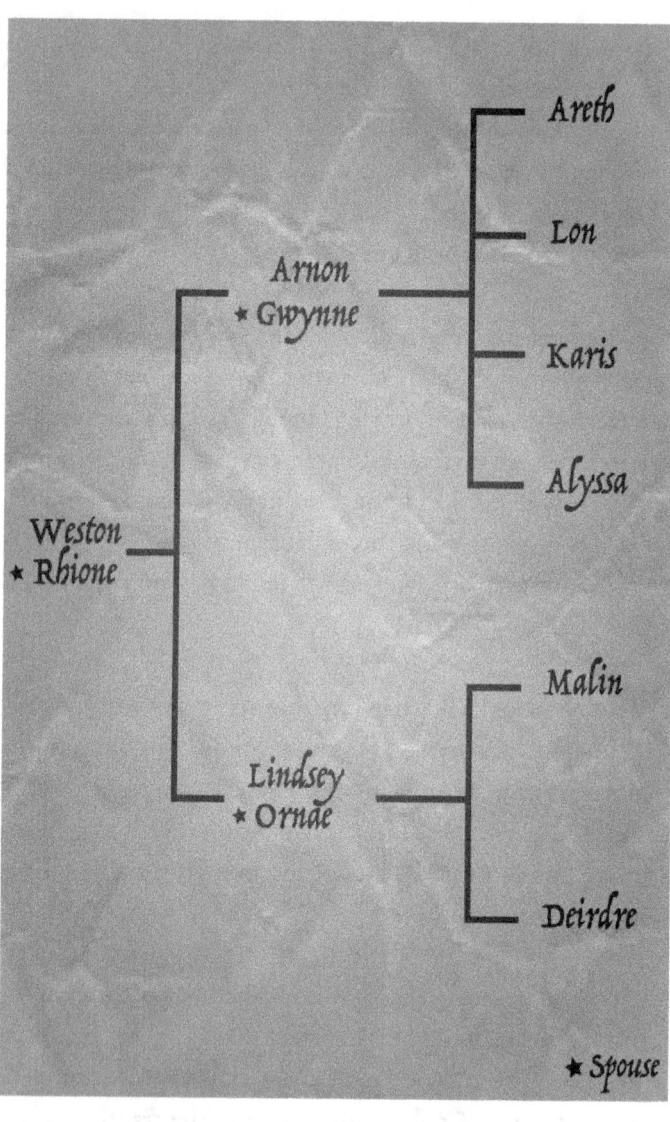

Areth

Lon

Arnon
★ Gwynne

Karis

Alyssa

Weston
★ Rhione

Malin

Lindsey
★ Ornae

Deirdre

★ Spouse

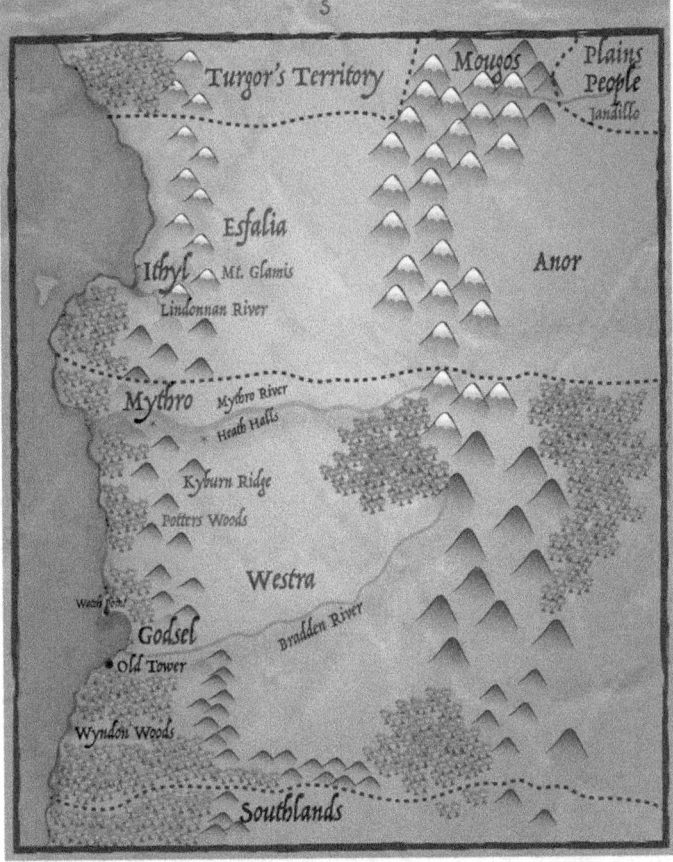

Map of the Westlands

N
W · E
S

Turgor's Territory · Mougos · Plains People
Jandillo

Esfalia
Ithyl · Mt. Glamis
Lindonnan River

Anor

Mythro · Mythro River
Heath Halls
Kyburn Ridge
Potters Woods

Westra

Wash Ford
Godsel · Bradden River
Old Tower

Wyndon Woods

Southlands

To my magnificent seven, who made it possible.

INVITATION

Seek for light
In a dark world
Honor the light
Defend the light
Become the Light

Table of Contents

1
Twin Ties

The night after Deirdre's coming out ball, the inhabitants of Tegyn slept deeply. Basil had not returned, but Malin, his wolf companion, Rilse, and his cousin Karis slumbered away. Their all-out encounter with the dark mage and his minions the night before had worn them out.

In addition, Malin and Rilse had spent the whole day from dawn until well after dusk scouting deep into the southlands. The result was two very tired bodies, both lupine and human, as it was well past the bewitching hour before they finally returned home to Tegyn.

Malin was so tired he sent his horse back to the stables at Oldsbury Hall, operating only on the mind instructions Malin had given him. More than once, Malin had regretted the lack of stables at Tegyn, and this was one of those times.

Both he and Rilse dragged themselves through the front door and down the hall to the library, where a light indicated that Karis was still up and waiting for them, half asleep in an arm chair before the fire.

"They've gone, those servants of the dark mage, pretty well all of them, south to where they belong." Malin was so tired his voice was almost inaudible.

"The riders?" Karis roused enough to ask.

"Yes."

"You say almost all of them?"

"A small party did not accompany the rest. We'll track them down tomorrow. But they are few enough in number to pose no real threat to Godsel."

Karis sighed in relief. "Well, then. We should sleep." He rose from his chair, swaying a little from weariness and inactivity. "Goodnight."

Malin caught his arm and steadied him. "You all right?"

Karis' smile flashed out. "The mage is defeated and his minions hightailing it for home. I'm just fine. See you in the morning."

The excitement was over and they could all finally relax. All three were sound asleep moments after they reached their beds, or as in the case of Rilse, after he reached his rug by the window.

Throughout the town of Godsel the excitement of the previous night had dissipated and everyone seemed to be sleeping more soundly than usual, with the stars bright above, and the winds almost still. In the harbor under the careful scrutiny of the watch, and through the streets of town, all was as it should be.

Until it no longer was, at least not at Tegyn. It seemed to Malin he had scarcely closed his eyes before Rilse arose to stand facing the bedroom door with a half-voiced rumble in his throat. Malin lifted one eyelid, then the other and tried to see what was happening. But he was so weary that whatever it was didn't seem important and he closed his eyes.

But they opened again almost immediately as Karis pushed the door open and plunged into the room, taut as a stretched bow string. "Malin. Malin. Wake up."

Malin meant to say, I'm working on it, but only a mumble emerged.

"Malin. We need to go, to ride north."

"What's happened?"

"It's Lon. He just woke me up."

"Who?"

"Lon. My twin."

"He's here?"

"No. Wake up, Malin. Listen."

Malin tried. But sleep clung to him like a stubborn tick. Karis shook his arm.

"Lon, my twin, woke me up."

"But he's miles away. Up north."

"Right. But we're twins. He connected with my mind and woke me up."

"Tell him hello from me." Malin closed his eyes and his head flopped back on the bed.

"Malin, wake up, I say. Wake up!"

Karis shook him again more vigorously, enough to elicit a low growl from Rilse's throat. "My family's in danger. We have to go help them."

Though Lon was miles away in the north in Heath Halls, the force of his presence, plus the sense of terrible danger around him had forced Karis awake. How could Lon reach him now, Karis wondered, since he had tried and not been able to connect with Lon earlier? Then he figured it out. His mother's stone. Lon was using the power in it to extend his own reach.

Awake now, Karis was flooded with Lon's desperation. But he was confused. He caught words, but tired and exhausted as he was, it took a few moments for him to put it together and comprehend what was happening. He had sat up in his bed, shaking off the deep sleep that encompassed him, and mind-listened more intently.

"Karis—prisoners—danger—come." Lon had sent.

Karis had reached out to strengthen the mind touch with his twin, in order to gather more information. One by one, he touched threads in Lon's mind. But they were so intertwined and bound together with intense emotion that he could not really piece the situation together. He caught a glimpse of a wasted king, his mother and sister behind locked doors, and Lon in the old passageways. Then the tie was broken.

Karis had been stunned. His family in danger? How could enemies reach the king himself? What was going on in Heath Halls? Desperately he tried again to reestablish the connection with Lon, but he could not. He mind reached once more, stabbing into the darkness of the north, but found nothing. Had he been dreaming? He tried again. Then in a sudden rush, he connected with Lon once more.

"Karis, come!"

Karis heard the words, felt the angst behind them, but could not really catch all the details. Then Lon was gone, his voice suddenly snuffed out on the last word.

But one thing Karis did know. Lon, his father and mother and younger sister were in immediate and serious danger. How could such a thing happen? Especially in Heath Halls, in the heart of their own seat of power at Mythro? Karis had remained upright in his bed in the darkness for several long moments, heartsick, trying to sift things out.

Then the practicalities touched him. He had to go north, and immediately. There was no time to waste. However, he would need help and supplies to get there and rescue his family. He would need Malin. He sprang out of bed and flung open his door, took the stairs down, two at a time. Seconds later he was bursting into Malin's room.

"Wake up, Malin," he repeated to his sleep-drugged cousin. "We have to go north."

A sleepy Malin thought about Karis' words. North. That was fine with Malin. North was as good a choice as any. Going was all right as well. However, daylight seemed a better time to discuss such things. Although he usually woke quickly and with a clear head, Malin was not quick this morning, in the deep dark before dawn. Their recent adventures had taken their toll.

"Malin. Sit up." Karis went around Rilse and snatched the pillow from under Malin's head and dragged him forward into a sitting position.

"All right, all right. I'm sitting." Malin struggled to retain his balance. "What do you want?" He resisted the impulse to add that whatever Karis wanted, it was not more important than sleep.

Karis repeated, "We have to go north."

"North? Why? Have you heard from Basil?"

"No. From Lon."

Malin stared glassy-eyed at Karis. "Your family? Are they with Basil?"

"No, Malin." Karis shook his cousin, and none too gently. "Wake up. They're in Heath Halls."

"Where is Basil?" Malin's mind was a little slow to grasp the essentials of their conversation.

Pushed beyond his limits, Karis made a flying leap for the water pitcher on the dresser, tripped over Rilse, who was standing in the way, and fell flat. The loud thud and Rilse's growls finally roused Malin. He blinked and focused his eyes, taking in Karis sprawled on the floor and Rilse standing over him.

Karis sat up, pushing Rilse away. "My family's in danger. There's something terribly wrong in Heath Halls."

"Heath Halls? That's miles away. How do you know?"

"Lon just reached me."

"Lon? But he's also in Heath Halls, isn't he?"

"Yes. We need to go north to him. To them. We have to rescue my family."

From those in his own halls? That doesn't seem friendly.

Rilse was right, thought Malin. That didn't seem friendly at all.

"Enemies threaten my father, my mother and sister."

All the news was bad today, thought Malin, but at least it was a family thing. "And Lon?"

"Him, too."

"How do you know?" Malin asked again. I had to ask it, thought Malin. Magic. That was how Karis knew. It had to be sorcery, probably Fainra, the Spirit Walks.

Just kin bonds. Not real magic, Rilse teased him.

Why does everyone insist on an opinion in the middle of the night? Twin magic. That's still magic, Malin told Rilse.

Touching another mind across the miles, Rilse noted. *Just like you and I do?*

Malin was brought up short. *Well, maybe.* So Karis had connected, in the mysterious way that twins do, with Lon, and though the images were not from a magical source, they still came from someone's mind far away.

"We're twins. That's how I know. We need to stop talking and leave. Now. Right now." Karis' voice was sharp and urgent.

Malin was aghast. "What are you thinking? That's a three-week journey. We have to gather provisions, clothing. Get horses ready. I'll have to talk to my father, and find Basil. We'll need troops to go with us. Now is not really possible."

Go on a fast ride north. Into the cold and the snow and the wild forests. Closer to other wolves. What are you waiting for? Rilse was ready.

Malin wondered vaguely if Rilse missed other wolves, as he sank back into the covers. Rilse and Karis had obviously concocted some sort of game.

"Malin." Karis' voice was low and grim.

Looking at him, Malin suddenly realized he looked haggard. It was no joke. Malin struggled upright once more, and swung his feet off the bed.

Karis continued. "If it's much later than now, it will be too late."

Then what's the point? Malin thought sensibly, taking care only Rilse could hear him.

"Malin." Karis' voice had grown hard, and he gripped Malin's shoulder so tightly it hurt, shaking him abruptly. "Malin," he persisted.

Much more of that and my mind will permanently detach from important connections, thought Malin. He stood up, knocking Karis' hand from his shoulder. "A winter storm is on its way, between us and Heath Halls. And it's still the middle of the night, or early morning. We have Basil to find and we have some more scouting to do."

"Malin, I know." Karis was desperate. "But now is all we've got."

"We would make better time if we waited until daylight."

We would be seen.

Malin turned to Rilse. *Seen? By whom?*

A few watchers are back, or maybe they never left.

In our wilderness?

Yes.

With horses?

No.

Close to Tegyn?

Yes.

Malin turned and gazed out the window, crossing to stand before it, searching the dark gardens, the woods just beyond. He could see nothing, but Rilse had never been wrong.

"What is it?" Karis was actually standing still, Malin noted. Progress, he thought.

"Rilse says watchers are back. At the south edge of these woods." Karis joined Malin, and they both peered out through the back garden into the darkness.

"We've no time for them, whatever they want. We must go." Karis' brief moment of distraction was over and he was back to the task at hand.

Who was Malin to tell Karis what he knew or didn't? Malin shrugged, gave in to the inevitable, and got down to the practicalities of such a journey. Even on horseback, as fast as they could go, they could not reach Heath Halls in less than two weeks. And in between Mythro and Godsel was a winter storm.

They dressed hurriedly in warm sturdy pants, sweaters and jackets. Karis had come in a long, black, winter coat, which he put on top of everything else. Malin looked through his stuff, and finally grabbed the thickest, longest jacket he had, thrusting his arms in and fastening it here and there. He could do the rest en route as they traveled, he decided. He collected a few pieces of extra clothing, that his senses told him they would need, and placed them in two stout packs.

Next came food. They would have no time to hunt or gather food from their surroundings as they traveled. Nor would they be able to take regular time to stop and build a fire. So Malin gathered food they could eat in the saddle and distributed it evenly in the two packs. The usual pack that came from the stables would not do in these circumstances, though they would take it with them to supplement what they had.

As he worked, Basil's absence meandered through Malin's head. What could have happened to him? Where was he? He paused to leave his mentor a note on the front hall table. He was more and more uneasy on Basil's behalf, but what he merely worried about took second place to what Karis knew, even if magic had brought the knowledge. And Malin did not doubt that Karis knew.

They left by the back door. *Enemies are close,* Rilse reminded them.

Malin paused, his hand on the door latch. *How many? Five. No, six.*

They slipped out the back, keeping to the trees until they were well past Tegyn, then they took to the road. Once they were out of sight of any watchers, they took to half running, half walking, but still searching any shadows they found, taking care not to make any noise. They made for Oldsbury Hall, or more precisely, for the stables there.

"I should have left Lanier at Tegyn, instead of sending him home a few hours ago," Malin complained. "It would have made this part of the trip a lot faster. At least we'll be wide awake when we get there. And maybe my father will even be up."

"We don't have time to talk to him. We only have time to get our horses and go."

"What are you thinking? We'll need his help. There's no way we can make it safely back here, even if we do manage to rescue your family, without help from my father and Godsel's guards."

Such urgency was on Karis, he could not tolerate the thought of the delay it would take to meet with Lord Lindsey in person and arrange for help to follow. "He'll take too long to wake up, and then he'll try to dissuade us. He'll request we wait, while he assembles a group of his guards and we'll not only arrive too late, but the guards will announce our presence. We might as well blow a trumpet and send a crier ahead."

Malin was stubborn. "You don't leave important information undelivered to the people who need it. There is no way we can rescue your family and return without being caught unless we have help from my father. He needs to know, and we need to know what we can count on."

"It won't matter if we don't get there in time. If my family's dead when we arrive, what good will his help be then? In fact, even if we leave now, we may still be too late."

Malin hesitated. Karis was beyond reason, but if they waited to speak to Lord Lindsey, they would be delayed, no question. But should that short space of time matter so much? Would an hour or two make the difference between life or death for his family? It seemed unreasonable, but what if it were true? In the end, Malin finally left a note for his father with the groom, grumbling a little as he did so, stressing its urgency.

"You must give this to my father as soon as it is morning."

"I will, Master Malin. You can be sure I will," the man promised, and he was well known to Malin for he groomed Lanier, Malin's horse. Malin sighed. He would have to be content with that.

"Where is Lanier?" he asked the groom.

"He returned several hours ago and we turned him into the big pasture for a rest."

Malin wished he could take his horse with them, but the poor beast would have been too exhausted anyway.

They left Godsel by the north gate where no enemies watched, or so Rilse informed them. Two hours before dawn, they moved silently through the sleeping town, away from any southern watchers, and away, Malin sensed, from the help they would need before the end. He sent a mental request to his father that help would soon follow, wishing he had learned to communicate with him that way.

At the gates, Malin was stunned to find they were guarded by four men, two of whom swung their torches to light the faces of the two young men. They had not been manned for many years, in fact, not in all the eighteen years of Malin's life, he thought. Rilse, of course, slipped through unnoticed. But as they recognized Malin, the guards moved aside with a respectful nod and let the two cousins pass.

"Evening, Master Malin. Some rare wild doings 'appening this 'ere night."

"You've got that right, Dab," he told the man, "right indeed."

He thought about leaving another message for his father, but on a sudden impulse, he said nothing. Until they knew who the enemy contacts in Godsel were, critical information should not be shared indiscriminately.

Beyond the gates, Karis pushed even with Malin, then crossed in front of him, heading west for the coastal road. Malin stopped his cousin.

"Not that way."

"Why not? We need to go as fast as possible. So that's the coast road, right?"

"No. The inner forest road is at least two days faster. Besides, it will also provide cover. We want to go unseen, as you pointed out."

"You're sure it's faster?"

"Positive."

"All right. Lead on." And a reluctant Karis followed Malin, casting a couple of hesitant glances at the road to their backs. "You're sure the other way is shorter?"

"Yes."

They went east, riding until they reached the road, where they turned northward on the forest way.

"We're heading into a snow storm," Malin warned.

Rilse was elated. *I like snow.*

I know, Malin grumbled. "We should be wise and wait," Malin warned Karis. *We're not wolves,* he added to Rilse.

Pity. Rilse grinned in his face.

"We must go now. We cannot wait, not even a few hours. And even then, we may be too late." Karis was determined. Blizzard or no blizzard, he was set on going immediately. Malin had never seen Karis so tense and rigid, so determined that it seemed nothing or no one could dissuade him.

But the loose ends worried Malin. They had not found Basil. They had not discovered where the small offshoot party of southerners had gone. Furthermore, there were the southlanders Rilse had sensed back near Tegyn. Perhaps they were afoot, their horses having tossed them off. At any rate, Malin was unsettled. However, his uncertainties paled beside his cousin's seemingly sure knowledge of immediate and deadly danger to his family.

And Karis could not survive such a journey without Malin and Rilse. And if Malin refused, he knew Karis would still go. Karis was determined. Rilse was excited, and Malin semi-willing. At least they would be out in the forest, riding.

So they went. Malin hoped with Rilse's help that he could shape their journey so they would all arrive alive and able to help Karis' family to escape their dire circumstances. But that was only a hope, not a certainty. And there were many miles to go and enemies between them and their goal.

2
Arrow in the Night

Weeks earlier than the ball, Karis' father, King Arnon of Westra, received a rather strange message. The king and Lon, Karis' twin, were alone at breakfast when the message came. It was a winter day, and though the room was cozy and a warm fire danced in the fireplace, the windows overlooked the Mythro river valley, now bleak and snow-filled under gray skies. Travel in winter was difficult, and sometimes impossible. Yet Lon held in his hand a request—no, a demand—for just that. Carefully, he read the message.

"To the heads of Esfalia, Anor, Westra and all subnations involved in the war:

"A council is to take place in the coastal city of Ithyl, two weeks after the celebration of the birthday of their king. This council has been called to discuss a proposition to shorten, perhaps even end, the current hostilities, thus alleviating further loss of life and destruction of property. This council is your opportunity to discuss terms and forestall further violence.

"The armies I have formed are vast, the forces arrayed against you are overwhelming. Be forewarned that if terms cannot be arrived at by the end of this council, my armies are poised to overrun yours in retaliation for the many injustices your varying nations have perpetrated on mine.

13

"Since the issue involves all the nations to whom this missive is directed, all those nations must attend the council. Non-attendance by any party named will void the council; any discussion of terms will be at an end.

"Signed, Turgor, Lord of the Northern Lands"

Surprised, Lon reread the missive his father had passed to him.

"What do you make of it?" The king asked, looking at Lon, the visual duplicate of Karis. The only way he could tell his twins apart was from the expression on their faces. Karis was always solemn and serious. Lon was usually smiling. And neither twin looked like their father. The queen's dark hair and fine features had come through the boys, rather than his blonde, bigger boned look.

"It's strange, isn't it? Turgor will never offer acceptable terms; this can only be a council for terms of surrender, but why would he bother to hold a council for that?" Lon was surprised and angry.

"No reason that I can see. Furthermore, we've never had such a request from Turgor before. This is strange even for him, arrogant and vicious as he is. He has to see some advantage in it for him, or he would never do it. That comment about 'the many injustices' really sticks in my craw," replied the king.

"He also insists here that all allied leaders be assembled before he shares his proposal." Lon looked up from the message he was still holding. "Doesn't he know that winter travel, especially through mountains, is difficult at best and often impossible?"

"He should. His lands are farther north than any of us," the king pointed out. "And if the meeting was there, we'd not consider going. However, Esfalia is our ally and longtime friend and we might relish a visit there. But why so little notice? That's just weeks from now. Barely enough time to get there, let alone make arrangements for the running of a kingdom."

"Exactly." Lon handed the message back to his father.

"And in the winter? When travel is more laborious and often delayed? It just doesn't make sense." The king shook his head.

"Right. It sounds like a trap. And is it even possible in that short of time?"

"Barely. But if the proposal is intended to end the war, and we don't go and the rest of our allies don't even get to hear about it because we're not there, that would not be good. He has us over a barrel."

"Who's invited. Everyone?"

"The messenger who brought this said all of the allies were invited, even the subjugated countries."

"How long a journey is it?"

"Let's see. I haven't been there in a long time." The king placed the message on the table and leaned back in his chair.

Lon laughed. "I've never been there, so I can't help."

"It's a delightful city, is Ithyl, nestled on the sea itself. If I remember right, it's a journey of three weeks afoot, and on horseback a little less than that. This time of year it can take longer, if the snows are deep in the mountains and the passes blocked."

"Will Ithyl have snow?"

"No, not likely. It hardly ever snows there. Its proximity to the sea keeps its temperature more moderate."

"But this time of year we can't travel by sea," Lon guessed. He was by nature thoughtful and intuitive.

The king rose and paced to the window. "Exactly. And by sea is our usual mode of travel. So why this time of year? What advantage is it to Turgor that the leaders from every country of his enemies will be together, and have to travel by land? Is he planning a military strike while our attention is elsewhere? And if so, where?" The king was trying to imagine all the possibilities.

"Good question. Do we have enemies in Esfalia?"

"Not unless they've been planted there surreptitiously by Turgor. Esfalia is our closest ally. We've been personal friends with their ruling house for long years. If that were not so, I would not even consider going. There are too many dangers already in winter travel, let alone in enemy territory."

"Agreed. Travel in winter is a problem, especially with a whole retinue. And that snow down there is just going to keep piling up." Lon joined his father at the window.

"Exactly. We'll have to travel light, and with just a small company. More would probably stir up avalanches to block the way and no one would get through." The king sighed. "And it will take at least a week to prepare affairs here before we can leave. But I guess we must go. If there's any way to stop the war a little sooner and save lives and homes, we must. Will you come with me, Lon? I'd like you to meet our friends there, and your insights into people would be helpful."

"I will come. But we must be wary."

"We must, indeed."

So it was decided. Mithrond, the king's chief and long trusted advisor would take over the affairs of the kingdom, with the help of Queen Gwynne, while the king and Lon journeyed north. A small company of the king's men would go with them. It was expected the journey would take three weeks each way, plus whatever time the council required and some visiting time with the royal family.

"We'll be gone over a month and a half, Mithrond, before we finally return." The king's blue eyes seemed troubled, not wanting to impose on the genial as well as competent and sturdy statesman before him, in the blue and silver livery of Westra.

Mithrond wasn't as tall as King Arnon, but he had a steadiness about him that was reassuring. He was experienced in the affairs of state and an honorable man, well known for his integrity. The length of his service was reflected in the silver at the temples of his hair, but there was no trace of balding. He still had a full head of hair, and a sparkle in his eye.

"We'll be fine, Sire. It's winter and less happens this time of year than any other season. There will be nothing we can't handle until your return."

"I'm sure you and Queen Gwynne will be fine. But this is such a strange request, and for this time of year, too. Be careful, Mithrond, be careful. Keep your eyes peeled for any unusual happenings."

"I will. And you, too, Sire. There may be real danger in your journey and the circumstances surrounding it. What if an attempt is made on the lives of the royal houses attending, while you are all gathered together?"

"We'll be careful. Besides, King Morland is a wise man. He will have taken great care. But you be wary, too, Mithrond. And may we both have an uneventful time until our return."

"Indeed, Sire. May you return with no unexpected events to mar your journey."

Two days later, Rast, with a small company of the king's guard and a few retainers, plus the king and his son, were on the road east to the inn where Lon met the minstrel. Just past the inn they turned north, taking the central inland road toward Esfalia. Lon thought briefly but regretfully of the good food and the minstrel's music the inn held. But their journey had just started and it was too soon to stop.

The day passed. Snows were deeper than usual for this time of year and progress was slow. Another day passed and they fell into a routine. Their stops were chilly, with no shelter except the thick fir trees close around them, which kept off snow and held back the wind. Brush was plentiful for fire, when they took the time. Food was simple, the king and his son eating the same rations as their men, with a hot drink to warm them now and then.

Nights they huddled together around a fire, before they retired to sleep in the three small tents they had brought with them. Lon watched his father, and though the king never complained, Lon knew his father felt the cold deeply. He would catch the king rubbing his shoulder or cradling an elbow that had been broken in a fall from a horse years before. They could only make slow progress, but the king had planned carefully and they would arrive in Ithyl on time, perhaps even a little early.

Day followed day. On some days they rode under a light snowfall, on a few they were holed up close to a cliff, huddling together inside the three tents for warmth, while the full force of a blizzard raged against them. Sometimes the trail was open and blown clear by winter winds, sometimes the horses were knee deep in snow. They moved silently and carefully through the mountain passes, fearful of possible avalanches, for the snow hung thick on the peaks. They moved as quietly as possible, the men speaking in hushed tones, but disaster found them anyway.

One of the pack animals brushed too close to the mountainside, scraping her withers. She whinnied in pain, plunging away from the sharp rock, but misjudged the space around her. Her right hoof left solid ground and she half fell, snorting and whinnying in fear and pain, her hooves scrabbling for the trail. Her shrill whinny rebounded from cliff to cliff, cutting through the cold air, as she stood trembling with all four feet secure once more.

The party stood motionless and silent, hardly daring to breathe, their eyes fixed on the snow pack on the mountainside above them. But the damage was already done. There was a rumble, a pause.

"Hug the inner cliff wall!" Rast called out. For long moments they fought to keep their places on the trail.

Lon felt himself lost in wave after wave of wet, heavy snow, full of grinding rock. Beneath him his horse screamed in terror, and it was all he could do to keep her near the rock wall. Briefly he hoped the rest were all right, but it took his full strength to remain there, fighting the elements that tried to scrape him away and hurl him down the mountainside they had just climbed.

Finally the noise stopped, the snowfall ceased. To Lon, it seemed that all the rocks in the world had thundered past them. When he found he could see once more, a pile of deep snow surrounded him. Ahead he could see Rast and his father. It would take them a while to dig out, he thought.

Then he turned and looked down the trail behind him. He could see several figures below, but the snow and rock fall was deeper the farther back down the mountainside it went. The whole look of the trail had changed as well, and Lon knew some members of their party were buried.

Rast knew, too. "Make sure you and your horse can breathe," he called. "Then try to dig out. Make sure the debris goes over the cliff side, because we still have to make it to the top and back when we return." Then Rast was crawling on his forearms and shins, trying to stay on the surface of the fall, crawling past the king, past Lon, trying to reach those below. Several of his men, who had been at the front, followed him, also trying to keep on the surface of the snow so they would not be buried in its depths.

Lon understood. If their party was not uncovered soon, those buried would smother, if they had not already been crushed by rock and the weight of the snow itself. He looked down at himself, at his horse. Near the rock wall, the snow was inches deep. But on the cliff edge, it was feet high and thick. The men were wedged against the wall by snow and rock. His own horse could not lift his right hooves, both front and back. But his head was well out and he could breathe.

Luckily for Rast and the few near him, thought Lon, the avalanche had thundered over their heads and down the mountainside. They were free to move and help the others below. Lon tried to count their numbers in his head, trying to figure out how many men were buried in the snow, how many pack animals had vanished.

The avalanche had been uneven, so farther down he could see a man or two, a pack animal or two. Certainly the calamity was not engineered by their enemies, but who knew whether those enemies had not counted on such accidents to lessen their numbers, perhaps even remove their heads of state? Travel in the mountains was always dangerous in the winter.

Lon went to work. Following Rast's instructions, he dug out around his horse, pushing the snow off the trail, which luckily or unluckily was quite narrow at this spot. He did not have as much snow to clear, but the force required almost plunged him over the cliff after it.

Then he moved up to help his father. The trail there was wider; however, both the king and his horse were deeply embedded. His father waved him away. "We can breathe. Go help those below."

Lon hesitated, then realized his father was right. He turned and crawled away, past his horse who had the good sense to remain still, on down the trail, following Rast's weird tracks. He started digging like those nearest him with whatever he found to hand, breathing in relief when he uncovered a face or a horse's nostrils.

Finally, they had done all they could, and the exhausted party took stock. One pack animal had been killed by a boulder that had crushed its head. The animal itself was finally uncovered and the supplies transferred to the other horses.

They had spent several long and frantic hours to find and uncover all the men. But by the time they found the last one, he was dead, smothered in the white killer that the snow had become. Silently they wound up to the peak and over the other side. They walked down and through the pass until they reached a spot where the mountainside overhung a wide stretch of ground that was clear.

Rast looked back. His men were exhausted and disheartened. The death of one of their number was a hard blow. "We stop here."

Camp was set up, a fire made, food prepared. The body of their comrade was wrapped in a blanket and buried in the snow. Large rocks were piled on top of him; in the current weather conditions, it was the best they could do.

"We have to return this way," Rast told them. "It will be different weather then. We can bury him properly on our way home."

It was a sober group that gathered to eat, and a sober group that entered the tents that night to sleep. The weather had joined forces with the enemy, Lon thought. Somehow it seemed unfair.

The next two days the party threaded up and over high peaks, with snow pack hanging above them, needing but little to send it plunging down upon them. Finally they were through and they all breathed a sigh of relief, followed quickly by a sigh of regret for the man who didn't make it.

Mile followed mile, day followed day, and finally they drew close to Ithyl. But nothing other than winter conditions interfered with their travel—no human element intruded. It doesn't have to, Lon thought. The weather had been enough.

"Not too far now," King Arnon told Lon, as they stopped about a fire for the night. "It will be good to be warm and comfortable and eat something else for a change." He looked at the dried meat and bread he was holding, the bread cold and partially frozen. "At least the broth is tasty and hot."

Lon tried to lighten the moment. "Onsgood would be appalled at our meals. He would never forgive our lack of propriety."

"Well, I won't tell if you won't."

"Agreed." They smiled together. Lon had wondered if they would, any of them, smile again before they reached Ithyl. But life went on, it seemed.

"It still seems strange," Lon mused aloud to his father, "this winter meeting of the heads of state."

"Agreed. We will not accept his demands for our surrender, nor will he cease his aggression against us. He wants more power and more land and resources. I see no good coming out of it for us or even for him."

"Exactly. That's the sticky part. He engineered this meeting, so there has to be something in it for him," Lon agreed. "We're missing something. But what?"

"Why does he want us all together? What does he hope to gain from a meeting that he couldn't do one at a time?" King Arnon grew silent, thinking. Then he shook his head. "It just doesn't make sense. However, if such a meeting could even remotely aid in an earlier end to the war, it is well worth the trip."

Then he continued in a more cheerful tone. "Besides, I haven't seen Ithyl's king and queen nor Anor's regent in a decade, and I've never met their boy king. We used to spend more time together, when the world was a happier place.

Maybe, some good will come of this trip for us, in spite of whatever Turgor plans."

Morning found them once more on their journey, the trail thick with deep snow. By late afternoon they crossed a windswept ridge where they made good time for an hour or so before they once more encountered heavy snow. They plodded on and through it, moving very slowly. Somehow being so close to their journey's end made the day seem even longer. They were all ready to have real shelter from the weather, good food and comfort.

By dusk they crested the summit of the last pass and wound slowly through it. The snow seemed even deeper there and both horses and men were worn and tired. They were all tense with the possibility of another avalanche.

Then the trail curved, and below them they could see a few faint lights in the far valley, just beginning to come into view. Finally, thought Lon, finally we're near the end. He smiled as their warmth touched his heart with new hope and energy.

The king maneuvered his horse to come alongside Lon, a smile on his face as well. "Those lights are Ithyl. As we round this mountain, we reach a wide valley and the rest of the city will be visible. We're almost there."

Lon felt relief wash over him. "None too soon, say I. We're right glad to see those lights." He glanced at the men behind and in front of them. "I'm sure the rest of the men would agree." Whatever perils they still had to face, this portion of the journey was almost behind them.

A few minutes later, the sun sank into the west, but its last rays lit up the snow above the jagged shoulder of Glamis Mountain. The moon was already visible in the sky, and promised to be full and bright. The trail they were on hugged the mountainside to the right, while the left fell away into a crevice between Glamis and the smaller peak beside it. The moonlight glancing off the snow gave enough light for the riders and their horses to make out the path, though it was narrow and thick with fir trees.

"Shouldn't we stop soon?" Lon asked his father. "Both men and horses are tired."

The king sighed. "I know. I just hate to stop so close to our goal. At any rate, we can't stop here. The trail is too narrow and steep. At the very least we have to find a spot where the trail widens or perhaps even descends to the beginning of the valley below. Another fir-tree-lined mile or two and we should be in the valley itself. Hope the light holds until that happens."

"Agreed. A trail this steep and narrow is dangerous to travel after sundown."

Lon was more right than he knew.

Ahead, their lead guard rounded a sharp curve that plunged downward for a few feet as it disappeared from sight. Somewhere an owl hooted softly. Seated on his gray, Lon could make out the figure of his father a few yards ahead of him.

Without knowing why, his mind went back to his last trip with Karis and Rast, though it had been closer to home. The watcher had ruined it, and sent Karis off to Godsel to avoid him. Lon missed Karis. They had done everything together. What fun he and Karis would have had together in a new city, a different court and palace, out of reach of the watcher.

They had heard from Karis just after he had reached Godsel. The watcher was gone, he said, but they had heard nothing since. Lon hoped the watcher was indeed gone and that Karis would truly be able to live.

Lost in his reverie, he vaguely saw the king rounding the same curve his men had, threading the path carefully. They slowed their horses, riding single file. Lon never did see what happened; the light was too dim and the trail itself dropped below his range of vision. But he heard a sharp whir. Ahead of him, the king cried out and slumped in the saddle.

Lon crowded forward until he was close behind the king. A feathered shaft visibly protruded from the king's upper chest through the thick wool of the winter uniform he wore under his cloak. Across the ravine from them, on the side of the smaller peak, Lon heard the snapping of branches and the thud of horses' hooves as their assailants fled.

Two of the king's men followed in pursuit. They didn't have much hope of success, Lon thought. They were separated by a chasm, and on a mountainside they didn't know. Long before they reached the other side, the sound of horses had completely faded.

Was this the why of the council? His father struck down before they even arrived? Were ambushes arranged for all the others as well?

It was too steep and narrow to stop, and there was no other way they could reach the king to assist him. Lon held his breath at the thought that his father might fall from his horse. If he did, he would almost certainly fall down the side of the cliff, to greater injury and perhaps death.

Luckily, the king kept his seat in his saddle. But they had to let the horses continue for many long minutes before they could finally dismount and run to aid him.

Lon was first, Rast was close behind him. "Father?"

But there was no answer. The king was slumped forward, his head to the left side, resting beside the arrow in his chest. His eyes were closed and blood seeped through his clothing until it looked black in the moonlight.

The whole night now felt that way, too, thought Lon. Black—in the moonlight.

3
Winter Meetings

The king's party finally reached a spot in the trail wide enough to help the king off his mount and attend to his wound. There had been no room on the snow-filled trail to do anything but descend single file. Lon was in a panic about this time. Every moment mattered to the wounded king. If he lost a lot of blood, he might even be knocking on death's door, though the wound itself was shallow.

Lon and Rast dismounted to attend to the king, passing their reins to their companions, as well as those of the king's horse. Rast reached for the semi-conscious king, wadding a strip torn from a blanket against the king's chest around the arrow to staunch the bleeding.

When they had done what they could, Lon and Rast looked at each other. The only way down that trail was on horseback and the king could not ride alone. It was not only a miracle he had remained in the saddle until that moment, but it was a second miracle that he remained there without his head ramming the arrow further into his body. They could not count on such fortune again. Roping him to the saddle would incur the same risk.

"I'll ride with him, Rast."

"He's a big man," Rast said.

"He's my father," Lon said simply. "I can hold him on until we reach the valley."

"I'll take your horse." Rast reached for the reins and looped them around his saddle horn, before he helped Lon onto the horse behind the king. Only then did he mount his own.

Lon reached around his father, pulling him against his chest, trying not to touch the protruding arrow, making sure the king's head was to the other side. He could feel the beating of his father's heart, its faint, erratic rhythm. He willed it to become regular, and deep, and it seemed for a moment that it was so.

In this fashion the party continued on down the mountain, for they could not stop where they were. After what seemed to Lon an interminable stretch of time, they finally halted at the foot of the pass in a small flattened section to the right of the trail.

Rast and the king's men lifted the wounded king down from his horse, and carried him several paces off the trail. They loosened his clothing around the arrow wound, which was high on the left side of his chest, and examined him carefully.

Lon knelt beside Rast. "How is he?"

"T'will not kill him. The wound is too high. If we can stop the bleeding and he gets help, he should be fine."

"Do we spend the night here, or do we press on to Ithyl? What would be best for the king?"

"He needs help we cannot give him, and medicines we don't have here. The arrow needs to come out and no one here is skilled enough to extract it. With it in, we cannot completely stop the bleeding."

"Then let's ride. And hope the way is short." Rast reached for the king, to take a turn holding him on his horse, but Lon shook his head. "This is mine to do."

Rast said no more, just helped him up and onward they went to Ithyl. He sent a couple of men ahead to alert the palace and allow them to make ready to attend the king.

"As I understand it, we're only about four hours away from Ithyl. We should be there soon," Rast told Lon.

"You call four hours soon?" Lon's arms were numb and he wasn't sure he could hold the king for one more hour, let alone four.

"Compared to what we've traveled, yes." Rast scrutinized the young man before him, noting the tenseness of his posture, the set of his jaw. "I could take a turn," he offered. "It would be an honor to serve my king in that way."

"I know, Rast. I just would like to do it if I can."

But that short way seemed longer than the whole trip to Lon; it was four hours to Ithyl with a wounded father before him on his horse, plus one more hour through the city itself to the king's palace. It seemed like forever.

Guards were sent from the palace to escort them through, and they brought with them a litter thick with furs to cushion the king and warm his pale, chilled form. Lon hesitated to let them take the king, but Rast whispered to him, "It will be better so. The king will be jostled less." So Lon acquiesced.

At the palace, King Morland and his queen, Elana, met them on the palace steps. The sturdy king gazed at his wounded friend, his brown eyes full of shock and sorrow, his brown hair still ruffled by sleep. "What has happened?" he asked.

"Just past the summit of Glamis Pass an arrow came flying straight for the king. Only one. It had to have been someone who knew we were coming, someone watching for us, for him, in the twilight." Lon's voice was low with weariness.

"Just the one?"

Rast answered. "Just the one."

"And straight for the king?"

"Yes." Lon answered this time. "He was right in front of me, and only one arrow was loosed."

The king straightened decisively. "Bring him this way." He ushered those with the litter inside the palace through several corridors to a comfortable room with a fire and a waiting physician. He looked down at the unconscious king, and back at the physician. "Do your very best. Whatever you need, we'll get for you."

The queen herself spoke to the attendants in the room, making sure all was in readiness, her slight figure a contrast to that of the king, her black hair scattered about her shoulders.

They placed King Arnon carefully in the bed and those assembled went to work to help him. Although it probably had a more formal title, afterward Lon remembered the room as the blue room, for the walls and the carpet and the bedding were all in different intensities of the same shade of blue, with white thrown in for contrast. Lon and King Morland waited nearby while the physician and his assistants worked on the king, who was still unconscious. The arrow was removed and examined carefully by one of King Morland's guard.

"Can you identify it?" King Morland asked him.

"It's not familiar to me, but I will give it to my hunters who are more experienced with arrows to see what they can make of it."

"Good. And let us know. A strange business, this," he said to Lon. "The whole thing is strange: the emissary, the message, the gathering and now this. What is really going on here? And why?"

"Exactly our questions. Who is behind this attack? Who stands to gain? What is so important at the coming conference that they want my father out of the way?" Lon sat tiredly watching as the physician finished cleaning the wound and bandaged it.

His father stirred, half sat up. "Lon, Lon?"

"Here, Father. Right here." Lon arose and went to stand beside his father, reaching for his hand.

The king opened his eyes and looked fully at him, then closed them and lay back.

"He will sleep now." King Morland touched him on the shoulder. "You should, too."

Lon hesitated.

"We will watch. My personal guards and physician will spend the night here. He will be safe."

Lon looked back at the king, noting the even rise and fall of his breathing, the faint color that was back in his face. Then he nodded. "I will rest."

King Morland led him from the room to the one next door.

Lon stopped him. "When is the council meeting?"

"In two days' time."

"Will my father be well enough to attend?"

"The wound is clean and not deadly. With rest and good care he may be more alert by then, but to move sufficient to reach and participate in the council is not only unlikely but ill advised."

Lon nodded. He had expected as much. "Then I will go in his place. We will be able to confer by then, he and I, so that I know his wishes. But I will plan on attending the council."

King Morland looked at him with new respect in his eyes. This son of his friend was a statesman as well as a son.

"Here is your room. Rest well. My physician has orders to wake you if there is any change for the worse. York, here," the king pointed to one of his retainers, "will attend to your needs. I'll see you in the morning." He started to leave, but turned back. "My guards will be outside your room as well."

"And our men?"

"They will be lodged with mine. Good night, son of my friend. I'm so sorry this happened."

Lon knew he spoke truly.

Shortly after, Lon, bathed and warm, slid into bed amid clean sheets and a thick coverlet. He sighed contentedly. Then his mind began to turn things over again, in spite of his best intentions to sleep. He and his father had been right to be suspicious. All was not well, and they had suffered an attack on the way. Who wanted the king harmed? Who stood to gain? Who didn't wish him to reach the council meeting?

Realizing the futility of pondering questions he could not answer, Lon slowed his brain and drifted off to sleep. His unanswered questions would have to be shelved until tomorrow.

Morning came. Light sifted through the edges of drapes hanging over two large windows, making rectangles upon the blue patterned walls. The room was a match for the one his father was in, Lon decided. In no time he was up and dressed and across the hall.

Rast was already there, watching the physician, who was watching his father.

"How is he, Rast?" Lon's whispered question reached only Rast, his red hair bright against the blue and silver of the dress livery of Westra.

"He's sleepin' well. Has all night. No sign of fever in him." He stepped close to Lon and spoke low in his ear. "They take good care of him."

Lon smiled his thanks. Rast would know. "Day after tomorrow is the council meeting. The doctor says he probably won't make it."

Rast shook his head. "He shouldn't be up and about that soon if he wants to heal right. He needs another few days in bed."

Doctor Haddon had heard them and turned their way, speaking softly. "He does well, your king. He has passed a good night, his body is strong and the arrow was not deep."

"Good news is always welcome." Lon relaxed, his natural courtesy coming to the fore. The physician rose and relinquished his place to Lon. Rast came and stood beside him.

"It was released too far away to lodge any deeper. They could not have killed him from that distance. So what was their goal?"

Lon did not answer.

Rast looked shrewdly at Lon. "Think that's the reason for the attack?"

"I don't know. But what other reason could there be for an attack at this time?"

"Kinda looks that way, all right."

"Will you come to the council meeting?"

"Sure I'll come. I'll leave a good man here, though, just in case someone tries something again."

Lon reached for his father's hand, but the king did not stir. His breathing was deep and regular, his body relaxed.

"He should sleep for some time, Prince Lon. Rest will heal the body faster than any medicine."

Lon caught the physician's subtle suggestion. He grasped his father's hand for a moment before he rose and let the attending doctor get back to his father's bedside. As he exited the room, he found York waiting outside.

"Will it please your lord to breakfast? The king has sent an invitation."

"I would be happy to accept." And Lon followed the retainer down the hall and deeper into the palace to the dining area. There he found the king who stood to receive him.

"He does well, your father?"

"He does well."

King Morland sighed his satisfaction. "That's good news. Join me for breakfast?" The king indicated a chair near him at the table. As Lon sat, the king continued, "Did you rest well?"

"I did."

"I'm so sorry such a terrible thing happened to my friend and your father in my kingdom. And, of course, the question we are all asking ourselves is who could have done such a thing and why?"

"Were you able to examine the arrow and place it? Did it have any distinguishing marks on it?" Lon was conscious of servants placing food in front of him, and a hot drink of some kind, but he found himself eating without really noting what. His mind was elsewhere.

"We did, but we really didn't find anything unique. The arrow is one that could be used by anyone at the front. If they really wanted to kill him, they needed to be closer to their target."

Lon agreed. "That's what Rast said."

"Or use one of the new rifles we have. We only have a few as yet, but we do have them. They could kill at that range."

"It doesn't make any sense. All I can think is that someone didn't want him at the council when it convenes. But I am here. His vote and wishes will still be shared."

"Maybe those who arranged for the arrow did not know you would be coming, or how capable you are." King Morland handed Lon a plate of muffins.

Lon grinned his thanks, both for the food and for the compliment.

Morland continued, "Perhaps whoever orchestrated this event hoped to lessen support in the council for the war. Anor's boy king is too young to have any real influence, and I do not know Lord Blandor, the regent," King Morland mused, stirring his eggs, buttering his muffins.

They were silent for some time, attending to the necessities of eating. When they were finished, the king stood to go.

"Though I have much to do to prepare for the council, while you are here, I hope you will make yourself at home. Your father will have our best care and the court is fully open to you. York will continue to wait on you and guide you wherever you would like to go." He paused and cleared his throat. "I know your father will not be well enough, but would you dine with the royal family this night? They would be glad of the chance to become better acquainted with you."

"I'd be pleased to."

"This evening, then." The king stood, extending his hand to Lon, then he was gone, striding rapidly through the door and out of sight.

Lon returned to his father, pleased to see him still resting comfortably, with Rast beside him.

He tapped Rast quietly on the arm. "Did those of our guard who pursued our attackers find anything?"

"No." Rast brushed his shock of red hair back from his forehead. "The cowards were long gone when our men reached the site. All they found were tracks."

Lon rubbed his upper arm, still stiff from keeping his father in the saddle on their ride down into the valley. "I expected as much, but hoped for more."

He stayed for a few moments, but feeling too restless to sit, he left the room.

York was waiting at the door for him. "York, did your men find anything unusual on the arrow? Or any clues to who fashioned it?"

"No, Your Highness. It was just an arrow from the area, nothing special about it."

Lon mentally chided himself, realizing he had been waiting for something out of the ordinary, something to explain the so far unexplainable.

"Would you like a tour of the royal halls?"

"Why not?" Lon grinned. "Time has to pass. It might as well pass agreeably."

York crossed the wide corridor just outside the blue room to the series of tall windows overlooking the grounds. "Through those windows you can look past the grounds, and over the walls around the palace. Just below them lie the abbey, several churches and schools, and the homes of the richer folk. But if you look beyond all that, you can see the sea itself."

Lon looked. York was right. The palace, the buildings, Ithyl itself, was amazing and beautiful, but the ocean beyond made it even more spectacular, the moving water a power lapping at the shore.

"Have you been here before?" York asked.

"No. This is my first visit here. But I hope it won't be my last." And Lon meant it. Ithyl, this city by the sea, was beautiful.

"At the end of these windows are the ancestors of the royal family, both recent and ancient. These two portraits are our current queen and king, whom you met last night."

"Yes. They were both up and waiting for us, even though it was very late." Lon stood looking intently at the king he had met last night, then he moved to the queen. He had been too focused on his father to really see her last night. It was a color portrait and the queen was a pretty woman with fair skin and dark hair, and eyes that were a surprising blue. A very dark blue.

He paused a moment, then followed York around the portraits, listening to his who's who, until he found himself standing before another woman with blue-black eyes and hair and very white skin who looked directly down upon him. He was suddenly aware that she seemed familiar, though he was sure he had never met her.

"Who is this?" he asked York.

"The queen's late sister."

"Late? The queen is still very young, so she must have been, too. How did she die?"

"We're not sure. She went on a journey with her family and they never returned." York moved on. "These are our queen's parents and over here are the king's."

He followed York for an hour, getting the lay of the palace, finding himself awed by the beautiful building and its expansive rooms and hallways, coupled with delicate and careful detail. Westra had nothing that elegant, he thought, nothing so large and lavish. No wonder Turgor coveted Ithyl's wealth. Then he found himself once more outside his father's room.

Rast was there, looking for him, Lon assumed. "Rast?"

"Your father's awake and wants you."

York understood. "I'll wait out here."

The king's personal guards from Westra in their blue and silver were posted within and without the room where the king lay, doubled by those in the gold and scarlet of Esfalia.

Lon followed Rast into the blue room. Inside, his father was indeed awake. A chair waited by the bed and Lon seated himself.

King Arnon reached out his hand to grasp Lon's. "When is the council?"

"Tomorrow."

The king's sigh of relief was audible. "We have not missed it?"

"No. We only arrived late last night."

"I was not sure how long I had slept." The king's voice was only a whisper, his face still white, with dark circles beneath his eyes.

"We have time."

"Something important must be happening there. If I cannot attend—."

Lon cut him off. "If you cannot, Rast and I will. Westra will be represented. Rest now. They've got the arrow out and the wound is clean. The physician says you should heal well." And quickly, he added under his breath.

The king relaxed and closed his eyes. In minutes he was asleep again.

Lon turned to Rast. "Glad you're coming with me. Maybe together we can figure out what is going on."

"Happy to do it. No one's gettin' away with this."

Lon sat for many minutes, watching his father's breath come and go, remembering how he had felt when he saw the arrow protruding from his father's chest. Then he stirred and stood, nodded at Rast, who followed him out the door. "Let's go see the council room, Rast. See if we can forestall any more skullduggery."

York was still waiting, and happy to guide them. Carefully he led them out of the family living quarters to the more public section of the palace. They came to the council room at last, at the top of a wide staircase on the second floor. York opened the double doors and ushered them inside.

It was a bright, cheerful room, a corner room with tall windows to the outside on two sides and the other two sides sporting shorter windows that opened to a hallway. The hallway itself curved around the front of the room before spilling into the wide staircase that led directly to the lower floor and the outside. In the room itself, tables and chairs outlined the circumference of the room. No secret cupboards, Lon thought. No sliding panels where unseen watchers could hide and listen. Everyone had to enter the same doors and be seen by all.

"What's down this hallway?" Lon asked, indicating the small hall that led from the council room on both sides.

"Libraries, small music rooms, smaller sitting rooms and such." York flung open several doors as they passed. "On the main floor below we have a large concert hall, which is used regularly. The queen's family is very musical."

In the room past him, Lon could see a variety of musical instruments. There were stringed instruments, woodwinds, and several small harps. A harp. That connected in his mind with something, or someone. He paused, looking into the small pleasant room. He almost had it. Then it fled.

Another small room had wall-to-wall bookcases with a few old scrolls in a case by the door. Others were just sitting rooms. Nothing to cause any alarm and none of them shared a wall with the council room.

"The council room stands alone," Rast pointed out, as York pushed on ahead of them.

Lon had observed the same thing. "The only danger is what we bring in ourselves." Satisfied, Lon called to York and they returned to the king and to lunch.

The king was awake this time. He drank a little broth from a cup Lon held for him, before he fell asleep once more.

The physician returned to note his progress. "He does well," he told Lon. "He even has color back in his face and the wound is healing quickly, with no sign of infection."

The day passed. The king slept and drank broth and took medicine. The physician paid several visits and all seemed to be going well. As evening came on, Lon slipped out of the room, where he found York waiting for him.

"Am I in time to dine with the royal family?"

"You are," York assured him. "They will be gathering in about fifteen minutes. Lots of time for us to reach the dining room."

"Who will be there?"

"The king and queen are absent with an envoy from the east. The oldest boy is off to the war, but you will meet the second son, Evan, and the two daughters, Bethlin and Marla. The king's uncle, Theron, may also be in attendance. It will be a small family group."

"Are others gathering for the council?"

"You and your father are the first. Those from Anor should come soon and will be housed in the palace. We have room also for our other allies. Turgor's men will be lodged in the town."

Lon grinned back at York. "A suitable division of your guests."

The dining room was not far from the breakfast room and Lon knew by the rumblings of his stomach when he was close. The smells from the room were delicious and reached all the way down the hall.

York had been right. There was an uncle, two young girls about seven and ten, and Evan. Lon found himself between Evan and Theron. He discovered Evan's older brother was with his brother Areth, north at the battle site. Theron was an older gentleman whose wife had already passed away. There was talk of the war, good food and laughter.

Then he returned to check on his father, and to sleep.

The next day came the council. Lon arose early to meet with his father. The king was stable. All bleeding had stopped; the wound was clean. But he was still weak and unable to move without reopening his wound and causing more bleeding. So Lon and Rast and several of the Westra guard went in his place, though Rast made sure at least two guards were left outside the king's door.

At the council, Lon and Rast found themselves scrutinizing those there, all their senses alert. With Rast's help, Lon identified the various heads of state, from the plains, from countries already overrun by Turgor, from Anor, and Nirson. The boy king for Anor was not far from them, his regent sitting beside him. The boy looked to Lon to be about ten.

Listening to the reading of the missive from Turgor, Lon felt someone's gaze upon him. He looked up to catch a man watching him, one of the company of the Duke of Blandor, the regent for Anor's king. The boy himself was watching Turgor's man, trying to fashion words out of the strange accent. But the man from Anor was staring at Lon, an avid look upon his face.

Rast caught it, too. "What's that all about?" His whisper barely reached Lon. He had made sure it would go no further.

"I don't know. I have never met the man before."

Then the meeting began. It was long and drawn out, the small rituals and motions of protocol dutifully followed. But as far as Lon and Rast could tell, nothing else really happened there that morning that explained the attack on his father. No new policies were decided, no new strategies evolved and put into place. Much pomp was given to Turgor's proposal of a system of vassals and tribute following their surrender, which the council rejected. But at the end of the day, after hours of deliberation, the current conditions were continued.

So why the attack? There had to be another reason. But though Lon cudgeled his brain, the answer eluded him. The only thing that had felt wrong was the regent's retainer staring at him. But a look was not a reason.

Lon returned to report to his father who was clear headed and in good spirits, and sitting up. A good sign, he thought. "The arrow, though painful, did little permanent damage," the physician told him.

But as he reported to his father the results of the council, with Rast's asides, his father, too was puzzled. What had anyone to gain by the attack on his person? What had anyone to gain from the council itself? It all seemed such a waste.

On the third day of the council, the king insisted the wound be bandaged and he be allowed up so he might regain his strength. Lon took him on a little tour outside the blue room to see the Esfalian ancestors on the wall. The queen had sent a messenger to invite them to a royal banquet that evening in the allies' honor and King Arnon wanted to be strong enough to go. "I'll exercise a little, then rest," he told Lon.

At the dinner hour, an honor guard came to escort them to the large hall. They stood behind the king along with his men from Westra to see that no harm came to him. Lon took his place to the right and looked around. All the allied leaders were there, though the messenger from Turgor was not in sight. Probably not invited, Lon thought, grimly pleased in spite of himself.

He turned to the king. "Have I ever been here before?"

King Arnon cleared his throat. "I don't think so. The last time I was here was just after Alyssa was born and your mother was home with you and Alyssa." Then he added, "I think Karis and Areth were here with me."

King Morland was on King Arnon's left, his queen, Elana, just beyond him. Puzzling over the events that had befallen them, Lon came up short suddenly, as he looked at the queen. There were the dark blue eyes and black hair, the white skin of the portraits in the hall opposite the blue room where King Arnon was staying. Once again there was that shock of recognition, though he could not place where he had seen her before. Or maybe it wasn't her, just someone who looked like her.

Dinner was all it should be, but Lon's eyes kept straying to the queen's face, unable to piece together the puzzle. As the dinner progressed, several musicians arrived to entertain them. One held a silver harp. Once more Lon was faced with midnight blue eyes, pale skin and blue-black hair.

Then his eyes went to the harp, a silver harp with a sweet, unforgettable sound. And he remembered the inn outside of Mythro, where the minstrel had played for the troops heading north, played beyond the power of one lone harp. And it too, had been silver.

As the dinner ended, and King Arnon left to return to his room for rest, Lon lingered behind and approached the queen.

As he bowed over her hand, he found himself asking about the music and those who played it. "Are they family to you?"

The queen smiled. "Yes. A brother and a sister."

"Are their harps of special make?"

"They are heirlooms of our family."

"I saw one like them a few months ago. A young minstrel was playing a harp like that at an inn in Westra for troops going north. Such power was in the playing that one of my soldiers became distraught and I had to intervene. That was powerful music, like this tonight. Do you have relatives in that area?"

The queen was silent, her face even whiter.

"Would you come speak with me in my sitting room?"

"Certainly." Lon was puzzled but willing.

"Brianne will lead you there." The queen indicated an older woman who had sat to her left at table. Then she turned and went out, Lon watching as she went.

"This way, Prince Lon." Brianne curtseyed, turned on her heel and headed out after the queen. "Her sitting room is down this hallway." She pushed open a door and ushered Lon into a small room with shelves of books and several musical instruments. "Take a seat anywhere, she will come soon." Then Brianne was gone.

A little surprised to find himself alone, Lon looked around the room, noting the instruments, the books, the photographs on the shelves in front of the books. He picked up one, obviously of the queen and king. He turned to another as the door opened and the queen entered with Brianne. Lon bowed, noting the queen's obvious discomfort. Sadness, he thought, wondering what he had done to cause it.

"The woman in that photograph is my sister, Reiha." Lon looked down at the picture in his hand. Though he could not really tell the color from the tinted pictograph, it appeared the woman had the blue-black hair, the midnight blue eyes and the pale skin of the queen and those of her family he had seen at the royal dinner.

"She looks like you."

"She disappeared years ago along with her child, a young girl. They were boarding a boat when a sudden wall of water came down upon them. Her husband, Jorik, was drowned, his body was washed up downstream from the dock days after. My sister was never found nor the child."

The queen was silent a long time, and Lon found himself wondering if she would even speak again. When she finally did, her voice was low and halting. "She, too, had a silver harp. Like the ones you saw tonight. The harp was never found either.

"Some months ago all the minstrels of the area were invited to play at the palace. The whole great hall was filled with singers and harpists. One after another, they played. But none like the ones you heard tonight. Then a man talked to the seneschal and mentioned there was another musician that had helped heal many of the soldiers who had returned from the war. They wanted to hear him. And so he was invited to perform. He sang and played a silver harp and broke our hearts. I sent for him after, but he had disappeared and no one could find him or tell me where he had gone."

"That sounds like the minstrel I heard in Mythro. Only the minstrel was not a man, but a girl, clothed as a man. And she played a silver harp. And power filled the room."

Lon caught the queen's sudden intake of breath. "A girl? How old?"

Lon thought. "About sixteen or seventeen, I think." He felt the queen's eyes burn into his.

"That would be about right. We do not know what became of my sister and her child. But they have to be somewhere. And somewhere they will be playing. My sister was a gifted harpist and singer. Her child may very well be the same. When you return, will you look for them? Perhaps my sister died and the child does not know who she is. Perhaps they both have amnesia. Perhaps——." She broke off. She could say no more.

"I will search and send you a message."

The queen smiled and Lon remembered how day felt when the sun suddenly emerged from the clouds.

"Thank you. And thank you for new hope."

4

In the Larder

The night of the ball in Godsel, Malin's tutor, Basil, continued to watch the southern riders battle their horses on the sandbar from his hiding place on the shore. He watched as the flagship moved away from the sandbar and headed back to the harbor. He saw the horses calm down and the riders leave the sandbar and splash through the water without the slightest attempt at concealment.

The riders gathered in a group just inside the trees. Basil listened to their conversation, but only caught a word or two, for he did not understand the language they spoke. He waited quietly, patiently, his keen eyes taking in all he could, watching both the riders and the course of the ship as it returned to the docks.

Distantly, he heard the flurry of sound as the guests, now free from imminent danger, came back on deck and prepared to disembark, enter their carriages, and head for their homes. The alarm would be given by now, Basil thought.

He looked at the riders. They still huddled in a group just inside the trees. The riders must know the raid had failed and the alarm given. Why did they stay? Basil could tell both they and their horses were nervous and wishing to be gone, but something held them. The horses were occasionally rearing and walking with stiff legs held by a very tight rein.

Then the group turned to face into the forest, and Basil could hear the sounds of a horse picking its way carefully through the woods. It was full night now, but the moon had emerged from beneath the clouds, its rays glinting off the now surprisingly calm waves along the shore. The riders parted, and the newcomer edged his horse closer to the shore, the moonlight suddenly spilling on a face Basil knew: Gray, one of Lord Norton's retainers. After a brief conversation, the bulk of the riders turned and headed south into the forest in the direction of the south wilderness. Probably to their cove and ship, thought Basil.

Basil picked up a few words of this conversation, for the retainer, of course, spoke the language of Godsel. One of the riders translated his words for the benefit of the others. Basil was sure he heard the words, "Thornton Manor." Were the riders going there? Was Lady Thornton involved or in danger? She was supposed to be in the country, visiting relatives for a couple more months. Had she returned early? Or was her empty manor a spot for a brief meeting with the riders and their Godsel contacts?

Basil waited until all the riders were gone, then carefully stood and just as carefully brushed himself off. What had he really heard? He straightened his tails and coat, then strode purposefully back toward the mare he had taken, determined to ride her close to Thornton Manor to see what else he could learn.

When he reached the spot where he had left the mare, she was gone. The reins must have been too loose. He could return to the town for a mount, but town was a considerable distance. Pity, he thought. A horse would make his task a lot easier. Maybe she wasn't too far away. He listened for the crack of a branch in the woods ahead, for hoof beats, for the sounds of a large animal moving through the trees. He was in luck. He could hear something breaking branches underfoot. The mare had not strayed very far.

He went after her, moving slowly, quietly, wishing he had more of Malin's talents. But she heard him coming and moved away from him as he approached. Keep talking in a calm voice, he reminded himself. Wasn't that how Malin did it?

There she was, stopped on the edge of the clearing ahead, cropping a mouthful. Basil approached her slowly, steadily. Talk. I must talk. But what do you say to a horse? "Nice horse. Pleasant little horse. How good of you to wait, instead of hobnobbing with the intruders. Pleased to make your acquaintance. Basil, here." It sounded like drivel to Basil, but who knew about a horse?

Still, he had to try. He went to work. He might just as well have been at a social function and the horse the newest guest he had to greet. His tones were sheer liquid, and he barely moved, slowly covering the ground to where the horse pawed nervously by the trees. Stooping slowly, Basil plucked a handful of sparse grass and held it out before him to the horse.

"I have a great admiration for your species, especially for the services they have rendered to mine. I refer to riding. Ah, yes. That moving forward steadily on the back of a gentle horse, a horse of exceptionally smooth gait and pleasant manners. Like you."

The horse, a dark mare with three white stockings and a white blaze on her forehead, was gazing at him, her mane and tail twitching, as was the skin on her neck. She swung her head around to watch him. Suddenly she lunged forward and chomped down on the grass in his hand.

"Wonderful horse. You've only bit the grass." Distracted a minute by her chewing, she didn't realize Basil had the reins until she felt him pull on them. She whinnied, gave him a white-eyed side glance, then finally allowed him to approach. "We will make a quiet social visit together, maybe find you a friend or two."

One foot was in the stirrup and the other was on its way over the mare's back before she realized it and shifted slightly. The foot was hung up for some time on the saddle horn as Basil no longer had the use of the mounting steps at the dock. "Yes, indeed, we have a visit to make. Lady Thornton has been gone visiting relatives for some months. Perhaps she has other company she doesn't know about? And what is Lord Norton's connection with all this? Why would a retainer of his be meeting southern riders? It doesn't look good."

Basil was fully mounted but the mare was resisting his attempts to guide her around trees and over logs. Woods were apparently not her thing. Perhaps the mare was only used to open trails. Finally, after several branches had struck him in the face, the mare settled down once more and they headed to Thornton Manor, but his voice and conversation didn't miss a beat.

"That was Gray, Lord Norton's right hand man. Lord Norton will know exactly where he is and what he's doing, though Lord Norton would probably deny such knowledge. Well, well. Associating with southern riders who attack Lord Lindsey's flagship. Could give a fellow a bad name."

His horse suddenly shied from a snapped branch in the path, and for a few moments he was busy trying to calm her. Malin sure had some useful skills, he thought. "There, there," he said to his horse. "Nothing to fear. Just a tree branch in the path. Yes indeed."

He reached the edge of the tree-lined road that led up to Thornton Manor and dismounted stiffly but carefully. He debated for a moment about whether to turn the horse loose so she would not give him away, or to keep her tied and accessible in case he needed her again. He chose the latter and went the rest of the way on foot. Not being a woodsman, and aware of his deficiencies, he chose the grass under the trees for his path. His feet made less sound there, and his moving silhouette would not be visible in the darkness of the trees.

He approached the hall carefully, going past the front, circling around the side to the back where he was finally rewarded by a small slit of light between the drapes on a large glass door. Because it was a December night and a chill was in the air, Basil slowly lifted his gaze to the closest chimney where, to his satisfaction, he found a small smoke trail curving into the sky. Someone was there and had been for some time, long enough to light a fire. He might be able to eavesdrop and pick up important information.

He leaned into the trees and stood listening for a long moment, as still as the trees themselves. Then the light spilled out as the drapes opened across the glass of the door. Just inside were three robed southern riders, with Gray, Lord Norton's retainer, in their midst.

Basil looked around. Where were their horses? He had not seen or heard them. Perhaps in the stables, to the other side of the manor. The rest of the riders had probably continued south. Basil resisted the impulse to hide himself more completely in the trees, knowing that movement would call attention to himself more than anything else.

"What is it that they do?" He whispered to himself. "A deed without a name."

One of the riders emerged, crossed to the far end of the house and turned the corner. Likely going for their horses, thought Basil, as the man picked his way through the darkness, for the door had closed and the curtains fallen back into place. Basil shifted, making sure he could not be seen from within, settling himself once more amidst a cluster of bushes, straightening his coat and tails, patting down his sleeves.

His waiting was not in vain. But unhappily the sounds of a shod horse striking the cobblestones came from far down the lane at the front of the manor, near where he had left his mare, and not from the direction of the stables. Then he heard the sounds of horses coming from behind the manor near the stables. The two should meet about where the wedge of light from the glass door split the night.

But Basil's mare apparently had forgotten the great confidence placed in her, the wonderfully nourishing mouthful of grass given her by her benefactor, and proceeded to whinny and thrash about until both Basil and the newcomer, maybe even the southern riders he had just seen, heard her. Pity, thought Basil. Now someone would come and look about and he would be discovered.

The single rider passed Basil, who hardly breathed, and continued to the back of the house and stopped, just in front of the door. The man from the stables reached there at the same time, leading three horses. The single rider dismounted. A knock, and once again light spilled out; the rider was Millicent.

Basil nodded to himself. Deirdre again. Malin's sister sure knew how to pick her friends. If there was trouble afoot, Deirdre seemed to always be in the midst of things. Millicent's filmy white dress was now covered by a dark cloak; and Basil could almost see the soulful eyes now narrowed and hard. Malin would be saddened, thought Basil, that she was involved with southern riders.

She gestured to the front of the lane, talking about his horse, Basil surmised. His time was gone. He had none left for listening. But to move was also to be discovered. Millicent handed her reins to the remaining rider and entered the manor.

The man with the reins tied Millicent's horse to a post by the door along with the others. While he was doing so, two other men emerged and headed up the lane to Basil's borrowed mare, still whinnying to Millicent's horse, standing by the door. Basil's hiding place was no longer safe. He had heard a dog inside and if used, the animal would ferret him out in no time.

Basil calculated time and distance. It might be possible between the time the riders were out of sight, and before anyone else emerged from the house, to reach one of the other horses and ride for Roswood and safety. It would be close. And there was no hope if someone else appeared. He waited precious seconds to see if anyone else was coming out before he took the plunge.

Out he came, straightening his attire as he went, his gait less smooth than usual, but certainly covering more ground. He reached Millicent's horse, his hands catching the trailing reins.

But fortune was not kind tonight. The door before him opened and another man stepped out. In an instant Basil turned Millicent's horse the other way, as if he were taking it to the stables. The other man stood watching a moment, then yelled something back inside and headed straight for Basil. Basil was trapped. There really was no escape, but he resolved to give it his best.

He bowed to the man who was attempting to stop him. "Wonderful evening, my good man. Out taking the air are you? Enjoying it myself."

Before Basil's words were finished, southern riders converged upon him. Shouts brought others, though Millicent and Gray were not among them.

Basil turned, shifting the horse as he did so, wishing he were younger and quicker that he might still attempt to mount and ride, but he was not adept enough. Instead, he put a bold face on the matter and began to walk back toward the door, the southern riders clustered behind him, the horse swinging about between them.

There would be time to devise other strategies, Basil thought. For now, his only refuge was in the habitual processes of social interaction that he had been teaching Malin.

"Evening, good sirs. A beautiful night for a stroll. I don't believe Lady Thornton is at home. May I be of some assistance?"

"Do the southerners want tutors?" Gray asked Millicent, his voice low.

"No. Just workers of magic. Basil is of no use to them and a real problem for us. Bring him inside. Let me look over the manor. Surely we can lock him away somewhere while we make our escape."

Gray protested. "But I live in Godsel. He will recognize me; he knows my connection to Lord Norton."

"I'll take care of that." Suddenly, just as Basil came fully into their view, Millicent clubbed Gray on the side of the head with her riding crop, knocking him unconscious. "Take this intruder and leave him unconscious and afoot well within the woods. See that he has no chance of getting back to town before we are well on our way." Millicent, Basil noted, had spoken carefully in English, which most of the southern riders could not speak. Clearly she spoke for him to hear.

At least two understood, for they hauled Gray off and out of sight. Basil found himself waiting with an entourage of southerners while Millicent scouted the main floor. "Bring him here." Her words were almost lost in the depths of the manor, but the southerners obliged, and Basil was soon face to face with her. Deirdre's Millicent, Basil thought to himself. Deirdre really had a penchant for trouble.

Millicent made no attempt at civilities. Gone was the young woman who had attracted Malin. The woman facing Basil seemed older, harder, her jaw tight. Even the voice had become severe.

"Put him in here," she indicated the larder, which could be securely latched from the outside. "That will teach him to spy." She turned a mocking gaze on Basil. "He will continue to be well fed, at least temporarily."

Basil was mocking in turn. "Madame," he bowed shortly, and with great dignity, walked past her into the larder, seating himself carefully on a barrel, spreading his coattails and brushing off his cuffs. His gaze returned to someplace over Millicent's head, as if she were of no further importance.

Angrily, she slammed the door, and Basil heard the latch fall into place. He heard the rattling of the door as they tested the latch, then their footsteps that gradually faded away into the empty corridors.

Basil was locked tidily away in Lady Thornton's larder, like a rather large delicacy, he thought to himself. It was night, and the single high window above him let in little light. He could barely make out the small room, with shelves on one side and larger barrels and containers on the other. There were bottles and the round shapes of cheeses on the shelves, as well as other foodstuffs that would not perish while the larder's owner was off a-visiting. There would likely be root vegetables, such as carrots, potatoes, rutabagas and maybe even some cabbages in a bin of sand, some dried meats, crackers, and dried fruits, probably apples. He certainly would not starve. He would have to wait until morning and more light to be sure of his inventory, but it looked as if there was more than enough food there to keep him in good form.

He tried the door. It was locked, and as he had suspected, from the outside. The only other way out was the small, high vertical window well above his head. He studied the outlines of the window for long moments, then gazed down at his own girth, pursed his lips and shook his head. He looked once more around the small room, noting wine kegs, pickle barrels, some small pails. He envisioned the makeshift ladder he would build, ending just below the window. But not tonight. He didn't wish his plans to be discovered before the enemy had departed.

He sighed, seated himself on a bucket, and listened carefully until he heard the others ride off into the night. He was patient and careful. They had elected not to kill him, but they could always change their minds. He waited for several hours more, until the first rays of the sun floated down to the top of his head from the high narrow window. It was morning. He waited until the breakfast hour arrived, but no sound or movement could be heard.

Well then, he was alone. They had fled the country. Millicent had attempted to provide an alibi for Gray by treating him as an enemy, but Basil had seen too much, so he was now safely out of the way, locked in the larder of an empty manor where few would ever look.

His captors couldn't have picked a better place for him, thought Basil. The larder was full. There were even some fresh breads probably left by the enemy. The bottles of wine on the shelves, as Basil soon ascertained, were of a slightly inferior quality than he usually drank, still they would sustain.

Besides, he had friends. Malin and Rilse would find him. In fact, Lady Thornton would eventually return, although that could be several months down the road. However it was not in him to sit and wait for rescue if there were something he could do. As long as Basil was in the larder, Lord Norton was free to carry out his plans, whatever they were. Basil found that idea singularly unacceptable, since it might also include sending someone to tie up a certain Basil-shaped loose end.

In the end, he considered all his possibilities and went to work on them all at the same time. It didn't matter which one did the job, as long as one of them did. He would work to get himself out, but not be too upset if Malin and Rilse found him before he succeeded. He waited until full daylight, then started stacking the buckets and barrels to make a safe pathway to what he hoped was up and out, at least to the narrow window high up on the wall. He would have to see about the "out" part of it. The makeshift ladder took some doing, for he was round and required substantial footing, but it was done at last.

Climbing was also a bit tricky, but slow and easy saw him through. In the end, he was carefully balanced at the top, gazing out the window directly in front of him. His worst fears were realized. His middle girth would not permit his exit through the window. No matter how he turned and squeezed, out was not in the cards. Close, but not there. He could see through the window to a small roof that jutted beneath it. Once out he would have no trouble getting down and away. Out was the problem.

Sadly, reluctantly, he climbed back down his "ladder" and seated himself on the apple barrel, on top of tasty apples as he had already discovered, the cores pitched in an empty bucket nearby. There would be little food in his near future, in spite of its plenitude. A bit of fruit to maintain energy, apples, a carrot or two, a sip of wine now and then to maintain body fluids, but he could not afford to eat bread or cheese if he wished to become thin enough to escape through the window. Malin and Rilse or Lady Thornton might come. But he needed to decide now if he were going to work on losing weight, just in case.

His last possibility was to get the door open. He looked around for tools to pry out the hinges, or jimmy the lock. He found a large nail, a bit of string, a fist-sized rock that had found its way in, likely with the potatoes. Well, he had nothing else to do. He would see what he might fashion.

He turned his back to the shelves of food, his face to the door. He would work on the locks and hinges several hours a day. The rest of the time he would gaze at the window, his goal, and recite. Only immortal lines from the literary greats could sustain him during this time of trouble. There, with his back to the food, he started in to recite some of his favorite lines.

"When in disgrace with fortune and men's eyes—."

He paused his reciting, drank a little watered wine, for he had found some water bottles with the bread left behind by the enemy. Most of the food he would have to resist until he lost enough of his belly to exit the window, but life was more than meat and drink. Wasn't it? The answer varied in its intensity as the days went on. The apples were removed from the barrel he sat upon and it became his toilet. It was the only barrel that had a tight lid.

A week passed. Every day he climbed to the top of his pile and tried the window, taking care to explore all angles to be sure to get his best one. Every day he climbed back down, and commenced reciting again. His voice became fainter, his tones less round as his belly became less full. Still, he ascended, tried, failed, and descended.

Every day he would chip away at the hinges on the door. He had found the end of a penknife and had actually removed several screws before it broke. However, the door was still locked and the hinges secure, much to his chagrin.

Two weeks passed, then three. He began to make up his own poetry, stringing words and sounds together.

"Round gold cheese come rolling by,
bring bread and wine for such as I,
round gold cheese my only friend,
yet apples are divine.
Turnips and taters, onions and cabbage,
favorites of my friend Babbidge,
Mustn't eat, must get thin,
oh what a pickle vat I'm in,
roast pig on a plate,
surely could my hunger sate,
plum pudding in a jar,
come out, come out wherever you are
and apples are divine."

Finally, on the evening of the twenty-fourth day, his mind would no longer hold onto words. Instead he whistled tuneless snatches of song, he, Basil, who never whistled. He was finding it harder and harder to ascend his tower of buckets and pails. He took a healthy swig of his second-to-last bottle of wine and began to climb once more. Up, up he went. He found the heights somewhat dizzying but persevered. Once more he tried his girth at the window.

He sighed and prepared to descend. He was getting thinner, just not fast enough. If he didn't lose enough soon, he might be too weak to take advantage of his freedom when he did escape. Maybe if he exercised, did some middle bends. He had heard that might be slimming. Not even a swig of wine would cross his lips, only water. And may the lords of society forgive my social lapse, he thought.

i

5
Coup d'État

Several days after the banquet with the king and queen of Ithyl, King Arnon announced over breakfast that he was ready to travel.

King Morland spoke to him, attempting to persuade him to linger a little longer. "What's your hurry? Give your wound a little more time to heal."

Arnon's eyes turned sober. "We've been gone longer than we planned already. I have a kingdom I'm responsible for."

Morland smiled warmly at his friend. "I know. But it sure has been great to see you and spend a little time together, even under the circumstances."

"A midwinter meeting, that accomplished nothing; a night arrow, that though painful accomplished little more." Arnon shook his head. "What is going on?"

"Beats me, my friend. I can't make heads nor tails of these events."

"Well, I feel we should be on our way, perhaps in the morning if horses and supplies can be made ready."

"Are you sure?"

"Yes, my friend. We must go."

"Then we will make sure things are ready."

So supplies were gathered, horses prepared and men made ready. Lon and his father met to say goodbye to their hosts.

"I'll look for the minstrel, and send you a message," Lon promised the queen.

She clasped his hand tightly and was slow to relinquish it. "Thank you," she whispered.

King Morland accompanied them outside to the palace court, reluctant to say goodbye. "You know you and yours are welcome anytime, for as long as you want to stay," he said gruffly.

"I know. But I've a queen and a kingdom waiting."

Morland smiled. "An old friend can't quite compete with that."

Impulsively, Arnon grasped him by the forearms. "Come visit in the spring. Any time. We don't need an occasion."

"If the war is over by then, I just might do that. What fun to let our families get to know each other."

As they rode out of Esfalia, Lon asked, "How long have you been friends?"

"Since we were children. There was no war then and ruling a kingdom was easier." His father paused then added, "And more fun."

Lon laughed. "I'll bet it was."

The journey back was a little easier than the one to Ithyl, for in many spots they had broken trail and warmer weather and light dry winds had improved the trail's conditions. They also made better time and their hearts were a little lighter. But as they reached the place where the arrow had struck the king, they were cold sober once more. They paused on the trail.

Looking at the trampled snow, Lon voiced his thoughts. "Why? Who got any good out of it? And why here?"

His father felt a sudden chill run down his shoulder blades. "If there were no reasons at the council, maybe the explanation is back in Westra. Let's go home."

Lon felt a tightness in his chest at his father's words. "What do you mean?"

"I'm not sure, but someone went to a lot of trouble to wound me, from a vantage point where they could not have expected to kill me. So why?"

Lon had to agree. "Exactly. Why bother?"

"If the queen were ruling in Westra alone, I might worry. Or if it were Mithrond alone, I might worry. But the two of them together should have been able to forestall any trouble." Still, if there were no explanations at the council, they had to be back in Westra at Heath Halls. A chill went through both of them and remained, for they had no answers, no explanations. But they pushed for home, suddenly and unexpectedly driven to get there as soon as possible.

Their return journey seemed endless in the cold, on a rough, uneven trail. Nights were long, but no storms forced them to hole up in their tents and wait until they passed over. There were no further ambushes, though Lon found himself tense from the waiting.

They reached the site of the avalanche where they found the ground soft enough to dig a shallow grave and take the body of their comrade from under the rocks and truly bury him. Rast and the king took time to say a few words about the man, for he was well known to them all and had been faithful well beyond mere obedience to the commands of authority over him. He had a wife and family, and his weapons would be carried back to them.

The king found the way long, though he said nothing. Lon could see the cold pained his wound, and though much healed, it sapped his strength and stamina. Yet he rode day after day, mile after mile. When they finally left the mountain passes, they breathed a sigh of relief.

All were glad when they reached the river road where they could make better time. South they went, picking up the pace, traveling a little faster, until they reached the inn. Lon assured them the food was exceptionally good and with his father's consent, they chose to stop briefly. But Lon had another errand there.

He searched the room for the minstrel, and though he knew the minstrel really only played at night, he found himself strangely disappointed when she wasn't there. He hadn't realized he'd been looking forward to seeing her, to hearing her sing. He had been pleased to have an errand from Ithyl's queen that ensured he would have to see her again.

As he placed their orders, he asked the innkeeper, "Does the minstrel still sing for you?"

"No, Sire. Not any more, she don't." He sighed. "She were great for business." Then he stopped, realizing he had revealed information not generally known. He stammered a bit, trying to cover his tracks. "I mean he." If the minstrel didn't want it known that she was female, he felt he should honor that. She had given much to his inn.

Lon let his slip pass, saying nothing.

The innkeeper continued. "All the farmers round about of an evening would bring in their wives for a little something and to listen." He was red-faced at his blunder, and stammered a little.

Lon touched his arm. "It's all right. I met her and knew," he said. "Such music."

The innkeeper relaxed. "She only left a few weeks ago. Going to Godsel, she said. We hoped she would stay the winter with us, but she were right restless. When the last group came through here bound for Godsel she went with them. Dreamed of the gold city she did, so my granddaughter said. Dreamed until it left her no peace and she had to go."

Lon was astounded, then things fell into place. So she, too, was gifted. That would explain the power of her playing. And the gifted were gathering to Godsel. The minstrel, his brother Karis, and he had heard a few tales about Malin. Why?

There was no one to ask. He sighed. He would have to send messages and inquire after the minstrel in Godsel before he could send any real information to the queen in Ithyl, who would be waiting anxiously. That was all he could do.

They finally reached Heath Halls and to their relief, found nothing that seemed amiss there. The queen took charge of the king. She made sure he was carefully helped into his own quarters, while fresh bandages were brought, as well as food and drink. Seated there, while the king listened from his great dark four-poster bed, Lon told his mother of the attack on his father. She shuddered and grasped her husband's hand more tightly.

"We'll soon have you as good as new," she said, smiling brightly to cover her dismay. Who had wanted her husband dead?

Lon finished his tale, ending with, "But we can see no reason for it."

"Some folk need no reason, beyond their own contrariness," his mother was quick, too quick, thought Lon, looking at her carefully.

So she, too, was uneasy, thought Lon.

"Well, at least you're here now, and safe." Queen Gwynne did not say that she had been worried when the news of the attack had come, nor that she had not slept a full night since. "I received word you were wounded just after Areth sent for reinforcements."

"Reinforcements? Areth?"

"Oh, yes. Our son sent us an urgent message, my dear. Mithrond brought it to me and we looked at it together. The message said they had a great need for fresh troops, additional troops to repel the advances of the enemy. The war must be going badly."

The king was having trouble taking it all in. Such a thing had never happened before, and shouldn't have. It was totally out of order, and did not follow the chain of command.

The queen continued. "It seemed a little odd, but it was Areth who sent for them. At least the message said so."

"What did Mithrond say about it all?"

"He seemed convinced that it was from Areth, and that we should do as it said. So he gathered up the last of the troops around Mythro, as well as some of the guards from the Halls themselves, and sent them north."

And there it was, the reason. Lon and the king stared at each other, stunned. "Sent them north? All of them?"

"Yes." The queen caught their reaction. She hastened to explain. "You left Mithrond in charge, and he said that Areth would not have sent for troops if there were not a pressing need. Based on his recommendation, we sent off all we could spare two weeks after you left. What's the matter?"

Two weeks? The king and Lon looked at each other. Worse and worse. The kingdom could fall in days with all her troops and part of the king's personal guard gone from the city.

The queen searched her husband's face. "What is it?"

"Troops are ordered and placed by General Rathman." The king's tones were measured, steady, but Lon could see the dismay in his eyes. The troops were ordered by the general; the requests arriving by formal dispatch. Areth did not have the authority to request troops, even as the king's son. Yet Mithrond was the oldest and most trusted retainer King Arnon had. If he had sent the troops north, he must have been convinced they were needed. Or – he couldn't voice his thought.

"Where is Mithrond?" Lines of strain appeared around the king's mouth.

Lon was already in motion and on his feet. "I'll send for him," Lon assured him, and in moments it was done. Still restless, Lon paced, then made up his mind. "I'll help. Two people looking might be faster than one."

As he left the king and queen, he spoke softly to the guards both within and without the room. "Let no one enter until I return. No one. And gather the rest of the king's guard and place them at the door of this room."

The guards' eyes widened in surprise, then narrowed in comprehension. With a quick bow of acknowledgement, two of them left immediately to follow Lon's instructions.

For his part, Lon raced down the left set of stairs that curved into the main hallway below. The king wounded and the garrison dispatched was too much of a coincidence. Yet Mithrond was a wise and trusted man. What did he know that they didn't? He had given his approval and issued the orders. Or had he?

Lon's goal was Mithrond's suite on the first floor in the left wing. If he were in the house or grounds, the guard would find him, but if not, Lon would. They had no time to lose. He rapped sharply on Mithrond's door. When there was no answer, he turned the knob and pushed open the door.

"Mithrond?" he called. Then again, "Mithrond?" There was no answer. Leaving the door slightly ajar, he stepped inside. The room was as he remembered it from a month ago: the same furniture, the same dark paneling, the same pictures of landscapes hung on the walls. He made one more attempt, "Mithrond!" There was no answer.

Lon turned to leave, but something drew him back. The room felt like his twin's room had when the dark mage was shadowing him. He walked past the sitting room to the bedroom. A quick glance told him no one was there. He continued on to the study and paused for a moment.

He took a step inside and looked around. Then he bent and picked up a picture that had fallen to the floor. He righted the picture and placed it back on the desk. He smiled at it. He had seen it there many times before. It was a hand painted portrait of Mithrond's daughter who had died in childhood.

Then it hit him. It was on the floor and had not been picked up. The Mithrond he knew would never have left it there, unless he had been in a terrible hurry, or had no choice. The taint of dark magic was heavier here, and Karis, the one with magic, was in the south. Was that planned, too? And by whom?

Lon left the study, a bitter taste in his mouth. The soldiers were gone, the king wounded, Mithrond under duress, perhaps even no longer alive. If the enemy, whoever they were, could attempt to murder a king, a steward would present only a small obstacle. Those who could oppose an enemy were neatly done away with.

Lon closed the door, making sure no one saw him leave Mithrond's rooms. His feet only skimmed the stairs on his way back up, but his mind was moving even faster.

He passed the king's guards. "No one has come, Your Highness."

Lon nodded his thanks and passed quickly into the presence of the king. He took the chair close by his father. "Mithrond is not in his rooms. They're empty right now. But I found his daughter's picture on the floor." He didn't need to say any more. His father understood.

Queen Gwynne also caught the undertones. That spot that hummed in the center of her forehead when things were happening was humming.

"Gwynne," the king's voice was low and urgent. "Take Alyssa and a few of my guard that were in Ithyl with us and flee south to Godsel. Now. Right now."

The queen caught his urgency and wasted no time with questions. She nodded. "I'll take the servants' stairs." She kissed him, touched Lon on the shoulder, and disappeared through the king's dressing rooms. They heard the light, quick sound of her footsteps that soon faded to silence.

"Father, I've ordered your guards to stand outside this door. That should be the rest of them that you hear. We should also see Mithrond soon, if he's all right." As Lon spoke they could hear the tread of feet on the stairs.

There was a rap on the door and a guard thrust in his head. "Mithrond comes with a company of men in the livery of Anor."

"A company?" The king was astounded. "A full company?"

"What is your will, Sire?"

"Send only Mithrond in."

As the guard withdrew, Lon whispered, "There are only ten of your guard. They cannot stand against a full company, no matter how valiant they are. Bring your guard in to ring your bed, then invite Mithrond in. Hear him out. It may be that there is a good explanation." But unlikely, Lon thought. Very unlikely.

At his father's nod, Lon sprang to the door, ordering the king's guard in before the company reached them.

"Send Mithrond in," he ordered, adding under his breath, though he didn't know why, "And let it be Mithrond."

The tramp of feet was heard now in the hallway itself, then the door was opened wide. A guard stepped into the space in front and formally announced, "Mithrond to see Your Majesty." And Mithrond was there, stepping in front of the guard, entering the room, visible, smiling, his presence assuring everyone that all was well.

Yet Lon knew the man standing inside the door was not Mithrond. The hair was right, the beard, the uniform. But the eyes were all wrong, narrowed and shifty, and the tight, controlled smile that ringed the mouth sent chills up Lon's back. Mithrond was open and warm, honorable. This man would not even meet their gaze.

Lon cast a quick glance at his father, and their eyes locked. His father knew as well.

"Your Majesty," the man before them gushed. "Welcome back." Almost mockingly he covered the space to stand by the king's bed. "We were so grieved to hear of your wound. What a terrible attack on the king we know and love." He bowed low and grasped the king's hand in his. "We're indeed glad to know you're recovering, that you're safe with us once more."

The emphasis on the word "safe" felt anything but safe to Lon.

The impostor Mithrond bowed and stood, his eyes met Lon's over the form of the king, his lips curled mockingly.

Where was the real Mithrond? Lon wondered. A prisoner? Dead? He could not say. But what he could say was that an impostor walked in his place.

Before they could even take another breath, however, Mithrond turned back to the doorway, and ushered another man into the room.

"Lord Tallon," he announced. "The Regent of Anor, the Duke of Blandor, has sent Lord Tallon and his men to assist us."

Lord Tallon stepped forward and mockingly saluted the king, lying pale and still in his great bed, the dark quilts emphasizing his pallor. "I am Lord Tallon. I bring greetings from the Regent, who has sent me to ensure that all is well here in your kingdom. We heard the king was wounded, and his city drained of men." He paused, his studied emphasis on the last words not lost on the king and Lon. "Our illustrious regent, the Duke of Blandor has sent this company, under my command, to assist you in keeping the peace, and protecting the royal family."

So that was it, Lon thought. The duke was ambitious. Anor would not countenance his deposing their boy king, but if he could have Westra—.

Lon looked at the man, dumbfounded. He knew him. He was the man who had stared at him during the council in Esfalia. He must have come directly here, not going first to Anor. And he had waited until the king and Lon had returned home. The wound would have delayed the king, giving the man and his retainers ample time to enter Mythro and prepare to take over. Then they had only to wait.

Tallon waved a hand behind him and two guards led Princess Alyssa into the room. She fled their grasp and went to stand beside Lon. His heart sank. The queen would not leave without Alyssa. He was right. A slight commotion outside the door and the queen was ushered in. The royal family, at least those members left in Heath Halls, was neatly caught.

Outside stood a whole company of men under Lord Tallon's command in the orange and rust of Anor. Inside the room were the last few members of the king's guard. There was no contest. Any opposition would result in a blood bath for the king's guard, and probably the royal family as well.

The fake Mithrond spoke up. "The palace guards have been given furlough. They have been working long hours since the departure of the troops. Your men also are weary; we'll provide them with rest. With Lord Tallon's help we can ease the burdens all around." The king's guard relaxed.

Mithrond was there, smiling; his presence confirmed that all was well. The king's own guards were given furlough, until further notice, and the soldiers from Anor took their place.

"We will escort you and the princess back to your rooms, Your Majesty," Tallon announced to the queen, "for your own safety. Don't worry about the king. We have a special physician with us to make sure the king is given good care, very good care, indeed."

The queen understood. There was no purpose in opposing those she faced. She would have to wait and watch for a better opportunity. She kissed the king and touched Lon on the arm as Tallon's men hustled her and Alyssa out the door and down the hallway.

Those remaining in the room watched her go, then Tallon turned back to Lon. "Prince Lon, my guard will escort you to your rooms. It would please us to have you remain there, for we will have need of your services, what with the king being ill and all. As for the king, he will remain here, for the time being, so we can best see to his care."

The veiled threat was not lost on Lon. What was going to happen to the king? To his mother and sister? To himself? He exchanged glances with his father, who shook his head almost imperceptibly. At the moment, there was nothing they could do. Whatever Tallon's plans were, they were in no position to resist them. They had no power, Tallon had seen to that.

So, just that quickly and easily, the royal family, except for Areth and Karis, became prisoners in their own palace. With one final changing of the guard, they had all become prisoners of Tallon, emissary of the Duke of Blandor, regent of Anor, to do with as he chose. And with that changing of the guard, Westra had fallen to Anor, without a single battle ever being fought.

6
Hidden Ways

When Lon awoke the next morning, and as soon as he was dressed and prepared for the day, the guards took him straight to an audience with Tallon. He found Heath Halls patrolled by Tallon's troops, men he had never seen and didn't know. Face to face with Tallon, he looked around for the fake Mithrond.

Tallon seemed to know who Lon was looking for. "The steward you left in charge is also exhausted. He's been ill and will be taking furlough with all the rest of your men."

Lon caught the emphasis on "all." So none of their own men would be left as guards, not even Rast. He had been hoping against hope.

Tallon smiled, his eyes hard. "The queen and the princess will remain in their quarters. Times are rough, and we wish to be sure they are," the man paused briefly, "safe." Lon felt the veiled threat, a cold spear of fear that pained all the way in. "The king will be well taken care of by an eminent physician we have brought with us. Arrow wounds can become deadly if the arrow was poisoned. We surely hope that is not the case in this instance."

Lon said nothing. There was nothing to say. Cold eyes searched his. Then, satisfied that Lon understood the situation, Tallon dismissed him to return to his rooms and closed the door upon him. Lon understood only too well that he was a prisoner, as were his mother, Alyssa, and his father. He also understood they were all in grave danger.

What did they want of him? He paced restlessly all day, worrying and waiting. Supper was a plate brought to his room; shortly after, he was once more escorted to the main salon to meet with Tallon.

"Since the king is unable to write his signature, we will need you to sign documents on his behalf."

"Unable to write?"

"Sadly, yes. The physician says a slow poison has begun to work and the king is," Tallon paused for effect, pretending to search for a word, "delirious."

"I don't believe it." Lon closed his lips angrily.

Tallon shrugged. "Take him to see," he ordered the guards. Then he looked back at Lon. "We'll need you to sign papers in the morning."

"What papers? Can they not wait for the king to become well?" He would make them show their hand, Lon decided, reveal their purpose.

Tallon's eyes gleamed; his lips stretched across his teeth. "Some of the holdings in Mythro need to be reexamined. Boundaries need to be changed; new nobles created."

Lon stared at him. They had to be very sure of themselves to go that far. Then he was hustled out the door, dragged to his father's rooms, and thrust inside.

His father lay before him, pale and white in his large dark bed, with red spots on his cheeks from a fever. His eyes opened and he saw Lon, but no recognition shone in their depths. Lon was sick at heart. Then he was pushed up the stairs, down the long, wide hall overlooking the central hall below, to his mother's rooms, where she and Alyssa were held. The guards left them alone for a minute.

Alyssa went flying to Lon, and he bent down and hugged her, reassuringly. "Lon, who are these strange guards, and why are they telling us what to do?"

"They're just new," Lon invented. "They have to learn how we do things here. They'll figure it out."

"Can we go riding tomorrow as we planned?"

"I'm not sure." Lon smiled at Alyssa and winked. "We might have to wait until they do learn."

She smiled and winked back. Then she leaned close, her blonde head beside his dark one, and whispered, "I hope they get better soon."

But his eyes, gazing at his mother over her head, were not reassuring. "Father is ill," he mouthed. When Alyssa went back to her books, he said to his mother, "They want me to sign documents for father. He's too ill." Both of them understood what that meant. If Lon refused to cooperate, his family would be killed. If he cooperated too well, when they no longer needed his signature, his royal authority, he and his family would also be killed. He could only hope to buy them a little time.

The guards were returning. "Try to reach Karis." His mother's words were so low Lon almost missed them as he hugged her goodbye.

There was no time for anything more. Lon was taken away, Alyssa shaking her head at the bad manners of these new guards.

Lon paced all day, waiting for an opportunity to try the old passageways he and Karis had discovered when they were about ten. The passages ran throughout Heath Halls, allowing those within to go almost where they wished. They had never been used in his father's lifetime, but he and Karis had played in them as children. There were rotted boards here and there, and if memory served him, in a section or two the passages were blocked. Pity his mother had not known about them; perhaps she and Alyssa might have been able to escape. Perhaps they still might be used for that purpose.

The passageways had been narrow and dark, as well as dirty and in poor repair. When the darkness of the black mage increased, Karis could no longer bear to enter them. So no one had used them or even been in them the last eight years.

Lon waited until full dark, then walked quietly to his door and listened. Hearing nothing, he crept noiselessly to the closet between his bedroom and the study. How had they opened the passageway? His hand traveled the smooth surface of the wall, searching.

So intent was he that he almost missed the noise of the guards approaching the door. Realizing they'd be doing a bed check, he scrambled across the room and dove between the covers. Why were they returning? He had thought they would leave him in peace until morning, but no. They actually entered his room to make sure he was there.

Throughout that night, the guards came at odd hours, making sure he had not left. They must have heard rumors about the passageways, he thought. Exploring the passageways would have to wait until Tallon's men were more sure of themselves.

He tried to reach Karis, but could not. Karis was just too far away for him.

The next morning, they dragged Lon down to begin his official duties and sign papers. "I will need the seal of the king," he told them.

"And where is it?" Tallon demanded.

"Only the king knew, and his steward. You could ask him." Lon stared into Tallon's eyes.

They were black with rage. So the steward they had removed and replaced with their impostor had come back to haunt them.

They returned Lon to his rooms while they searched. But the seal was not easily found.

Lon took advantage of the focus on the king's rooms over the next few days to search out the passageways, electing to do it in the early hours of daylight, when no one was about and any light he carried would not be noticeable. Starting in his closet, he opened the panel by twisting a section of the wainscoting to reveal a small knob that turned.

He followed the labyrinth of narrow halls connecting one room to the next, all inside the walls. Most of the passageways ran along the outer walls and Lon had to stoop to get through. He wondered how a man the size of his father would fare. He stepped slowly, carefully, knowing any sound could be heard and give him away.

His first foray was to his father's room, but guards were there and he didn't dare emerge. He listened in the passageway, but could hear nothing. His second was to the queen's rooms. He timed his visit so that Alyssa would be sleeping and only the queen would be awake.

Once again he had to move slowly, avoiding creaking floorboards and actual holes in the floor, watching for splinters and nails protruding from the walls. In the passage outside his mother's sitting room he waited for a long time. He could hear the guards speaking and he wasn't quite sure where the sound was coming from. Finally they moved away, and he slid the wood panel aside and slipped into the room, closing it behind him.

His mother's quick intake of breath let him know she was startled, then she smiled. "The old passageways. Do they still work?"

"Yours does," he smiled, brushing the dust and cobwebs from his clothes. "They haven't been cleaned in a long time, though." He added, "They're not watching me as closely. They search for Father's great seal. Do you have it?"

His mother shook her head. "The last I saw of it was before he left for Ithyl. He was using it in his study, but I don't think it's there now. I think he left it with Mithrond."

"Then they might never find it, unless Mithrond is alive and well somewhere." They were both silent a moment, heavy with thoughts of their friend and steward.

"The guards came and asked me where it was, but I truly didn't know."

"I told them only Mithrond would know. Tallon's eyes changed when I told him; they went black. I don't think Mithrond is available for questioning. He was the only one, other than the king, who would ever use it."

The visit was heartening for them both, but Lon dared not stay long. In the next few days he traveled through the passages, one at a time, finding where they led, and if they were still functional.

Pushed for time, he also searched in the late afternoon, when the halls were less active than they were in mid-morning. Enough daylight filtered through the cracks in the walls that he could find his way. He also began to search at night. He was nervous that those in the rooms might see the light he carried and become suspicious, but time was running out.

Last on his list, Lon checked the passageways in the rooms taken over by Tallon. Perhaps he could pick up information, or even help his family escape. He passed through with no problems until he came to the section that opened into the study. Before him was a large enough hole in the second story floor that he could not step across. Jumping was out of the question. The floor wood was weak, and he might crash through. In any case, the noise would alert the guards. He would have to exit the passageway and enter the study itself, then cross the room, use the regular door into the hall and into the library beside it to enter the last section of the passageway.

He found himself trapped. The study became occupied while he was beyond it, and he could not return. What if the guards checked on him? He was so agitated that he almost missed the conversation happening just outside the passage walls. He was not sure what finally caught his attention, but something did. Words trickled into his mind and snapped him fully awake and focused on the conversation.

"They're going to be sent to Esfalia, as soon as the extra guard unit comes. Tallon says it's too much work to guard them all."

"Who's going to be sent?"

"The queen and the child. For their safety, you know, what with the king being so ill, and all."

"Safety." The two guards laughed. "There's safety and then there's safety."

"They planning a little reception? Near the woods where the king got his?"

"Could be. A nice, special reception." As the men left, Lon was already slipping through the passage to the study and back into the passage on the other side. A few minutes later he was in his rooms, listening to the guards pacing the corridor outside. He breathed easier. Obviously they had not checked and discovered his absence, or there would be a hue and cry going on while they searched for him.

He climbed into his bed and tried to calm himself, reaching out again for Karis with his mind. He knew he was too far away, but he had to try. If he waited for Karis to reach him, it could be too late. He lay there in the darkness, the guard's boots on the hall floor a background, his heart drumming with urgency.

"Karis." He focused all his thoughts on his brother, his face as he had last seen him, flushed by his hopes and his fears. "Karis." Nothing. Why hadn't he asked Karis to teach him a little magic? In case it was ever needed? Finally he fell asleep, to be awakened by the guards the next morning.

They took him down to see his father, twisting in fever and pain, his features sharp and thin under translucent skin. "He refuses to eat," one guard told him, mockingly. And Lon understood they were not feeding the king. "Just takes a bit of water now and then, and of course his 'medicine'."

Lon reached out a hand to touch his father and they jerked him away. "Come on, now. You've work to do." With a mocking laugh they took him to the audience hall.

There were several men of the kingdom there, for the king would meet with any who needed him on certain days of the week. They had come and been turned away, and returned. Their anxious faces relaxed a little as they saw Lon, for all trusted him. He greeted them, then went into the small chamber where they would meet with him one on one, in the presence of Tallon, of course. Lon's thoughts were bitter. They would give him no opportunity to reach out for help.

He heard his people's concerns. He had often assisted his father, and besides, he had taken time to get to know their people, especially the common folk. As he said to his father, we get to know the nobles, but unless we make the effort, those really working in the kingdom are bypassed. He had studied the families and their genealogy; he had spent time watching how they spent their days, and what it meant to the kingdom. He could tell the working men how to better run their farms and make them more productive.

His greatest ability, however, was that he could truly read the hearts of those who came before him. Those that were just angry or greedy, he laughed with, helping them find themselves again, seeing their neighbor's perspective. Those in sorrow or need he reached out to and gave them advice or aid before he sent them on their way. As they left, Tallon gazed at him with grudging admiration. "Well done, for a spoiled king's son."

The guards returned Lon to his rooms, to lunch and rest before being taken again to the audience hall. He could tell Tallon was planning an alternative to the great seal, perhaps creating their version of it. He had to reach Karis soon if there was any chance of escape. Lon could perhaps get them out of Heath Halls through the passageways, but they needed help to reach safety, which was miles south of them in Godsel.

And soon, tomorrow or the next day or the next, they would come for him to sign their documents. After the signing, how much longer would Tallon have need of him? He tried to focus on Karis, but he kept seeing his father's wasted face, the now pale waiting faces of his mother and sister. He had to get through. He had to. But two hours after he was returned to his room for the night, he still had not managed it.

As he prepared for bed, he remembered his mother. She, too, had gifts, though not as strong and controlled as those of Karis. Perhaps she could help. Before the thought was fully formed, he was in the passage and on his way to her rooms. He found her sitting in the dark, her face white against her black hair, the pale moonlight sifting down from a high narrow window above her. She was rocking back and forth, staring at the wall before her. Alyssa was asleep; only the tread of the guards could be heard outside in the corridor.

The queen started as he emerged from the passage, a shadow moving among the shadows of her room. Lon caught her arm, then slid to her hand. In silence, he showed her again how to access the passages, how to find and turn the knob.

She might need them soon.

"How is your father?" Her low whisper barely reached his ears, and certainly would not carry to the guards outside.

"Ill." Lon didn't say how ill. The queen could do nothing and worry would not help.

"They poison him." Her tone was flat, matter of fact.

Lon nodded, then moved quickly to his reason for being there. "How can I reach Karis? I've tried, but he's just too far away."

The queen thought a moment, then lifted a long chain from around her neck with a green stone on the end and placed it over Lon's head. "This will help. Your reach will be longer."

There was a soft cry from the bed. Instantly the queen was beside Alyssa, her hands smoothing back the silky blonde strands from her face, her voice speaking reassuringly. "Sleep, my child. Sleep."

When the child was silent and sleeping once more, she lifted her face to Lon. "Alyssa seems not to know of our peril, but at night she dreams dire things."

"What things?"

"When she wakes, she does not remember. But she cries out often in her sleep. And she wakes already worn and pensive before the day really begins."

Lon reached out and touched Alyssa's hand. "It is sad when men make war on children."

"Indeed," his mother continued. "If we were both to try and reach Karis at the same time, your efforts might be stronger."

"I dare not stay to try to do it together. But I will try as soon as I return to my room."

Lon stood and gazed at his little sister, hugged his mother, and was gone. He would try once more to reach Karis, and this time it just had to work.

7
Winter Ride

It was night a full ten days later when Karis and Malin came to a halt on the outskirts of Mythro. Their horses were worn and trembling with cold and fatigue. Karis' dark eyes burned with a desperate energy that kept his body going long after it should have dropped. So great was his sense of urgency, of time running out for his family, they had ridden through a great winter storm, up through the wilderness of the forest road, with a minimum of provisions and clothing.

Malin sat his horse, tired but relaxed, his clear eyes alert. In the first few days, he wondered why he had come. He soon had an answer to that question. Karis would never have made it. Sheer force of will could not have done it, nor magic. Karis lacked the wilderness skills for survival.

As they traveled north the weather became colder, the storms more bitter. Without the help of both Rilse and Malin in finding food and shelter and keeping them on the trail, the journey would have ended in disaster within the first few days. Malin wondered if Karis knew that, but it didn't really matter. His cousin needed him.

Rilse caught his mood and agreed. *We do good work. We are here very soon. And we still live.*

Malin laughed. We are here very soon. *Usually this trip takes much longer. With your help we have found food and shelter, and yes, we still live. The forest has been good to us.*

We are good to us.

Malin smiled at Rilse's matter-of-factness.

The horses stood uneasily in the deep snow, their breath curling white from their nostrils. In spite of the length of the ride and the fierce pace pushed on them by their riders, the horses were restive and on guard. Malin and Karis dismounted, catching the reins close to the horses' heads to avoid any harness noise.

Karis took the lead, his black hair frosted where it showed under the edges of his cap, his booted feet silent in the powder of snow. Even the horses could hardly be heard as they left the main trail to take a smaller one branching right that would skirt the town of Mythro on the south. They went single file now, the white woods reaching out to them on either side as they threaded their way carefully, avoiding branches, leaving the mounds of new snow lying along them almost untouched.

Rilse left them and went deeper into the woods on the left. *Stay in reach,* Malin sent after him. He knew they would need Rilse.

I'm here. Looking out for you.

Cheeky creature, Malin teased. But they could not have done it without Rilse. Briefly he worried about Basil, but Basil could handle anything. He now knew his gifted cousin could not. How difficult to be driven to accomplish things you didn't have the skills for.

A quick smile of satisfaction touched Karis' face, lighting the darkness of his eyes for a moment. There it was, what he had been looking for. He stopped and Malin's eyes followed his pointing hand. Below them, through the thin screen of trees that remained, was their immediate stop, a cottage set in the hollow on the edge of the woods. Around it were several rough buildings that stabled horses and held feed. These were the holdings of Rast, huntsman and housemaster to Karis' father. If anyone outside of those in the Halls knew what was happening, it would be Rast, and his loyalty would never be in question.

As he stood there in the night, Karis thought wryly of the twists of fate. He wondered if he should ever have left Heath Halls, if whatever was happening to his family could have been prevented if he had remained here, even haunted by the black mage as he had been. A load of snow falling down his neck and the scraping of stirrups on tree bark brought Karis back to the present. "Ifs" were never very fruitful, he thought.

He spent a few moments listening, then, satisfied that all was well, he led them into the small meadow, hopefully hidden from all other eyes. When the horses would have whinnied a greeting to those within the stables, Malin kept them quiet.

The connection Malin had with animals was amazing, Karis mused. The red hound that sprang to meet them and lick Karis' hand did so in relative silence, with only a faint whine of welcome. In past days, even though he knew you, the hound would set up such a baying that the moon might blush. Not tonight, not with Malin along to hush him. No one in the cottage, let alone anyone in the surrounding area would know they had come.

It was also amazing to Karis that Malin had been willing to come along on this mad journey, in view of their rather rocky beginning. They had not started out as friends, though they were fast gaining a mutual respect for each other.

Rilse was far enough away to cause no consternation, noted Malin, which was good. If anything about this mad trip was good, he thought. He looked at Karis, unshaven, unwashed, with great hollow eyes from lack of sleep. He smiled wryly to himself, knowing he looked the same. Why, if they were lucky, in a few hours they would be permitted to do it all over again, in reverse.

The cottage itself was dark. And no light appeared while the two figures unfastened and removed the gear from their horses and rubbed them down, making sure they had fresh hay and drink from the central water trough in the horse yard, though they had to break the ice to do it. They left their horses in the warmth of the nearby stable. Still in silence, they crossed to the cottage itself.

Rilse.

I'm watching. No men out tonight. Only wolves.

Other wolves? Besides you?

Yes.

Are they friendly?

All are friendly to the gytrash. I'll check them out. But I'll be close when you need me.

Karis lifted the latch and pushed steadily at the door until it opened; he slipped inside and pulled Malin in behind him. Malin froze. There was a sound from within that sounded less than human. He listened as it came again. "What is that?" he whispered.

"That's Rast," Karis whispered back in relief. "Snoring. He is here. I was afraid he might be away." Karis moved toward the sound. "Rast," he hissed. "Rast."

A muffled voice answered. They had to strain to hear it. "Huh? What? Whosat?"

Malin stepped forward beside Karis. "Wonderfully expressive, isn't he?"

Karis' smile flashed out, as close to a grin as Malin had seen from him their whole journey. He actually didn't look too bad when he smiled, thought Malin.

They heard the thump of stockinged feet hitting the floor, and in the glow of the coals on the hearth, saw an old weathered, irate face, with a thatch of reddish hair on top of an incredibly long, skinny body.

"What's happenin'? What do you mean wakin' good folk in the middle of the night?" He towered over the two young men, and for a minute Malin thought he was going to cuff their ears for them.

"Come, where's your hospitality?" Karis stepped forward, closer to the glow cast by the fire. "Is this the way we greet visitors now?"

"Lon?" He looked closer. "Well, I'll be. Karis. There's no mistaking the sharp planes of thet face. And on a night like this. Thought you'd gone south. Get yourselves in and outta the cold." He bent over the table and soon the flare of a lamp lit the room. His shrewd old eyes took in the two, their faces red with cold, their unsteadiness from fatigue. "Set yourselves about the fire."

Karis did as Rast instructed, Malin followed, more slowly, carefully latching the door behind him, warily searching the corners, taking in the square table with its four chairs, the bed off in the alcove, empty now. Then, feeling the quiet confidence from Karis, he relaxed, realizing his gifted cousin would know if there was danger here.

"Hungry?" Rast read their expression correctly. It had been days since any warm food had entered their stomachs. "There's still a bit in the supper pot, might even be enough for two, with a warm drink to wash it down." He took out a round loaf, cutting two large hunks from it which he placed on the table. Thick slabs of cheese followed.

"You've journeyed up from Godsel," he guessed. "How long have you been on the road?"

"Ten days."

Rast sat and stared at Karis. "How many? I thought you said ten."

"I did. It seemed like forever, and if things go right, we'll soon do it all over again, only going the other direction." Karis' voice was suddenly grim. "And we'd better hope for ten on the way back as well."

Rast looked from Karis to Malin and back again. "That trip takes three weeks. In the summertime."

"Well, we were in a bit of a rush," Malin admitted.

"You'd better set. Here, at the table." Rast studied Karis. "King that ill? He took an arrow in the shoulder a while back, goin' to Esfalia, to council with Anor and Esfalia about the war, but twern't deep. He was able to ride a few days later. It should've healed just fine." Rast, quicker than Malin would have thought he could, placed dishes and utensils on the table, and a pot of barley drink on the coals to heat.

"It isn't the wound."

"What then? Mithrond and the queen, Lon, they'd take good care of the king. And the kingdom." Rast turned shrewd eyes on the two young men. "Haven't heard anything since we returned, but if there was trouble, Mithrond would've sent word."

"Who's Mithrond?" Malin was trying to keep things straight.

"The king's oldest and most trusted advisor. He's been steward as long as I can remember. The soul of honor," Karis informed him. Then he turned back to Rast. "You've heard nothing? No rumors of trouble in the Halls?"

Rast rubbed the top of his head, patting down the hair sticking out at strange angles. "Nothing." He thought a moment. "The old guard are on furlough. They did double duty while we were gone. I did hear new troops came in, from Anor. Mithrond sent most of our regular guard north." Rast stopped suddenly, realizing how strange that sounded. Why had he not realized it before?

Karis understood. "I see. Mithrond sent most of our troops north, after a supposed message from Areth. Then two days later, a full company from Anor enters the city and takes charge."

"From Areth, whom we hadn't heard from in almost a year." Things were becoming clear to Rast.

Karis continued. "Because it was Mithrond, no one questioned what was happening."

"Someone should have," Malin added, thinking of his father's garrisons. Not one of his troops or retainers would have stirred a foot without his father's direct orders.

"So you're thinking someone sent them away on some tomfool trumped-up errand, so the troops from Anor could just take over. What about Mithrond?"

"Well, if Mithrond was out of the way, Anor would be running things."

"But I saw Mithrond—he gave us our furlough."

"All of your guard went to their homes?"

"Yeah. I just live closer than most. Some of the queen's servants too, I hear. Maddie, the queen's maid, stopped to visit on her way home."

"The Hall's servants?" Karis couldn't quite seem to grasp the situation.

"Yessir." Rast's voice was firm. "It sounds funny, but Mithrond would've sent word if things weren't all right."

"Unless he couldn't."

"Couldn't?"

"Couldn't. If he had been replaced—." Karis didn't finish his thought.

"You mean removed and killed. That's what it would take. Mithrond would have to be dead to fail in his duty." Rast didn't mince words.

"Exactly."

"Who?"

"Who came with the troops?"

"Tallon, Duke Blandor's man."

"So. The boy king's regent is getting hungry."

Karis continued. "I was hoping there would be some friendly soul still in the Halls. It would make our work easier."

"They hatch a plot?" Rast studied Karis.

"My family are prisoners in Heath Halls, my father is being poisoned. Mithrond is gone."

A gust of wind caught the door and rattled the latch. Rast secured it, went to the fire and brought out the kettle, pouring drinks into the old tin cups.

Karis continued as if to himself. "So then only the new steward and his men keep the Halls, but Anor is supposedly our ally. It doesn't make sense." He dropped his hands in frustration on the table. "But no matter how or why, my father is dying, and the rest of my family is in great danger."

The old man's eyes were bright. "Poison, you say?"

"I think so."

"So it's a rescue. Where will you take them? If all the troops belong to the enemy, there's no safe place here."

"Exactly. We go south." Karis and Malin had covered all the possibilities on the long ride up.

"Is Areth still at the front?"

"As far as we know."

"So the enemy uses his name. I just hope someone from his own troops doesn't cut him down from behind."

Karis paused a moment, remembering his older brother as he had last seen him two years ago. Areth had clapped him on the shoulder as he rode off with the forces to the northeast, to stop the warlords there. He could still see Areth, his hair bright in the sunlight and his eyes, gray as the water of the seas in a storm, narrowed with purpose.

Rast spoke again, half to himself, as he crossed to the hearth and stirred up the fire. "A fine mess it is, when a king's not safe in his own castle, so to speak." Then he grinned, his eyes sparkling and his sleep-tousled hair an unruly halo atop the long, thin body. "What is the plan? For if I know anything Karis, my boy, you've a plan."

The simple meal over, Rast removed the bowls and cups, the utensils, and wiped off the table. He found some paper and Karis went to work, showing Malin the layout of the Halls.

"Here are the abbey ruins I told you about, just below the Halls. I tried to send Lon a message that I would come there, but I don't know if he got it. Here's where the tunnel emerges from the secret passages. Too bad an earth fall has blocked it. We can use the passages in the house, however, which will make our task easier." In his mind he added, "possible."

"Are the hidden ways keyed to open by magic, like the one at Oldsbury?" Malin tried to quell the queasy feeling that hit the pit of his stomach at the thought.

"No. Just hidden ways made by the carpenters as they built the walls. Pressure in the right place opens and closes the panels as well as the outer sections of brickwork. But it's old and has not been kept in good repair. Until this war started, there seemed no need."

"Pity we can't go in that way." Malin said, deliberately keeping his tone light. "We'd be much less likely to be caught."

"Well, if we're lucky, we'll at least have access to the passages through this end of the halls, at the southeast corner. There's a stand of trees close by, and the servant's entrances are there." Karis didn't mention the possibility of guards being thick about, but it was in all their minds.

"Sounds better to me than that drainpipe climb you mentioned to me on the way up. Wonder if there are some passages at Roswood. Aunt Aila would be quite miffed if we were to find them and she had never known they were there."

Rast stared at Malin and shook his head. Malin was too much for him.

"Rast. Do you still have that old mail carriage that used to go between Godsel and Mythro?"

"Sure. The old carriage is in running shape, though for how long I can't say. She's in the last shed."

"And horses? At least six?"

"Horses I have, but not as many as before. The war's taken most of 'em. I have my old gray, and your mother's and sister's ponies. Then there's the two matched browns I was sending to old Duke Astor next week to replace his that were stolen. They could pull the carriage. Then there's two others you and Malin could use."

"We want the carriage for the king. He's too ill to ride, and the mail carriage will not be noticed as much as another. Tell me," Karis' eyes were almost black in their intensity, "Will you drive the mail carriage south with the king? Past the watch point and down the coast road?"

"Will I," Rast chortled. "You just bet I will." He had stacked everything in the empty stew pot which he took and set beside the hearth to be washed later. "Haven't had no fun fer a while now."

"Lon'll ride with you and care for the king. The rest of us will take the forest road."

"That'll be hard. The ponies aren't too fast."

Malin's heart misgave him as he heard the plans. Ponies? Women on ponies? They'd never get out of Heath Halls.

"My old gray and your horses can fend for themselves until I return, or someone comes," Rast went on. "There's plenty of hay and water in the yard, and I'll leave the outer stable door open for them, for warmth. The browns are pretty fair horses. They should give anyone trying to follow a good run for their money. And I have a couple of others that should work for you two."

He looked at Karis, whose eyes were closing in spite of his efforts to stay awake and alert. "But you need sleep. You rest here for the remainder of the night and during daylight hours tomorrow. We'll work on getting into the Halls tomorrow night."

Karis jerked himself awake. "There's no time, Rast. We go tonight. Pray we're not too late."

Rast opened his mouth to demand more information, looked at Karis' face, and shut it again. Then he went to work.

Out of a bin he took two sacks and several small loaves of bread and a great chunk of cheese which he broke in two. He placed half the food in one sack and handed it to Karis, the rest went into his own. Two small bags of roasted barley followed.

"Provisions for the journey." He chuckled. "You might see into the future, Karis, but you were never very practical." Malin had to agree.

Karis grinned at Malin. "True, but Malin, here, is pretty fair. He even left messages, so we hope help will be already on its way north."

"Messages?" Rast was appalled. "You didn't tell people directly?"

Karis reddened. "We were in a hurry and had to go. We're still in a hurry."

Rast shrugged. "Better hope they got them. Sounds like lives may depend on that." Before they left the cottage, Rast pulled a great warm coat off a peg and wrapped himself in it. Then he looked at Malin, in his Godsel jacket, suitable only for the south. Karis' coat was thick and warm, but Malin's was woefully lacking. "You come all the way in that?"

Malin shrugged. "We rode fast."

Rast was appalled. And Karis saw for the first time the inadequacy of Malin's winter attire and flushed.

Malin caught his look. "I have warm sweaters under it."

Rast went to a chest and pulled out another coat. "Used to belong to a friend of mine. Here, put it on. It should fit you."

Malin changed, putting his jacket into the chest, a broad grin on his face. "This will be great."

On a sudden impulse, Rast grabbed an old pair of trousers and another jacket from the chest, as well as an old blanket. "Can't tell. Might need 'em," he answered to Malin's questioning look. Then they were out the door.

"Wind's rising in the east," Rast noted. "'Twill be a rare cold night."

Malin nodded in agreement. "Another storm's on its way."

"A storm?" Rast questioned.

"Heavy winds, dumping snow. We've about an hour or so," Malin explained.

Rast scrutinized Malin. Karis saw his look and answered it. "He just knows."

Rast looked at them. "Two with gifts, eh?"

"That's nothing. Wait 'til you meet his wolf."

"His wolf?" Rast was incredulous. "No one owns a wolf."

"I don't own him. He just—."

"Comes when you call and does what you ask, and sometimes does things for us that you don't ask." Karis was getting back some of his own.

Malin was embarrassed. "No one owns Rilse," he mumbled.

"Rilse? You've named him?" Rast was unbelieving. "You're sure it's a wolf?"

"It's a wolf," Karis asserted. Then to Malin he added, "Is the way to the Halls clear? Is it safe to ride? Ask Rilse."

"Ask him?" Rast was incredulous. "Ask a wolf?"

Malin reached out to Rilse, the tips of his ears red. *Anyone about?*

No riders out. No walkers either. Just wolves. They won't bother you.

"All clear," Malin reported back. The others had a hard time hearing the words. Malin was not comfortable performing in his new position.

At his words, they headed for the horses and carriage. Rast deposited the clothing in the carriage, beside the mound of old mail sacks. He held one up for Karis to see. "There's plenty of them still here. They're empty, of course."

"Is there something we can stuff them with?"

"Straw. I've plenty of that just inside the barn." Together the three of them stuffed a goodly number of mail sacks with straw. "We'll have to hope that no one looks very closely at our letters." Rast grinned as he spoke. "Ready?"

Karis grinned back. "Ready."

The matched browns were skittish about the night's activities until Malin calmed them. Even Rast, their owner and breeder, stepped back out of the way to watch and commented to Karis, "He has a rare way with them, doesn't he?"

Karis nodded, a sudden grin on his face, as a feeling of family pride in Malin touched him. Rast muttered to himself. "A wolf. I'll be jiggered."

Behind them, Karis' and Malin's horses whinnied. They were protesting being left. Malin hesitated.

"They're great horses." Behind him, Rast's voice grated against the wind. "But they're already tired. If we have to make a run for it——." Rast didn't finish. They all got the message. "Say. If the stars like you, Karis, you might find your old black in the Hall's stables. Your mother couldn't bear to part with him."

They hitched the browns to the carriage, Rast driving. Malin and Karis mounted up, leading the rest of the horses, and sped by the cold. It was not a night to stand and savor the weather. The carriage creaked as it rolled on its way. Just past the hollow where Rast's cottage sat, they picked up a wider trail that had been used to send horses back and forth to the Halls. Soon, the ruins of the old abbey loomed ahead, a darkness in the white world about them.

They slowed their horses to a walk, guiding them carefully into concealment and shelter in the lee of its walls. Ahead of them, on the crest of the hill, were the Halls.

Rilse?

Here. Where the wind brings me your smell. I'm close.

The abbey ruins proved empty and Karis' heart sank. He had not realized how much he had hoped he might find Lon there. His twin was not great at sending and even poorer at receiving over long distances. He probably had not received Karis' message. Even if he had, he probably did not have the freedom to reach the ruins. He dismounted in the shelter of the walls. "We'll go on foot from here."

Rast nodded at Karis' words. "Do you think we need to leave someone with the horses?"

Karis hesitated. They would need all three of them to help the captives escape their captors, but it would do no good if their horses were not waiting there for them when they returned. So many lives depended on him. What if he chose wrong?

Behind him, Malin spoke up. "Rilse will watch them."

Rast snorted in disbelief. "A wolf? Guarding horses?"

"This wolf will, Rast."

Karis nodded, relieved.

Malin pulled the horses as close to the old abbey walls as he could, both for protection from the storm and to keep them hidden; he secured them to a few saplings growing beside the tumbled walls.

Close by a wolf howled.

Rast couldn't help himself. He turned to Malin. "Yours?"

"Not mine," Malin said flatly. "But it is Rilse."

"Let's go," Karis urged. Before them the north wind was rising sharply, and snow had started to fall. They were facing full into a winter blizzard, now, not just into a southern storm.

And who knew what else awaited them in the halls? Malin thought, as they trudged forward. The wind and snow were really the least of their worries.

8
Enemy in the Halls

As he listened to Rilse howl behind him, Malin felt himself relax. The horses would be watched. They could depend on the white wolf, and the black one if it came to that.

Any guards about? Malin asked Rilse.

No, no humans. They don't like the cold. Rilse sounded contemptuous. *Just wolves.*

"Rilse says no humans are about in the night."

"Only we are dumb enough for that," Karis said. Then his grin flashed out. "Only we."

"And the wolves," Malin added.

Because we're dumb? Only humans can't take care of themselves in the cold. Only humans.

"Will they harm the horses?" Rast was concerned.

"No. They've fed recently, and they run with the storm. But I sense something else." The others waited for Malin to continue, but he stopped, then shrugged. "Maybe not." *The gytrash, Rilse. I almost feel the gytrash.*

Strange. After I met with the wolves, I went back to the white wolf. I was only the gytrash for a few moments.

"There may be dogs." Rast cleared his throat. "Some came last week, with the new troops. I've not seen them, but it's rumored they're dogs trained to kill an enemy."

"That would be us," Karis said soberly. "They may be penned up for the night. The storm is fierce enough to keep anyone inside."

Malin reached out around the Halls, checking for animals. He found small creatures, the horses and animals in the barns and stables, their horses in the ruins, and Rilse, but nothing else he recognized, except the madness of the gytrash, in several locations.

There's something, Rilse. Something like the gytrash and there's more than one.

I will watch.

"Rilse says he will watch."

Karis wasted no time questioning Malin. Their journey north had given him tremendous respect for his cousin who, ironically, hated magic. He took a deep breath, and into the storm they went, up the hill and toward the Halls. The wind whipped at their clothing; snow stung their faces. Twice more they heard a wolf howl, but by the time they reached the southeast corner of the Halls, there was no further sound, only wind roaring through eaves, shaking windows.

Malin and Rast stopped and waited for Karis to take the lead. Karis longed to attempt to mind reach Lon, or the queen, but that would drain him of energy that might be needed later on. Besides, he might connect with Lon and distract him at a crucial moment, perhaps a fatal one.

He was also reluctant to announce his presence by using his magic until he had to, just in case. The queen had intuitions sometimes, though they were never under her control. Perhaps she would know they were there. But they could not afford to wait until that happened.

Below them, Malin felt their horses turn into the wind, where their manes would offer them some protection. He soothed them once more, just for luck, sensing Rilse upwind of them, close by. The wind was rising and would continue to increase, Malin noted. At least it would cover any noise they made, if it didn't freeze them first. He was glad for the warmer coat, the scarf around his neck and the collar up around that. His gloved hands were thrust deep into his pockets for extra warmth.

Karis searched the brickwork for the entrance to the secret passage. It had been seven or eight years since he had been in that way, and who knew if it still worked. He tried several places, without success. In the dark and the storm, he couldn't tell if he had the right place and it no longer worked, or if he was in the wrong place. He grew more tense and worried, if that were possible. They had to find it. The drainpipe was too open and climbing icy walls and pipes could injure them before they even found his family.

He bit his lip and tried again, going over the same sections more carefully, moving several feet beyond where he had tried in the first place, but though he pressed and pried and mumbled imprecations at walls in general, nothing worked; time and cold were working against him. His hands became stiff and numb. Beside him, Rast and Malin stamped their feet to keep circulation going. Karis thought regretfully of the secret passages, then stood away from the walls.

"The drainpipe it is," he told them. They followed him around the side to the northeast edge of the building, hugging the walls as they went, for they could not risk running into any guards so close to their goal. Rilse and the horses were now quite a distance away. The cousins and Rast ducked below any windows, not wishing to be seen even as shadows moving against the storm. The wind was strong and increasing in fury.

In this way they reached the north side of the hall where Lon and Karis had their rooms on the second floor. Karis hoped Lon was still there, but if Lon were imprisoned elsewhere, he hoped his rooms were empty, since this seemed to be their only option. Karis thought briefly about his medallion, sure it would not work so far away from Tegyn, its power source. He led the way to the drainpipe.

A flimsy ladder, Malin thought, if he ever saw one. It might hold Karis. It might even hold Rast. But he was afraid it would break loose under his weight.

Karis started up, his booted feet and gloved hands scrabbling for purchase against the cold brick and icy metal. Below, Malin scrutinized the pipe carefully, watched it shift and strain under Karis' weight, but it held. Karis was level with the second floor windows now. His feet found the ornamental bricks that protruded from the wall, his hands clutched the frame work around the windows. He released the pipe, and Malin watched him tug on the first window. It didn't move. Again Karis pushed. He didn't dare exert too much pressure because he would lose his balance.

Both Rast and Malin had their eyes fixed on Karis. They didn't see the form that launched itself out of the storm upon Rast, aiming for his throat. They heard only one snarl before it closed with the woodsman. Instinctively, Rast thrust up his arm to protect himself. He felt the fangs of the creature fasten on his arm and the flesh of his forearm tear. Above them, Karis felt the commotion and looked down, losing his grasp upon the upper frame of the window. Desperately he lunged for the drainpipe, feeling it sway dangerously beneath his hands.

Malin felt for the mind of the creature, but there was only a red fog there, a madness and a desire to rend and slay whatever it came across. Men had made their own gytrash out of dogs. Only torment and abuse could have done it. Malin could find no way to connect with such a beast, and he withdrew, shaken and sick. The creature was savaging Rast. Malin drew his knife; one stab and it was over.

Karis clung to the drainpipe. Rast stood, shaken, clutching his arm. Malin stepped back from the body of the dog that had attacked them. Were there more of them? Malin reached out, now knowing what he was looking for.

He had to warn Rilse. He paused, gathering his thoughts and aiming them in what he hoped was the right direction.

Rilse.

A very faint *Here* came in answer.

Malin gave his warning. *Dogs about, gytrash dogs. Rast is wounded. Can you help him back to the horses? And guard them all?*

Yes.

"Rilse is coming to take you back to the carriage. Do you have something to bandage that arm?"

"In the carriage." The wind had risen and it was almost impossible to hear.

"Go." Malin nudged him back the way they had come. Rast understood. He could no longer help where they were and the carriage and horses could use more protection. He plodded back into the storm.

Grimly, Malin looked at the figure of Karis above him, releasing the pipe and trying once more to open the window. Karis couldn't do this alone. His father was too ill to walk, and Karis too slight to carry him. King Arnon was built more like Malin himself. Once more Karis tried the window. Again and again he pushed against it, to no avail.

Malin sighed, circled the pipe with his hands and started up. It looked like Karis would need his help to even get the window open. The cold weather had tightened it.

Suddenly, Malin was aware of red fog once more; one of the dogs must be near. He lunged upward, trying to climb above the reach of the dog before it could get to him. He hoped the drainpipe would hold. He had not yet reached safety when the dog sprang upward, throwing its weight against the drainpipe. Malin felt the pipe shift, straining against its fastenings. Three times the dog leaped. Malin felt its teeth graze his boot.

To the side of Malin, frozen in place, Karis clutched the window frame, resisting the impulse to see what was happening, realizing if he lost his balance and had to clutch the pipe, it would probably come away. There was no way it would hold both their weights. And then they would all be at risk.

Malin heard a wolf snarl. Rilse was below, the gytrash Rilse, with the huge black body and the red eyes. A quick snap, and the red haze faded from Malin's mind. He scrambled up the pipe until he too clutched the frame.

Thanks, Rilse. Rast all right?

Down here with me.

With the gytrash, Rilse?

The gytrash is shifting. Rast may have seen that.

The horses?

Wolves guard them. From a distance, he hastened to add, as he felt Malin's objections forming. *And only while I'm here. They're not hungry,* he assured Malin. *The man and I will return and wait there until we are needed.*

Karis looked down at Rast. He remembered that Rast's rheumatics, as he called them, always kicked in when the weather was colder. Now he was wounded as well, and their adventure had just begun.

Karis looked across to Malin. He knew in his bones that if they were caught, the royal family would not live long enough to see any help that came out of Godsel. But they had to try.

Rast followed the wolf down toward the old abbey, the wolf that changed shape and color. He shook his head. The wound must be giving me more trouble than I know, he thought. Getting delirious already. The wind wailed and moaned. He pulled his fur-lined leather cap close about his face, the flaps down over his ears, and angled into it, leaning as he went.

He followed Rilse down the hill and into the carriage. He shredded an old mail sack, bandaged his arm, and settled himself to wait, eyeing Rilse through the window. It took some getting used to, he thought, walking and talking with wolves, wolves that changed shape and form. Wolves that were more like dogs, and dogs that were more like wolves.

Back on the walls, Karis and Malin worked together to force open the window. In the Halls themselves, no lights or movement could be seen, no sound except the wailing of the wind. When the window suddenly gave and swung open, both grasped the frame tightly to keep their balance. Then one after the other they tumbled into the room and shut the window before the rush of air could alert anyone to their presence.

Karis leaned against the wall before him, trying to focus. He was grateful for the stone that grated against him and for the cold that cleared his head. Lon's rooms felt empty. Karis hesitated a moment, wondering if Lon had been moved and was under guard somewhere. No. The rooms still held only Lon's presence, not that of anyone else. The rooms were also well placed. From them he and Malin could reach both the king's and queen's rooms, and if they were not there, scour the place room by room, if need be, to find Alyssa and Lon.

The two cousins were grateful for the shelter of the small study they were in. Karis walked quickly into the bedroom, Lon's bedroom. Malin lingered behind him in the doorway. A tramping of feet in the corridor made both of them freeze in place. Then Malin dodged back through the doorway into the study.

Karis mind read. An inner watch and bed check, for Lon. He could scarcely believe it. In a few seconds the guard would march into the room to make sure Lon was there, and Lon wasn't.

Well, if it was Lon they had come to see, then they should see him. Karis hoped there was no snow visible on him or on the floor. At least, he thought with satisfaction, the window was shut. He had just enough time to yank off his cap, climb into bed and pull up the covers before the guards were there. The door was shoved open without even the ceremony of a knock. Karis was jarred.

What had happened to bring such things to pass? Lon was a prisoner in the halls ruled by his family since the dawn of that age, now subject to such disrespect.

He had no time for further thoughts, except to hope that Malin had enough sense to be quiet and stay out of sight. A rough hand grasped his shoulder and shook him.

"Eh, he's real right enough. If he was making the dogs jumpy, there's no way he could beat us back here."

"Are you sure it's him?"

Karis' head was raised and yanked into the pool of light that spilled through the open door and onto the pillow.

"It's him. Couldn't mistake those black eyes and hair."

By now Karis felt a word or two was in order. "What's wrong? What's happened?"

"Nothing you need worry about. Nor any of your family for that matter." The rough hand holding Karis suddenly released him and he fell back on the bed. The man before him had been no retainer of his father's. His coarse features and manners would not have been permitted in his father's halls for one minute. So whose man was he? Who stood to gain?

The door closed behind the men, and almost immediately, Karis heard a soft click that came from neither Malin nor himself. He heard his cousin move toward the sound in the study. Malin's ears and reflexes were definitely keen, thought Karis, for even as he opened his mouth to speak, two figures struggled in the doorway.

"Malin, stop! Malin! It's Lon." Karis' sharp whisper reached the two, and sheepishly they pulled apart. "Lon, let me introduce you to your cousin, Malin."

"Lon. Of course it's Lon." Malin was chagrined.

"They've been and gone," Karis spoke, correctly interpreting Lon's apparent anxiety. "You were nestled all snug in your bed where you ought to have been." Lon's face was shadowed, but his relief was obvious, even to Malin, who did not know him.

"How did you know the guards were coming to check for me? Never mind. You and your magic." He grasped his twin's shoulders and gave a squeeze. "Father still lives and Mother and Alyssa are also in the Halls. Thanks to your timely appearance, no one is alerted and won't be until my next bed check, a full two hours from now. We have at least that much time."

Malin listened, amazed. Even their voices matched.

"Into the closet." Malin and Karis did as they were asked and went into the closet. Lon came behind them with a small lamp which he proceeded to light.

"I'm still useful to them. I have more legal papers yet to sign. They have taken longer than they planned to rework boundaries and ownership of the estates."

"Legal papers? When did would-be-assassins worry about papers?"

"These do. In case the king dies, which they will see happens, I am the acting head of state and my signature is needed to smooth the way. No one can contest the changes if my signature is on the deeds."

"And then?" Karis asked, already knowing the answer.

"Then I'm on my way to Achenshead, in Anor, supposedly to council. Mother and Alyssa are to go, too. They were to go earlier, to Esfalia, but the weather in the passes has delayed things. Now they go to Anor. We can guess what the enemy has planned."

"An ambush. And if you were to return, the king would be dead by the time you got here."

Lon gave a quiet smile. "I'd forgotten how it feels to have two minds work almost as one. Welcome back, twin." For a moment their hands clasped and their eyes met. Malin found himself feeling left out, wishing he had a brother.

Don't get greedy. Rilse's voice was very faint.

Malin smiled. *Anything moving?*

No.

"Who stands to gain?" Karis asked.

"As I've been listening through walls I have heard the name Duke Blandor, Anor's regent for their boy-king. The regent apparently has dealings with Turgor of the Northern Lords. In exchange for opening their kingdom to Turgor, for not opposing him, and for not aiding their long-time allies in the war, Blandor is to have Westra."

"Anor is not a possibility. The people of Anor would never countenance the deposing of little Edwin and would not allow his murderer to hold power," said Karis, thinking aloud.

"Exactly," Lon responded. "But Westra, now that would be enticing. Westra holds the seaports and the trading centers for the goods for both countries. Esfalia would be left alone to battle Turgor on three sides, with no allies. Tallon is here to secure Westra for Blandor, as well as lands and position for himself. With all the troops gone north, there is really no organized resistance to oppose him."

"Just us," Malin interposed.

Lon looked at Malin, startled for a moment by his comment.

Then a smile flashed across his face, so like the rare one or two Malin had seen from Karis. "Just us," he agreed.

"Was that you in the lower halls just now?"

Lon nodded. "That's how I get my information. I took the secret passage there, but the coming of Tallon, the current steward, startled me, and I shut the panel too loudly,

alerting the dogs. Naturally, their first thought was of me."
Lon suddenly grinned. "I have given them a spot of trouble,
you know: An open window and papers ruined by snow and
rain. A locked outside door swinging open. A mouse in the
stuffed duck. Little acts of unkindness, just to keep them on
their toes."

Karis' grin matched Lon's. "Well, let's give them a spot
more."

Then Lon added soberly. "You know Mithrond is
missing?"

"Yes. I understood that from our mind touch."

"They replaced him with one of their own. No one
knew." They were silent. "He was a great man."

Karis caught the past tense. "They went that far?"

Lon nodded. "Yes. I'm sure they did."

"So they'll stop at nothing," Karis said slowly. "No one
who happens to be in their way is safe. Let's remove their
prisoners and whisk them away as fast as we can. Are all the
old passageways still open?"

"Not all. I was almost trapped just now. The section
between the great study and the lower hall is blocked. The
connecting doors will not open. I had to leave the passage
in the study and re-enter through the library and was almost
caught by the guard. I barely made it, and as you saw, I didn't
make it in time. But the passage runs to the southeast corner
and will still open to the outside."

"I couldn't find where to open it, so we came around.
Is the passage to the queen's apartments still open?"

"Yes. She and Alyssa are there," Lon assured Karis.
"They're guarded. I don't know about a nightly bed check."

"And Father?" Karis could not help the lump that rose
unbidden in his throat as he thought of his father, king and
strategist, slowly dying of poison, brushed aside like so
much dust.

"In his own apartment, but he cannot walk. He does not even appear conscious. I think most of the time he doesn't know us, or what's happening to him." Lon dropped his head and fell silent.

Karis and Malin waited for him to continue, not willing to disturb him.

Lon cleared his throat and continued. "After we rescue the family, if we are able to accomplish all that—."

Karis interrupted. "We can't think 'if' only 'when.'"

"When, then, I have some papers to destroy. I wouldn't want to leave my autograph around."

They went to work. Karis and Malin and Lon disappeared into the dark through an open panel that closed behind them with a snick. Lon led the way to the queen's apartments. They hadn't gone far when they saw a faint light descending the narrow inner stairs; the queen and Alyssa were coming to meet them.

In the queen's hand was a clear stone that gave a pale glow. Both Alyssa and the queen were wrapped in warm coats and carried small bundles. "Karis. Thank the gods you've come." The queen's voice was breathy, audible to only those almost touching her.

Karis touched her arm and led the way. Then they were slowly, silently, threading their way through the passages. The queen's light was all they could risk, for the passage was old, and in some places cracks in the wall would reveal their presence. The storm's noise covered any they made.

The group picked their way carefully, circling round and finally ending on the bottom floor by the servant's quarters to the east, close to the stables, and facing the ruins. Karis found himself strangely content, even in such dangerous circumstances. He was home, with his family. The dark mage was nowhere around, and action was always a better companion than waiting.

Just before the outer door, they paused. Lon could not resist asking the question in all of their minds: "How long until your absence is discovered?"

The queen smiled and her face, still beautiful, was suddenly young again. "Tonight we shall not be bothered. In fact, we should not even be checked until late morning. Look!" She whispered. She pulled back Alyssa's hood from her face. It was swollen and blotchy.

"I have the mumps. I'm very contagious." Alyssa whispered, and smiled at Karis.

A small sound came from Lon, and Malin instinctively drew away, but Karis started to laugh, then clapped his hand over his mouth.

"Well done, Mother. Well done, I say." Her smile matched his. The others looked on, wondering.

"No, the pressures haven't unhinged our minds," Karis assured them. "It's an illusion. Great work, Mother."

Queen Gwynne shook her head. "Only occasionally and at great need will the power come, and then it comes in the form it wills, not at my bidding. Alyssa was clear until just before our last bed check. Then she became as you see her. They will not check again until the guard changes and someone new is on duty. That won't be until morning."

In the passageway the group pushed on silently, single file, until they stood at the end of the blocked passage, with Lon peering through a small crack.

Outside, the wind howled even louder, if that were possible.

"It looks clear. Mother, you go first." Lon slowly opened the passage door that let them into the study.

"No. Take Alyssa." Lon felt his mother beside him, rock solid and unmoving. She would not be persuaded and time was short. He took Alyssa's bundle and her arm and sped her across the study, to the hallway just outside, and into the empty library. Scant minutes later, Karis and his mother followed.

Then it was Malin's turn. He stepped out only to hear footsteps coming down the hallway. He retreated, closed the panel and waited. A late night guard, pacing the halls? The footsteps continued.

When he could no longer hear them, Malin once more opened the panel. At least he tried to. He was sure Karis had pushed just there. It took him long, precious minutes fumbling in the dark, before he got it open. He poked his head around and listened. Nothing. With a sigh of relief he closed the panel, slipped through the doorway and down the hall into the library. Lon had the panel open there, waiting for him.

As they reached the end of the passage, the queen gestured to Karis. "Are there outside guards?" she whispered.

Lon answered her. "There is no need. We are still prisoners as far as anyone knows."

"No guards, just the dogs," Malin added.

"That's right. The dogs. How did you get past them?"

"We managed." Karis grinned and looked full at Malin, as a wolf howled somewhere in the hills. He opened the passage, where Rast and Rilse waited outside. "You all right, Rast?"

"I'll be fine."

Malin had sent Rilse a call from the study.

"Mother, Rast will take you and Alyssa. Wait for us in the ruins."

The queen hugged him. "We'll wait. You can count on that."

Malin held Rast back a moment. "How's the arm?"

"It will mend just fine with only a scar or two."

They went to work. By the light of the queen's stone Karis showed Rast where to put pressure to open the passage. He took advantage of the moment to whisper, "Lon has some business to do. Malin and I will get Father. If we are not back in an hour, get Mother and Alyssa to Godsel." He didn't need to add that if they weren't back by then, they would not be coming. Tallon would have his hands on them.

Rast bobbed his head. Despite his injury, Karis knew he could rely on Rast. There was no further talk as Rast shepherded the queen and Alyssa, battling wind and snow, down to the carriage. The huntsman swiftly flung open the carriage doors and ushered the queen and Alyssa inside, climbed in after them and closed the doors, grateful for some shelter from the elements. When they were inside and seated, he draped a blanket over them. "There," he said. "We'll wait out of the weather."

Behind them at the halls, Karis and Lon held the passage open a little longer, watching until the three, followed by Rilse, disappeared into the darkness and the storm. Then they turned and the door clicked shut behind them, blocking out the wind that whistled around the walls. They had more work to do.

9
Illusions

"Lon, will there be more bed checks for you this night?" Karis whispered. Lon had to strain to hear over the two chimes of the clock in the servant's quarters.

"Two," said Lon. "At three and six. For the king, too."

"You're joking," Karis was astounded. "I thought he was so weak he could not go anywhere under his own power."

"Exactly. They use it as an excuse to mock us, to gloat over our weakness and their power."

"Pursuit organized as early as these watches would soon find us prisoners back in Heath Halls," Malin spoke aloud for all of them.

Karis smiled grimly. "I know. We'll create an illusion of both of them in their beds. That will buy us a little time."

"Two? You're daft." Malin could tell from Lon's face that he knew what that would cost Karis. "Two illusions in the same night, one right after another? When you're already exhausted? What are you thinking?"

Lon had seen Karis exhausted after one. Yet, what other choice was there? Wordlessly, Lon turned and began to lead them back the way they had come.

"Will Mithrond's impostor sense your use of magic? Does he have enough power to sense its presence?" Malin's question stopped them.

"I don't know. Usually, yes. With the medallion on, I don't know, though I also don't know if I can work with it on. I never have, but I suspect it only damps the field around me, not interferes with what I'm trying to do. Anyway, we have to try."

Malin agreed. They did have to try. They stopped at the study before separating out to their individual tasks.

"Be careful," Lon whispered.

"We will." Karis' reply was almost lost as the two parties separated.

Below them, downstairs in Mithrond's quarters, someone tossed restlessly in the bed, troubled by dark dreams. A bald head glistened in the pale light showing through the drapes. On the table beside the bed rested a wig. Mithrond had boasted a full head of hair, even at his age, and anyone replacing him had to have one. A uniform of the king's livery was dropped beside it. Since the man was now officially on furlough, "Mithrond" would have no need of it. The man lying there seemed oblivious to any activity around him. Apparently his magic did not extend that far.

Malin and Karis continued their journey back into the passage, around the curve, and up the narrow stairs to the second floor where the sick king lay, slowly wasting away. They moved in silence now. They could not risk being heard by the guards on the other side of the wall.

When they finally stood by the king's bedside, Karis found he was not prepared for what he saw. Even in the shadowed chamber, the king's face seemed thin and fragile, his form lost in the huge bed. The three weeks of "care" had done their work.

Karis reached out his hand and touched his father's face. It was damp and cold to the touch. He drew back the blankets, wrapped one around his father and lifted him up and into Malin's arms, amazed at the lightness of what had been a strong, solid man.

Malin answered Karis' questioning glance and nodded. "Yes, I can carry him," he mouthed.

"Take him to Rast."

Karis half-closed his eyes and tilted his head. Malin knew he was light-reading, listening with light to the placement of the guards. Then he spoke. "Now. The guards are gone on rounds. Careful of the library."

Malin hoped he remembered which room was the library. He shifted Karis' father, making sure the king was solid in his grasp. A thump in the walls would not be helpful at this point. "And you?" he asked Karis.

Karis' grin shot out. "Lon and King Arnon will be gone. Someone must fill their beds." Karis fairly pushed Malin into the passageway. Then he turned back to the bed and Malin, watching, saw him sag against it a moment, his face tense and pale, his body taut.

Then Karis straightened and sounds came from him—strange sounds, half chanted. His body seemed to grow, reaching upward. Around it gathered a half light, half haze. The substance grew, swelled to man-size, and moved to a horizontal position on the bed, a figure half of light and half of mist that shimmered between being and nothing.

A moment it was thus, then King Arnon lay upon the bed. Karis swayed, then stumbled. His hands reached out to catch himself, reached out through the figure that lay there to the solid bed beneath. Anyone watching would have seen a white-faced young man up to his elbows in a king. His hands could not be seen.

In Mithrond's bed, Fardon the impostor stopped thrashing about. He sat up suddenly, rigid. Sweat trickled down the back of his neck; his face flushed then went cold.

"Magic," he muttered. "Someone's using magic. Tallon said I would be the only one here with any magical ability." He sputtered with frustration and helplessness. He realized only too well how little magic he had. Not enough to offer any competition to someone with real magic. Just enough to create a glamour around the uniform and the wig to fool simple people nearby.

He listened, but only the wind moaned outside. He had felt something; he was sure.

I should probably tell Tallon, he thought, but Tallon would be angry at being awakened. He had tried that once before. And for what? Probably it was nothing. Certainly there was no trace of anything now. He hadn't really been awake enough to sense where the magic was coming from, if it was nearby or a great distance away.

He shoved the covers aside and stood, but his room was cold and chilly. The banked fire in the grate didn't produce much heat. He pulled a chair to the hearth, and sat, wrapping a blanket around himself as he did so. Gloomily he stared into the glowing coals.

Why had he ever agreed to impersonate the steward? He had not intended to get involved in such plans. He liked to entertain, to please those around him, but there was no pleasing Tallon. And what had they done with Mithrond? Tallon and his men had come in the night and dragged Mithrond from his bed and taken him who knew where? A nasty business indeed.

He leaned back in his chair, feeling quite sorry for himself. The fire had reached him now and he was comfortable and toasty. His head rested against the back of the padded chair. He closed his eyes halfway, then completely. In minutes he was sound asleep again.

He would not have been so comfortable if he could have seen what Karis was about. Karis straightened, shook his head and looked for a moment down at the illusion of his father that he had created in the bed. An astonished Malin still stood in the passage, blocking it, with the real man draped about him. Malin shut his gaping mouth, collected his wits, and headed down the passage. Karis went in the opposite direction, toward his old rooms.

Malin mind called to Rilse. *We have the king. Everything all right?*

No one and nothing stirs. We wait.

Can you lead Rast back to the passage entrance?

Yes.

Malin reached the blocked end of the passage and found Lon there. Together they made the study loop and returned to the passage with no mishap, for no one was about. Reaching the outer end of the passage, they found Rast waiting. Malin handed the unconscious monarch to Lon and Rast.

"I'm going back for Karis," Malin announced.

Lon was torn. Father or brother? By the time he had resolved his hesitation, Malin was gone. Rast could not carry the king alone, not with his wounded arm, so Lon's decision was made for him. He shifted his hold, making it more secure, and out they went.

In the darkness of the passage, Malin paused a moment to slow his breathing, then retraced his steps. Around the loop he went, with no one the wiser, then back toward Lon's room.

Suddenly the madness was teasing the edges of his mind. A dog. One of the dogs was somewhere close. He couldn't pinpoint the location. Lon and Rast were sitting ducks. Rast couldn't use his right arm and hand, and they were carrying the king. Malin could not get there in time. He would have to hope Rilse was nearby. He reached out for Rilse, caught a faint response, and sent a warning. That was all he could do.

His thoughts moved forward to Karis. The guards would check the king's room first, and that would buy Karis a little time to replicate himself. Enough? They would have to see. He could hear the tramp of the guard's feet on the stairs. And what if they again pulled the face on the pillow into the light to make sure? Illusions were not solid; they would discover the deception.

Karis, standing by Lon's bed, heard the guards and suddenly laughed. Bone weary and stretched to his limits, he felt reckless. In his mind's eye he could see the guards' faces as their hands passed right through Lon's head resting on the pillow, and he laughed again.

Malin, just emerging from the passageway, saw Karis just standing there, grinning like the village idiot. He's lost it for sure, he thought.

They could both hear the tramp of the guards outside the door. They weren't going to see the king; they were coming for Lon. Was their time gone so soon? Karis tried to think, but it was as if everything was moving outside of time. He had not the strength to weave another illusion so quickly upon the heels of the first.

Malin disappeared back into the passage and closed the door.

I caught the dog just before he reached them. He will hunt no more. It was Rilse.

Are there others?

One. I will take care of him, too.

The guards were at Lon's bedroom door.

On the other side, Karis stumbled against the bed and remembered. Why, he could just lie there, himself. Exhaustion made him clumsy and he struggled to pull back the quilt, climb in, and cover himself.

Then the door opened and the guards were there. The corridor lamps spilled light into the room, casting shadows, larger than life, across the figure in the bed.

"Make sure, Tallon says. Waste our time's more like it. The kid hasn't moved all night and won't." The first guard, beefy and belligerent, paused in the doorway.

"If he says make sure, we make sure." His companion was smaller built, with a quick, darting look. "They go tomorrow. We mess up tonight and things go wrong, we won't live to be rich dukes in his new Westra." So saying, he walked the few steps from the door to the bed. His hand reached down, paused, then he turned back to the door. "Get outta the light." Then he turned back, looked at the head on the pillow, grunted once, then turned away. Seconds later the door was shut and grumbling voices continued down the hall, curved with the stairs, and faded into the darkness.

Karis climbed out of the bed, leaned on it for a moment, then straightened and seemed to grow once more. Malin moved to where he could watch, finding himself unpredictably fascinated. Karis' hands moved, as did his lips, though Malin could hardly hear anything this time, Karis' voice was so weak. Shadow formed. Light played about it and mist curled through it as once more a chant, though faint, trembled in the air. Then the standing figure was also lying in the bed, and none could have told them apart.

In Mithrond's rooms, Fardon still slept in the chair before the fire. Suddenly he staggered to his feet, tripping over the blanket, trying to collect his senses. "It's magic again," he muttered, his face white under its redness. "Magic and it's close. Too close. Somewhere in the Halls. Tallon's not going to like this."

He dragged himself to his clothes and put them on. At the door, he stopped suddenly and returned to the table, snatched up the wig and put it on. Then he paused for a moment, settling his illusion about him like a cloak. He straightened, squared his shoulders, and opened his door. He had to tell Tallon this time.

Karis slumped over the figure of himself that he had just made, before he wavered toward the concealed passage. Malin emerged, grabbed his arm and half-dragged, half-carried Karis into it. Luckily the study was dark and out of use for the night. They struggled through the passageways, into the study, out into the hall. Voices. There were voices coming down the hall. They went back into the study passage and closed the panel behind them. The voices were closer; they must be coming to the study. Malin eased Karis onto the floor and waited.

"I have to see him. It's important. Tallon will want to know immediately."

The guard was not impressed. He yawned. "Tallon will come when he wishes, not when you decide he should. I will tell him and we will see what he will do. It better be important." The guard vanished into the hall in the opposite direction. Fardon could not sit still. He paced the study. Suddenly he went after the guard.

"Guard, guard! Tell him it's about magic."

Malin looked at Karis, but his cousin had not heard. He was only semi aware, so deep he was into exhaustion. As soon as the way was clear, Malin slid Karis over his shoulder and almost ran through the hall and the library, into the passage itself, and through it to the outside walls. If what he had heard was right they had no more time.

Are we done? Rilse asked.

We are. We're heading south.

Lon was waiting. "I have one more job to do," he told Malin. "Tallon was to have Heath Halls, as a bequest from Westra's late king. I've found and destroyed the other papers, but that one is missing. I have one last place to look."

"Be fast. They may soon know about us." Quickly Malin explained what he had overheard.

Lon understood. He brushed quickly past Malin and Karis on into the passage once more.

Outside in the storm, Malin carried Karis down the hill, and with Rast's help, placed him in the carriage. The queen tended both Karis and his father, giving them something strong to drink, trying to strengthen them. She never noticed Rast and Malin had left until they returned, bringing Karis' black from the stables. Lon came out of the passage behind them.

"Hand Karis up," he told Malin. "The black will keep him on." In short minutes, Rast had secured Karis to the saddle. Malin had his work cut out for him for a few minutes, trying to settle the horse with an unconscious Karis on board and a white wolf nearby.

Could you go farther away? He asked Rilse.

Could you be nicer?

Initially, Queen Gwynne protested when she realized she was not to go in the carriage with her husband, but she understood. Lon could help drive. If they were to have a chance, there must be no riders. The carriage was slow enough as it was, without any added weight. Furthermore, only two went with the mail. Any more would excite suspicion. Besides, Alyssa would need her.

Malin cornered Lon. "What did you do back there? Did you find the paper?"

Lon grinned. "I did. And so did a broken bottle of ink. A window blown open in the storm, I expect. I'd have burned the paper, but the fire had died down too far." He shrugged. "There's nothing left with my signature."

Rast interrupted as he pulled on his cap. "We're going to have some unhappy people soon. We'd better ride."

"We need to give Karis a little time. He can't ride like that," the queen protested.

"They know about the magic. We have less time than we hoped." Malin didn't expound.

"What do you mean?" The queen's voice trembled and Malin was half sorry he had spoken.

"We heard the impostor sending a guard for Tallon. He didn't know exactly what had happened, but he knew magic was involved. The illusions will not hold them if they go truly searching now. We hoped they would not be alerted and would not discover them until morning."

Gwynne paused in the rude shelter of the abbey ruins, trying to comprehend everything that such news might mean. Even partially sheltered, the howling storm still gusted around them, driving sleet and snow into their faces as it found cracks and fissures in the walls. Karis was dazed and groggy, even the bitter cold had not revived him. "So pursuit could come almost immediately."

"Yes."

Rast finally broke the silence. "We must be on our way. Karis will be safer anywhere but here. Can you manage his horse?" He looked at Malin.

Malin nodded and went to work, touching the black's mind, replacing his fearful images with calm ones. In minutes, the black had calmed and turned into the wind, Karis on his back.

"If you've gotta rest, do it in my cottage. Lon and I and the king better be on our way. We can't move as fast as you and we'll need all the time we can get."

Rast turned and bumped into Lon. For a moment he studied Lon, looking at his attire. Then he reached into the carriage and pulled out the trousers and jacket he had brought. "Put these on. You look too much like a prince. And put some dirt on yer face. Remember, we're just two mail yokels on the monthly mail run."

Lon did as he was told. Rast had a better sense than he of the challenges they might face. "How's this?"

"Much better. You might even be a mail yokel far's anyone could tell."

As he finished buttoning his jacket, Lon slid off the pendant his mother had given him and handed it to her. "Take this with you. It has done its work."

The queen looked at Karis. "It has indeed. You reached him, he came, and just in time." She slipped the pendant quickly over her head.

After giving his mother a quick embrace, Lon took his place in the carriage with the unconscious king. Rast climbed on top, shook the reins, and the carriage was on its way. The king was tucked inside, a large parcel with blankets wrapped around him, and a warm drink in his stomach.

The queen watched until the carriage disappeared into the driving snow, while Malin helped Alyssa on her horse, battling the wind that threatened to blow her off, securing her with some rope Rast had brought.

When she turned to see, the queen was concerned. "Will she fall off?"

"The horse will give her no trouble. Our biggest problem is sleep. If she falls asleep, she will forget to hold on. But even so, the rope should keep her in the saddle." Malin was keeping their horses calm and quiet in spite of the storm. The child's pony as well as the queen's turned out to be sturdier beasts than Malin had anticipated. With their smaller riders they should have no trouble keeping up the pace.

Karis was leaning forward on his horse, only half conscious.

"Can we do the same for him? Can we tie him to his horse?"

Malin looked at Karis. "Yes." He arranged Karis in the saddle, and tied him there; as they traveled, he would work with the horse to smooth out its gait to keep Karis from falling off.

Malin checked all four horses, their equipment and their riders, plus the ropes that secured Alyssa and Karis to their respective mounts. Malin reached to help the queen up, wondering if he should secure her, too. But he found her alert and awake, and when she settled into the saddle, she was steady on her mount.

Malin climbed on his horse and they were ready to ride. He looked around at the small child, his half-conscious cousin, and Gwynne. May the fates be kind, he thought. What on earth are we thinking to take such a group out into the teeth of a blizzard with pursuit just a few hours away?

He led off, taking control of the horses' minds, making sure they followed him. Then they turned inland and headed into the storm. Tonight it was their friend as well as their enemy and would hide all signs of their passing. The wind covered all noise and was already filling their tracks with snow.

Malin placed Alyssa behind him, followed by Karis with Queen Gwynne last.

Karis roused enough to protest. "I should ride rear guard. I'll follow you, Mother."

His mother looked at him, as he swayed in the saddle. "And who would make sure the rear-guard stayed with the party and on his horse?" She didn't have to mention the time they would lose searching a back trail for him.

So Karis moved into third position and sat dozing on his horse through the blizzard. With Malin's help, Karis' black stayed right behind Alyssa's horse, and Karis stayed on.

They would go several miles inland to meet the south roadway. In that storm, they were invisible and they would leave no tracks. Besides, the road would be faster than struggling through the woods.

Long before daylight, they reached Myrrha's inn, skirted it and turned south. They planned to follow the inland trail straight down to Godsel. Malin hoped he could see well enough to follow it, for the snow-filled way was deceptive.

Rilse?

I'm here.

Anyone after us yet?

Not close.

Can we make it back in ten days?

I can. Not sure about this "we."

I know. Stay close. Keep me on the trail. Malin meant to ask, Do you really think we can? But he didn't.

Rilse caught his thought and answered anyway. *Why not?*

Queen Gwynne had similar concerns, but she bit her tongue and rode south.

Malin watched her handle her horse and face into the wind, checking her daughter and son. Not too many members of the royal family would dare such a feat, Malin thought. Takes a mother.

For a moment he thought about his own mother, wondering what she would have done in such a situation, wondering what it would have been like to have known her and grown up with her presence in his life. Then he squared his shoulders and once more took the lead. He had a job to do.

Little Alyssa flashed him a smile as he went past her. He was grateful that to her this was an adventure, even though it might be a difficult one. He reached down and adjusted her scarf. He glanced back at Karis, saw he was still on his horse, but only half aware. Behind Karis he glimpsed the queen and caught her lips moving, but the roar of the wind was too loud for him to hear. He rode past Karis and back to her.

"Thank you. Thank you for this chance for my family. I know we may not make it through the storms, and the king may never recover from what they have done to him, but without you there was no chance. Karis would not even have made it back to us without you and your wolf. Nor would we have escaped from Heath Halls. But now we have a chance. Thank you."

Malin squeezed her hand, unable to speak. She's one courageous woman, he thought. She had a clear grasp of the situation, yet still she went forward. Then he wheeled his horse and once more took the lead. They had no time to waste. They had a long way to go and soon there would be enemies on their tail.

And so the royal family of Westra, a house that had ruled their people well for generations, left Heath Halls, by carriage and horse, vanishing into darkness and cold. They were swallowed by a raging winter's storm with the promise of enemies soon to follow. It was uncertain whether they would survive the storm. It was also uncertain if they did, whether they would survive the hunt by their enemies. Still, they went.

10
Carriage Ride

O n the coast road, Rast, the cantankerous mail driver and Lon, his scruffy new apprentice to the mails, were on top of the carriage. Inside, the only things visible were the old mail sacks.

"They made the trip to Heath Halls in ten days. How long will it take us? Can we make it back in ten?" Lon asked.

"Not with this carriage. Horses and riders can move faster. Perhaps, with luck, we can make it in fourteen or fifteen days. Mail carriages usually take at least three weeks, but the drivers stop to eat and rest. We'll do that on the way." Rast shook out the reins.

"Will the horses make it?"

"Maybe."

"Sure you want to be in on this?"

Rast shrugged. "Haven't done nothin' fun fer a while. Life needs a little doin', ya know." Then he added more soberly, "Besides, they're trying to kill my king and his family."

"This might be more than you've bargained for."

"Mebbe, mebbe not."

The carriage struggled along the narrow trail for another mile before slowing at the crossroads where it joined the wider coastal road to Godsel. This was a point of danger, for if they were seen coming onto the road, they would be hard pressed to explain their actions.

Quickly Rast led the horses onto the main road, not even pausing to brush their tracks away from the snowy side trail that could be seen. "The blizzard'll erase 'em almost faster than we can make 'em." He slowed the carriage. "You get inside and care for the king."

Rast watched Lon jump off the carriage, grasp the door handle and turn it and open the door. Rast nodded in approval as Lon opened the door just wide enough to let himself in. The boy had some sense. They had to keep the heat in to keep the king warm. Jackets and blankets were good, but saving heat was essential.

As the horses settled into a steady pace, the woods and the small hills beyond them faded into a snow-filled sameness, buffeted by the wind. The rhythmic gait of the horses was muffled in snow, the creak of the carriage itself lost in the wind. Anyone watching would only see a shadow moving beyond the falling and drifting snow of the night.

Inside the carriage, Lon cradled his father's head against his chest and spooned the warm liquid they had brought into his mouth. Then he tightened the blankets and settled him back as comfortably as he could, the mails sacks around him. Anyone peering in the window would see only the sacks, if they could see anything, but Lon saw only his father's pale face. Would his father make it?

He wondered when the guards would discover that they were gone. Would they brave contagion to find out his mother's ruse, or would they first check on him? They would be annoyed—even angry—that the queen, prince and princess were missing, but when they checked the king's room where the guards paced before the door in a constant pattern, then fear perhaps would touch them when they found it empty. He could almost see Tallon's face when he heard the news.

Lon basked in the satisfaction of his daydream and dozed, his mind and body in a lull after the quick action at the Halls. His face smoothed out in sleep. His dark hair fell from under his cap against the rough collar of his coat. His shoulders, leaning against the carriage door, reflected the movement of the carriage itself, but he slept on untroubled. Action and decision were better lullabies than a bed at home watched by the enemy.

Lon roused as the carriage slowed. Taking advantage of the moment, he fed the king more broth. Although the king did not really wake, or become aware of his surroundings, Lon felt he at least looked stronger.

As the carriage drew to a stop, he arranged the mail sacks once more to cover his father and climbed out. He would join Rast on top, one driving the carriage, one watching the road for pursuit.

"The rocking of the carriage is putting me to sleep," Rast said, handing Lon the reins. "King all right?"

"As all right as he can be, now."

They settled back into their steady pace, and Rast dozed off. Lon grinned. He glanced at Rast, making sure he was not so soundly asleep as to be in danger of falling off. Finally he shook him. "Why don't you sleep inside? I'll wake you when I need you."

Rast looked at him in surprise. "In the carriage with the king? Never thought of it."

"Get on down with you and take good care of him."

Rast shot him a grin, then he was inside and the carriage once more creaked and complained on its way. The king slept; Rast slept. Lon tried not to.

It felt right to be riding again with Rast and his father, Lon thought, though the present circumstances were far from ideal. If it hadn't been for the war, and the dark mage, he and Karis would still be spending time with Rast, hunting and riding and fishing.

In fact, far south, past the borders of Westra, was wilderness. King Arnon had planned an expedition there to explore. He said it was a new kind of world to experience. But who could say when there would be time for such things again? Lon sighed. First they had to save the king and the kingdom.

Lon, too, drifted into dreaming, leaving the horses on their own. He did not see the first faint rays of morning reach to color the pale snow before them, to touch the sky's edge and the white line of the road. Snow still fell about them, but softer and lighter now, a dusting over their dark jackets and trousers. The wind had lost some of its force.

But Lon was dreaming of wrath-filled men who rode in ever widening circles out from the Halls, searching for the fugitives' trail, but weather and wit had defeated them, for they could find no trace. It was as if the king and his family had never been. Lon smiled.

Back at the real Halls, Fardon waited for the guard to wake Tallon so that he could warn him that magic was afoot. The guard returned finally. "Yer to wait 'til full morning," he reported. "Tallon says no inept worker of magic is going to deprive him of his sleep." The guard was delighted to stress the word "inept."

Furious, Fardon turned on his heel and retired to his chambers, too angry to sleep. He paced to and fro for the next hour or so. Then he suddenly stopped himself. If something is wrong, it's Tallon's problem, not mine, he thought. Deep inside Fardon knew something had gone wrong. He smiled. Tallon would get his. With such pleasant thoughts he fell asleep and slept soundly.

Unlike the events of Lon's daydream, the king's absence was discovered first. An hour or so after breakfast, the physician who daily administered the "medicine" to the king came bringing the cup. He reached for the sleeping king's head to raise it up, and his hand passed through the head and came to rest a foot before his face. His mouth went slack and he stared at his hand in silence. The old woman with him gave a great shriek and fled the chambers.

Within minutes the guards were there, and soon Tallon himself, rubbing the sleep from his eyes. In great anger he entered, strode to the bed and grabbed for the king's body. His hands, too, found nothing. Then as they watched, the morning rays of the sun reached into the room. The king wavered a moment, became a shining rising from the bed, larger and larger, and then he was gone.

In a fury, Tallon led the guards to the queen's chambers, his short sword in hand, only to find them empty. What he might have done there, he did not say. Lon's room was searched with the same results. Tallon stormed to Mithrond's chambers and found Fardon there fully dressed, sitting before his fire, waiting for him. Even Fardon was not prepared for this Tallon. He had never seen him so icy and cold.

"You should have brought me the message yourself, instead of trusting it to a mindless lackey."

"He was your guard, sir. He was not willing that I should enter without your permission, which according to him, you did not give."

"How far away are they?"

"They?"

"The prisoners. Magic was used to make replacements, at least illusions."

"The last time I felt magic was just past two this morning."

Tallon glanced at the clock. The hands were almost at nine o'clock. "Six to seven hours head start. Someone will pay for this."

Fardon understood that someone would. Just as long as it isn't me, he thought. Cold with rage, Tallon and his men met in the large salon to discuss the lack of royal personages upon the estate. Tallon planned the search.

To the first group he said simply, "You will guard the king."

The men looked puzzled. "But the king is gone, sir."

"Of course he is, but the people don't know that yet, and we can buy ourselves a little time. No one is to be allowed in to see him. No one. Guard in shifts. Post a relief guard so the regulars may rest."

The second group was to search Mythro, looking for the royal family. "Enemies have taken the queen and her daughter." His white teeth shone below his black moustache. "Find and rescue them, and bring them here to me."

He turned to the third group. "You are messengers. The family might head for safety toward Godsel. The coast road would likely be too open and dangerous, but in case, three of you ride that way. Inform the way stations to watch for a party of riders, one of them the queen. Tell them that for her own safety she must not travel alone but wait for our guards. We will keep her safe." Again he smiled. "Yes, we will keep her safe.

"Three more of you are to head to Anor, to Duke Blandor. Warn him of the situation and bring back his orders." As he spoke, the searchers and messengers saluted and left about their business.

As the newly appointed guards withdrew, the steward turned his attention to the fourth and last group. "You are my hunters. Harad, you are to take your twelve and search the wood's trails. If you find them, it is not necessary to bring them back. The woods swallow up many things without a trace, it seems." His words hung in the air between them and Harad saluted, his pleasure at his assignment obvious on his flat features.

"You can depend on my woodcraft, my Lord, and on my hounds."

"I hope so, Harad. I hope so." They looked across at one another, the physical darkness of Tallon a contrast to the blondness of Harad. Yet somehow they seemed the same.

As the last group departed, Tallon spoke to the few soldiers left in the hall at their posts. "It is essential that we overlook nothing. Go through the Halls again, the stables, the servants' quarters, everything. Look through every inch of these halls, on peril of your life. If you miss something, you will pay. Find me the king and his family. Now."

Finally Tallon was alone. For some moments he fingered the parchment lying on the great table. Then he seized it and wrote, sealing the note with his own seal. Rising, he called for Racar, called by some the Fox, a private messenger of unknown allegiance. When Racar entered, he handed him the message. "You know where it is to go."

"Yes, my Lord."

Perhaps it was because he was insubstantial, but Racar seemed like a claw of something larger than himself. Even Tallon breathed easier when Racar was gone. He leaned back in his chair and took a deep breath.

Then Tallon thought about Fardon. He would plan something special for him. Guard or no guard, Fardon was happy about what had happened. Tallon was not one to leave others happy at his expense.

The changed gait of the horses woke Rast. They were climbing the long hill that led to Brandon Heights where the first way station sat between Godsel and Mythro. It was both lookout and guard post to watch the seas, to give warning of stray raiding parties from the north. Rast glanced right, to the sea, gray and wild in the winter storm. It was high tide and below the hill the open sea roared and crashed on the rocks. He smiled, a little grimly. Pursuit would not come from the seas this day.

The storm had not stopped since they left Heath Halls in the night and it was now morning again on the following day. If pursuit were to catch them, it would be shortly. Yet there was no place to turn off, no woods even close to this part of the trail. If Tallon were to catch them here, they would be helpless.

Rast banged on the carriage roof to alert Lon, and then climbed up beside him. "Brandon Heights is over the next hill. Hold yourself ready in case of something amiss and get that hat over your face. Some of them will have seen you."

"Not me they haven't." And while Rast watched in astonishment, Lon wadded a bit of rag and placed it in his mouth, changing the whole shape of his face until it was unrecognizable. His jaw went slack and his eyes took on a vacant look.

"No, sor. They haven't seen me. 'Appen I've not been this road before, riding the mails. No, sor."

Rast chuckled. He could see no sign of the king's son in the sorry creature that sat beside him, grinning mindlessly.

"Look to yourself, sor. 'Appen some might know you."

"They might, but I've only to tell them that the regular driver and carriage are out of commission and I've been asked to go. If they know me, they'll believe me. If they're Tallon's men, they won't know me and it won't matter. I hope," he added, under his breath.

Rast knew no messenger had passed them, but pursuit was a possibility and many a backward glance he gave to the road behind. Then they were at the top and planning and worry were things of the past. They would win through or be stopped here. It was not under their control.

"Who comes?" It was the traditional question asked in the proper way and the one who asked was only half awake in the pale chill of early morning.

Rast was ready with his answer, had been ready since the carriage first touched the coast road. "Mail. If this carriage can make it." He said no more. Who knew when the last mail carriage had come?

The guard grinned in sympathy. "She does sound as if each turn of the wheels might be the last. I'd like to go to Godsel myself. Or Mythro. In spite of the trouble up north and to the east there'll be some doings there for the year's end celebrations." The guard was awake now.

Rast nodded and Lon beside him spoke for the first time, winking slyly at the guard as he did so. "Yes, sor. Only way they got us. Jest the feastin' and the mimes. Wouldn't leave 'ome in this weather else." He dug his elbow into Rast's side and laughed loudly. "Right?"

"Hold your mouth, you, or there'll be no feast for you." Rast shoved Lon away and turned, complaining loudly to the guard. "Cain't get proper help these days. Just lazy loafers who only want to spend their time on women and drink. You know, sir."

The guard sighed his sympathy and waved them on. Only two mail yokels off early for the year end fun. He wished heartily that he was in Godsel instead of half asleep in the cold dawn at a guard station that saw no action. King's man he was and Rast recognized him from past years, but he showed no signs of placing Rast and little interest in doing so.

Then suddenly the guard stopped, turned about and sprinted after them. Rast caught his breath, looked down at his hands holding the reins and hesitated, then shook himself. What am I thinking? He muttered. No way this carriage can outrun any one.

The guard came up beside him.

Rast looked at the rifle the guard carried. At least it wasn't pointed at him.

"Would you stop for a hot drink and a bite of bread this dawn?" It was a polite offer.

Rast sighed in relief. "And be late for the doings? Naw. We'll go on. But thankee."

"Good day, then. Drink a round for me."

"Right you are. Good day." A few creaks and groans of the carriage and they were past, over the ridge of the hill and starting down the other side. Rast looked at Lon, doubled over with laughter, trying to keep his face straight.

"You should have seen your face back there. Good thing the guard didn't get a good look. A little worried, were we?"

For a moment Rast felt irritated. Then the moment caught up with him and he grinned. He roared and slapped Lon on the back. "Ya should've seen yours." And then they were both hard put to drive the carriage, they were laughing so hard in relief.

When their laughter subsided, Rast glanced behind. They had a good lead, but men on horseback were much faster than their old carriage, though they had pushed the horses hard.

Rast handed the reins to Lon, needing both hands on the brake now, for the old coach could not take the rough road at any speed without coming apart. That they could not risk. Besides, the road was slippery with snow and ice, even though the storm had ended. By the time they reached the bottom, both men were sweating from nerves and fatigue, but Lon was jubilant.

"We've done it, man. We've done it. Taken the king right from under their noses and past the guard station. We've nothing between us and Godsel now but open road."

Rast didn't fully share his enthusiasm. His face was red with cold, and almost as red now as his hair. "Aye, Lon, we've passed the guard and made it down the hill but we're a long way from Godsel. We've days yet to go with an ailin' king, and that's not the worst of it."

His face grew sober. "There'll be riders coming behind us. Mebbe they won't bother to chase an old mail coach, but then again mebbe they will. Even with the start we got on them, we can't outrun them. No, sir, we can't outrun them. And if they were to stop us and search—." Rast fell silent. "But we can outthink them." He brightened. "Just around the next bend, where the road is hidden from the hill, we'll tend the king once more. And then, well, we shall see. I've got me an idea."

Lon was curious, but already they were into the bend and the carriage was pulling to a stop. The two made fast the reins around the post and lost no time in jumping down to open the carriage. It was the work of minutes to shift the mail and assist the king to swallow some warm broth.

Perhaps the warm drink early that morning had done him some good, as well as missing his daily "medicine," for the king's eyes were open, and he seemed to recognize Lon's face bending over him. Lon could never have lifted his father in his normal health and vigor, for he was a big man, but now, he had no trouble lifting the king to rest half on the seat and half on the mail sacks full of straw.

Lon tucked the blanket around the king and pulled out a flask of broth and herbs, to which he added liquor from Rast's cottage. The king was conscious, so Lon fed him bits of bread moistened in the broth as well as the broth itself. "Rast, if I shift the mail sacks, I can ride here while I feed the king. He's doing better."

Satisfied that the king was in good hands, Rast again took his seat on the coach, kicking the wet snow off his feet as they went. Overhead, clouds had thickened, the wind had risen, and snow was falling once again. The storm had ebbed a little with the dawn, but it was returning with a vengeance. Rast gauged the snowfall and the rise of the wind with a practiced eye, then with growing astonishment. This storm was coming from the south, the first storm he had ever seen from that direction in the winter time.

Rast scratched his head in amazement. Then he got down to business. "Well, well. Our tracks'll be gone in 'nother half hour, and then they can search for us until doomsday if'n they like," he muttered to himself. One of the horses whinnied, and Rast raised his voice so that Lon, who was still inside the carriage with the king, could hear him. "If I remember rightly, there's an old hunting lodge just into these woods. They'll be looking for us on the road today, mebbe even tomorrow. If'n they don't find us then, they'll not look farther. So we'll hole up fer a bit. The day after, the road'll be ours. This weather'll hide our trail and none'll be the wiser."

"And the king will have time to recover."

Rast grinned. "Ya got it." Then Rast was working the reins, urging the horses to the limits of the coach's ability. "This old carriage'll get us there yet," he said hopefully.

But it was already difficult to tell where the edges of the road were. His eyes were stinging from the wind and snow, his skin red where it was open to the weather. Midday came. Rast removed his scarf to gnaw the small loaf of bread and chunk of cheese he had brought with him. Hours passed. Though the day gave no indications of what time it was, it seemed to be growing darker. Suddenly he stopped.

"Lon! Lon!" A dark head poked out of the carriage. "Can you leave His Majesty? I need you up here. The snow's so thick it takes an eye on each side to see the road."

"Aye. The king's fine. He's fallen asleep again, but his color's better. And Rast, he recognized me!"

"Well, come up here, before we're snowed in."

Although the comment was meant as a joke, the carriage did have its troubles pulling away from the road where it had stopped. The snow was so thick it was difficult to see, and the temperature was dropping fast.

"Watch for the stone cairn they use for the signal fires. The turnoff should be just past it and to the left. And," he half muttered to himself, "it will be hard for even us to find, let alone someone not watching for it. But we've got a chance now, and a good one at that." He grinned. "And it's gettin' better all the time."

The wind was howling around the cliffs and gusting through the rocks. In the few lulls, they could hear the crashing of the waves against the cliffs and on the rocks, for here the road ran especially close to the sea. The creaks and groans of the carriage added to the noise of the storm.

"Let it be soon," Rast muttered under his breath. "It better be soon. We can't ride no further in this weather nohow." It was difficult to see through the thick snowfall from the overcast skies; only gray surrounded them now.

Lon concentrated on searching for the cairn of rocks until his eyes burned with the effort. The wind bit and howled at them. Once, Rast had to stop the horses so that he and Lon could warm and dry their noses where ice was beginning to form. They resisted the urge to check on the passenger in the carriage, knowing that if they opened the door, half his warmth would be blown away.

On his way back up to the seat, Lon glanced back down the road. Hurriedly he grasped Rast's arm, his lips close to his ear. "Look back."

There behind them was the cairn of stones, the marker they were looking for. They had missed it, looking as they were into the teeth of the storm. Rast got down again, turned the carriage, and walked beside the horses, feeling for the road with his boots. No trail could be seen in the solid whiteness. Even the coast road itself was now only a faint outline.

Finding at last what he sought, Rast carefully turned the horses inland where trees soon surrounded them. They were grateful for the protection from the wind but they were also grateful to leave the fury of the whirling, drifting white behind them. Even better, in short minutes, no trace of their coming or leaving the road would remain.

Rast led the horses farther and farther inland, forging steadily southeast. Lon closed his eyes, feeling the beginnings of warmth come to his fingers and toes. Sleep. How he wanted to sleep.

He didn't notice the carriage stop, or hear Rast call to him. He was unaware of anything until he felt himself being shaken.

"Get down, Lon. Get down and walk. Stamp them feet. Don't stop moving or you'll freeze to death."

Reluctantly, Lon let himself be hauled off the carriage and up and down the trail a few times. "Slow down, slow down," he protested to Rast.

"Slow down, by my granny. You just get thet body of yers movin'."

When Rast was finally satisfied Lon wasn't going to freeze to death, he set him beside one of the horses, where he clung and grumbled mentally at Rast's grouchiness, still not fully aware of his peril.

Then they were there. The lodge loomed up before them, a solid lump in their white world. Rast maneuvered the carriage until its door was facing that of the lodge, and in minutes they had carried the king inside and placed him on a rough bed which they dragged beside the fireplace. Rast took the carriage and horses to the stable just beyond the lodge, almost stumbling over several large boulders by the door.

The horses snorted and reared back before they would let Rast lead them to the stables. Vaguely Rast wondered why, but the cold and their need drove other thoughts aside. The stable was warmer and empty and had plenty of hay, though it was a little old. A trough inside supplied the water, outside it would have been ice. Soon the horses were cared for.

Within the shelter of the lodge itself, Lon started a fire, for one was laid in the hearth and wood was by it. Returning circulation was making his hands and feet prickly and sensitive, but he persevered. He and Rast hung their coats by the mantle to dry and dropped together onto the rug by the king's bed, right in front of the fire. For long minutes they lay close to the fire, just letting the warmth soak in, and the dampness dry out. Time to think made Lon realize the situation he had been in.

"I came close, didn't I?"

"Yeah, too darn close." Rast looked hard at Lon, remembering how concerned he had been, then got up and barred the door.

Lon's eyes took in the action and narrowed. "Expecting company?"

"Never know. This storm should keep all enemies away, but you never know. Don't hurt to be careful."

Then they slept, sheltered within the lodge, warmed and comforted by the sweet-smelling wood of the fire. Outside the storm continued, the wind piling up the falling snow against the walls of their shelter. Before it ceased, no trace of the travelers remained, not on the coast road, and not in the inner fastness of the woods.

The three horsemen who rode down in haste from Brandon Station on lathered horses passed by the cairn of stones and the woods trail without knowing what they passed. There was no sign the travelers had left the coast road, no sign in fact that there was another road. They did not find what they sought.

Hours later when they returned, the land still held its secrets and their poor mounts toiled back up the hill to the station with much ill temper from their riders, for they returned empty-handed.

"It was just a mail carriage anyway," one of the horsemen remarked. "And certainly neither the king nor the queen were with them. The guard would have seen them and told us. It was just mail."

"They probably went off the road and were lost in the storm. Frozen to death," another responded. And so they agreed among themselves not to mention the mail coach to Tallon, for it wasn't important, and not finding it would make them look bad.

Back in the lodge, Rast tried to rouse himself, conscious of a strange odor that seemed to be coming from the fireplace. He should scout the surroundings, he thought, but a strange lethargy overcame him. He had trouble lifting his head. Other things ate at him, and his uneasiness grew. But he found no matter what he did, he struggled just to move his head and eyelids. Then he couldn't move at all. He could not lift his head, nor move his hand. In fact, he could not even blink his eyes. In his mind he was back in the forest with Karis and Lon, and a dark mage was having his fun. Then his eyes closed and took his mind with them.

All through the rest of that white winter day, and into the night, Rast, Lon and King Arnon lay stone still, in an unnatural sleep, unaware.

11

Fainra

A couple of hours after the inland group passed the inn and started on the main road south, Malin stopped to have the riders dismount from their horses and walk them around. They couldn't afford to risk frostbite, having no real way to deal with it. With pursuit close behind them, there was no time to stop and make a fire for a hot drink. The best they could do was a warm brew the queen had brought with her to aid circulation, though Malin couldn't help but think that Rast's medicinal bottle might be more effective.

He walked Alyssa, while the queen helped Karis. Then they swapped. Gwynne walked Alyssa and Malin took Karis, for he was too unsteady to walk without a lot of help. But he did rouse enough to try. They stamped their feet and worked their hands and fingers, feeling their noses and covering them with scarves. The storm was still about them, for good and ill, Malin thought.

"When could we expect pursuit to start?" he asked Karis quietly, out of earshot of the others.

"We probably have three hours," Karis told him as they walked.

"Well, we can go slowly and carefully, taking time to try and cover our trail and pray they don't bring dogs, or we can trust to speed and hope to get there first." Malin was blunt.

Karis shuddered. "Those dogs. Do they have more?"

"There were more in the pens beyond the house. Rilse only killed the four roaming loose."

Alyssa and Gwynne reached them in time to hear the end of their conversation. "Someone killed the dogs?" Five-year-old Alyssa's voice was tragic.

"It was a good wolf, dear, and bad dogs. It's really all right. The good wolf will be close by to help us when he can," her mother consoled her.

"What does he look like?"

"White. With silver on his ears and tail," Malin told her. Unless he's huge and black with red eyes, he added only to himself. "His name is Rilse."

"Can I meet him?"

"Perhaps later, dear," her mother told her. "Right now, we're going riding again." She had read the situation correctly, Malin noted.

At his nod, she helped Alyssa back into the saddle and followed suit. Malin had his hands full doing the same for Karis, who was weak and not really strong enough to bear his own weight. But Malin took advantage of their moment together to speak to him.

"Fine animals damaged, children and women hunted. This is a different game from that we played in the south." His voice was grim. "With time, this storm will cover our tracks. But the closer they come the more danger we're in. Those dogs are killers, trained to hunt, and we're the game. They will find us. Our only real hope is speed."

"Speed it is, then." Karis looked at his mother, already worn and pensive. At least this ride would be so hectic she would not have time to worry.

Alyssa, his sister, smiled at him, but her smile was tired. Like we are, Karis thought wryly. Like we all are. Except maybe Malin. Karis looked at Malin, springing on his horse, taking a moment to mind touch with all the horses, using that way to gather the group and lead them through the storm. Malin seemed to thrive on action.

Afterward, people spoke of that wild ride through a storm that wouldn't stop. The wind howled around them and whipped at their clothing, and snow crusted their eyelashes and hair. Then things grew worse. The storm shifted until it came straight from the south, until they had to face directly into a bitter wind that took their breath away.

Like Rast, Malin wondered at this, for most of their winter storms swept down from the north, where this one had started. He had no time to dwell on his discovery, however. Wind snatched the thought from him like a piece of paper, swirling it, lifting it high and far, before burying it under a pile of snow. The tasks before them erased all other concerns.

Onward they rode, silently, for conversation was impossible. The storm was noise enough to drown all their attempts at speech. Besides, the ride took all their energy. Malin brought Karis up beside him, hoping they and their horses would break trail and reduce the force of the wind for the queen and Alyssa. As they faced into the wind, they gasped for breath, the wind driving the cold into their lungs until they burned.

An hour or two later Malin pulled them into the lee of a cluster of trees, where they each took some broth from a flask they had brought, that was still warm to the touch. Then they adjusted their hoods and caps and scarves until only their eyes were open to the weather.

As he fixed her scarf, Karis spoke softly to his sister. "A rare ride we're having, like the ones we used to have when I was home."

"That was in summer," Alyssa said, shivering. They were both silent a moment, remembering the fresh forests and the warm winds sweet with the scent of fresh berries. Then Alyssa lifted her face to him and smiled, her blue eyes bright and trusting.

"Will we make it to the castle at Godsel, Karis? Before the cold gets us? And before the bad dogs find us?"

Karis looked down at his sister. They had always, as a family, been direct and truthful with each other. He decided that hard moments were no reason to change. "I hope so. I think so. If the fates are kind, we will." He gave her a quick hug, and once more they were on their way, Malin in the lead, and Karis close behind him.

They rode all night and through the next day, with only a few short stops. There was no shelter, and they dared not stop longer without building a fire which would be a beacon to those who tracked them. When the queen's brew was gone, they used the "medicinal" liquor they had brought from Rast's cabin to warm them, watered down for Alyssa. And they ate in the saddle, dismounting only to stamp their feet to keep circulation going.

Malin reached out for Rilse, but found only the red rage of the gytrash. Surprised, he tried again, but he could not push past the presence of the nightmare black wolf to reach the inner Rilse. The burning eyes harbored a killing frenzy he could not penetrate.

By nightfall after a day, a night, and a morning without stopping, Alyssa was so weary she flopped in the saddle, even tied there. Karis wasn't much better. Malin was grateful for Karis' black, who kept on at a steady pace under him, straight down the trail into the heart of the storm, no matter what Karis did.

The situation was urgent. If the storm raged on, they could not survive the night without shelter. They were spent and could not continue to ride. If Malin left the trail to seek for shelter, the others would be left stationary in the cold. Yet they had to stop. If only he could penetrate the gytrash to reach Rilse. Rilse would find shelter for them.

Urgently, he reached out once more for his friend, but only the gytrash was there. An hour passed, then another and still he could not reach Rilse. Doggedly he pushed on, trying again and again. When a response came, it was so faint and unexpected he almost missed it. It came from a Rilse exhausted by the rage, the almost madness of the gytrash.

Rilse, are you all right?

I'm better now.

I couldn't reach you past the gytrash.

I know. I've been working. His voice, though tired, was smug. Malin caught an image of trackers and dogs being sidetracked, of several dogs not returning, of horses running away in terror and supplies being lost. *It will take them another day, maybe another day and a half to regroup.*

Malin sighed with relief. *That may just save our lives. But we need shelter. It is too cold to stop without it.*

Yes it is—even for wolves. I will look.

It was at least an hour later when Malin heard back from Rilse, an hour in which they had slowed to a stumbling walk, and finally stopped to reposition Alyssa, who had slid under her rope to the side of her horse.

Just off the trail there's an unused cave. It's big enough, even for horses. You could eat and sleep. Be warmer.

Rilse, if anyone ever casts aspersions on your mother, you just tell them the gods themselves must have picked her. You are one marvelous wolf. Maybe two, rolled into one.

I know. The cave is off to the left, just where that huge tree stands.

Malin got a picture of the cave and its location. He tried to rouse Karis, who was nodding on his horse, with no results, so he simply took the more direct route. Mind touching the horses, he bade them follow him, off the trail to the west, through dense woods that barred their way and winds that whirled snow about and blinded them. The image of shelter that Malin kept in the horses' minds was strong enough that they kept going until they reached the base of the hill and the cave Rilse had found.

Malin reached for Alyssa, wrapped her in an extra blanket, carried her in and laid her down close to where he planned to build a fire. Together, he and the queen lifted Karis down and placed him beside Alyssa.

Malin quickly built a small fire well inside the cave, and breathed a sigh of relief when the smoke drifted past him to the rear. He followed its path with his eyes, watching it dissipate as it traveled upward. He took a moment to step outside the cave and search for any visible smoke rising. There was none. The storm had its uses, Malin thought, although he suspected that even if the weather were clear, the smoke would not be visible from that cave. It must have airways deeper into the hill.

He melted snow for the horses, fed them oats and left them grazing on the dry weeds showing through the snow at the cave's entrance. Then he brought them inside as well. The cave was large enough for all of them. They could not have asked for anything better suited to their needs.

The queen was busy on her own. She had a pot and was putting things in it. When it was hot, she gave some broth, made with the dried beef that Rast had given her, as well as the herbs she had brought, to both Alyssa and Karis, who immediately returned to sleep. She brought some to Malin and joined him by the fire, just as an exhausted Rilse emerged from the storm.

"Will we need to keep watch?"

I'll watch. Rilse stretched across the opening behind them.

Malin turned, catching the wolf smile on Rilse's face. "No. Rilse will stand guard for now."

They drank their soup, wrapped themselves in blankets and fell asleep.

They slept through the afternoon and all through the night, with only a few short periods of wakefulness on Malin's part to replenish the fire. The horses had not moved. They were glad to be out of the storm and warm, and they were calm and quiet. Just before daybreak the storm began to dwindle and Malin awoke.

Rilse? He felt the wolf stretch and yawn.

No one comes. Since you're awake, I'm going hunting.

Malin hugged the curve of the cave wall until he reached the entrance. Kneeling, he peered out. He realized what was different. The noise of the wind was gone, the sounds of the storm. He looked upward and couldn't help feeling relieved as he noticed the snow had also stopped. He saw blue sliding beneath the clouds and at the edge of the trees, the first rays of sunlight sifting through them. His heart lifted in spite of himself, even though good weather would increase their danger.

Behind him, Karis stirred, and sat up. "How did you find the cave?"

"Rilse."

"We'd have been done for without it."

Malin nodded. "We would indeed."

They let the queen and Alyssa sleep on while they packed their blankets, took care of the horses, and got out their food supplies.

"Is he still around?"

Malin raised an eyebrow. "Rilse?"

Karis shrugged his shoulders. "Of course, Rilse. What other 'he' is there?"

"No one we would welcome."

Karis fell silent. No one indeed. The black mage, Tallon's hunters, their other choices were all bad.

Malin added, "He's hunting now, but he's been our guard while we slept."

"How far behind are they?"

"Probably just beginning again on our trail. Rilse scattered their horses and attacked their dogs. They lost their supplies and had to return to the Halls to start over."

Karis sighed in relief. "At least now we have a real chance."

Rilse turned up with a rabbit for the stew pot, and Malin was kept busy with the horses while he delivered it. Rast's horses were not used to the white wolf as Malin's had been. Alyssa stood up and ran to Rilse and hugged him.

They love me, Rilse licked her face.

Quite pleased with yourself, aren't you? teased Malin.

"Breakfast stew is the best food I've ever had," Alyssa said afterward, wiping her mouth with her fingers. "And Rilse is wonderful."

The queen smoothed back Alyssa's blonde locks, tucking them under hat and scarf, and hugged her. "He is indeed wonderful, that wolf."

Alyssa's eyes grew big. "He's really a wolf, isn't he?"

"Yes," Malin assured her. "He's really a wolf."

Minutes later they loaded the last supplies, stamped out the fire, scattered loose dry earth over the coals, and mounted up. Even the horses took heart, and the whole party went with new energy onto the trail south, in and out of forests, over hills and down valleys, following the west side of the Mythro River.

Four hours down the trail, they stopped and dismounted to stretch and eat the loaves and cheese Rast had packed for them. Food renewed their strength and gave them heart.

As they climbed back on their horses, Malin whispered to Karis, "Tallon's men are seasoned riders. They will make our pace seem as nothing,"

Karis' worried look told Malin he understood.

The clouds had returned overhead and sealed off the sun; in gloom once more, they fled south. Whenever they crested a hill, Karis and Malin would look back over their trail, watching for dark figures in the white world around them, for splashes of color in the gray of the day. Malin would listen for the baying of hounds, the sudden beating of birds' wings in startled flight.

In the early part of the afternoon, Malin reluctantly pulled them to a halt. The horses were spent, and the queen seemed ready to fall off, though she did not murmur or complain. Surprisingly enough, Alyssa seemed in the best shape. Her spirits had improved as they journeyed south.

Once more both Karis and Malin scanned their back trail, watching for signs of pursuit. In spite of their great speed and only one night's rest, they were still at least six days from Godsel.

"Shouldn't we be meeting troops from Godsel by now? Surely Lord Lindsey or Basil would send help." Karis' voice was so low only Malin could hear it.

"If they got our messages." Malin hadn't been pleased with leaving such important details up to someone else. "I hope they did, but we don't know. Grooms are not always reliable. We don't even know if Basil received our note." Malin couldn't resist reminding Karis, who had been in such a rush he would not wait to deliver their messages in person. "But if they got them, then it's possible we may meet help later today. I hope it's in time."

"Can you reach Rilse?"

Malin looked at him, then once more down their back trail. "No. Not since the cave."

They stopped and made a small fire. The queen sat nodding by it while Alyssa fed it with small twigs, careful to use only the dry ones Malin had collected from the back of the cave and brought with them. They were worn and silent. Malin rightly judged a stop with a small fire would warm both their bodies and hearts.

The cold bread, with a bit of cheese, was brought out of the pack and shared. Malin added a little dried fruit hoarded from their Godsel stores. The queen melted snow in a container Malin had given her to provide water for the horses.

Karis was uneasy and paced about the small clearing at the road's edge. He checked their supplies. He stepped away to view the smoke from their fire, but it burned invisible, even in the damp clouds that closed them in. He skirted the edge of the brooding forest but did not enter. Finally he came to rest by the fire, close to Malin.

"There is something close. I feel it, waiting and watching, yet not Tallon and his men."

The queen had overheard. "I know. I feel it, too."

Karis started as a small cluster of crows took to the air down the road from them, watched them fly off, then settled back as nothing further broke the silence. On this road, set back in the forest to either side, were some small villages, but they were few and far between. They were also small enough that they would be no match for what was pursuing them. There was no help close they could access.

Then in quick decision, Karis spoke again to Malin. "I must risk the Spirit Walks. Something is very wrong, and I need to know what."

"To the Spirit Walks now?" The queen voiced Malin's thoughts exactly. "When you are so spent?" The queen's preoccupation with her own thoughts was broken. "If Tallon's men find you in that state, you would be easy prey. Not only that, but we cannot travel or move you until you wake."

"I know."

"And what about the dark mage? He almost overpowered you from Fainra before you left for Godsel. What if he's waiting there again?"

Remembering the gray shapes that had walked through him in his own short time in the Spirit Walks, Malin shuddered.

The queen continued. "Going to the Spirit Walks would be a blazing signal no magician would miss."

"Away from the gray hordes are places of seeing, farseeing." Karis seemed to guess Malin's thoughts. "Something is happening we need to know about."

"Queen Gwynne is right. What about your watcher? What if he's there waiting?" Malin wanted to know.

"That's a risk I'll have to take."

"Why?"

"Because my instincts say to do it, just as yours tell you the weather."

Malin was silenced. Not convinced, just silenced. "How long will it take?"

"An hour. Maybe a little less."

The queen was troubled. She turned to face Karis. "All day we have walked in shadow, a growing menace that comes out of the south. The storm also came from there, too, you know. Have you ever known a winter storm to come from the south?"

Malin answered quickly, the pieces suddenly coming together in his mind. "No, never."

Gwynne persisted. "But knowledge is not worth the risk to your life, Karis."

Karis reached forward and touched her arm. "I only take what risks I must, Mother."

The queen smiled her rare quick smile, so like Karis' own. "I know."

Pressed by a feeling of urgency, Malin interrupted their conversation. "Perhaps the queen and Alyssa should start on their way. I can wait for Karis and we could catch up when he wakes. Our horses are faster than yours. That way we would waste no time."

The queen hesitated.

Karis turned to her. "Mother? That sounds like a good plan."

"I don't know. It almost seems I should wait. What if you are unable to return?"

Karis laughed. "My friend and cousin would fish me out as he did once before."

"You've been through Fainra?" Alyssa stared openly at Malin.

Malin laughed. "Perhaps it would be closer to say that Fainra had been through me." He cleared his throat.

"Is it nice, or horrid? I know Karis thinks it's nice. But it sounds horrid." Alyssa seemed genuinely curious.

"Horrid," Malin agreed, trying to lighten the mood. "Just a bunch of gray things that keep brushing against you, and they are cold as an old skin made of fog."

"I will wait a little while." The queen was hesitant, not sure how to proceed.

"Malin, when my cheeks have color, I'll return shortly. Don't wake me before, or my mind may be left behind."

Malin nodded, being sure not to look in Karis' eyes, remembering the last time. "I will keep watch," he said, solemnly.

Karis lay on his blanket beside the fire. At first his breathing was slow and even, and he seemed only to sleep. Then all color fled, and he lay motionless as one dead, save for the faint breath that could be felt near his face.

We watch and wait, Malin thought, wishing Rilse were nearby. Just in case, he tried once more to reach him. *Rilse?*

There was no response. So, he thought. We wait, while the enemy and their mad dogs come relentlessly behind us. He turned and gazed toward their back trail. But the woods surrounding them hid everything. He could do nothing but keep watch as he had promised.

12
Harad's Hunters

As they waited and watched, Alyssa found herself feeling cramped and restless. She stood and walked to the edge of the clearing, peering into the white-shrouded woods. They made her shiver. Finally, she found herself walking in the hoof prints of the horses, following them backward to the road. The cold bit at her and she hopped and stamped a little as she went to keep herself warm. The dark brown of her cloak rippled around her, a sharp contrast to the gray stillness.

Reaching the road, she looked up and back as she had seen Malin and Karis do, and suddenly her day had purpose. She could watch for the enemy while Malin and the queen watched over Karis. Quick as a squirrel, she scurried down the road, then up and over the last rise, where but an hour since the two young men had scanned the back trail.

At first she thought it was just a brown patch on the winter road, but then she noticed that the brown patch was moving and growing larger. In sudden fear, she turned and sped down the rise, across the short stretch of road to the clearing and the small fire where Karis still lay white and unmoving. The queen was pacing by the fire. She gave a quick nod of relief when she saw Alyssa, until she saw her face.

"What is it?" The queen's voice was low and quiet. She pulled the child over to the road's edge, away from her son.

"They're coming! They're coming, Mother. Down the road."

"How far?" Queen Gwynne was suddenly breathless.

"A long ways, back where we curved around the river. But they're coming fast." Alyssa, too, was short of breath. "Will they catch us?"

"I don't know, love. Wait here." Gwynne went to Malin, fluid in her motions and so quiet he needed her touch to rouse him. Quickly she motioned him away from Karis.

"The enemy comes. You will know better how many and how far the moving specks on the road may be. I will watch while you go and look."

Malin went, fast as Rilse on a hunting trail.

Gwynne seated herself on the ground by Karis, her keen eyes searching for signs of his return, but he was unmoving. No trace of color showed in his face. Even without the approach of Tallon's trackers she would have been anxious. He had been longer than the hour he planned, and he had been weary when he began. Had the dark mage caught him in Fainra? Every minute brought certain peril to Karis, both from behind and within, yet she dared not disturb him. To do so might bring madness, half-wittedness, even death.

Malin and Alyssa ran into the clearing. "Two hours, maybe," Malin's lips shaped the words, "before they reach us." The queen was horrified. She stared down at Karis, willing him to wake, but he lay motionless.

While she watched, Malin put snow on the fire, and he and Alyssa gathered up what few things they had and re-packed them on the horses. They had not unsaddled so it was scant minutes before all was ready.

Still no movement showed in the form near the now cold fire. No warmth colored his face. The queen touched his hands. He was icy, but the fire could not be rekindled.

She wrapped the blankets tighter, breathing with him, unconsciously urging him to return. Finally, she spoke.

"Karis." Her call was soft, yet insistent.

"Karis." There was no response. Once more she tried. "Karis." She bowed her head, troubled and defeated.

Malin spoke in her ear. "You must take Alyssa and go. Fly for your lives down the south road."

Gwynne shook her head, her eyes empty. "I can't leave my son this way. The wolf. Can't he help?"

"I can't reach Rilse, though I've tried. Maybe he will harry them and buy us some more time, but he's not here now, and they are."

Still she lingered. Malin touched her shoulder. "As soon as he wakes we'll be on our way." He paused, then continued. "There is no need to risk four lives. You may have already waited too long."

"Mother." Alyssa mouthed the word only, not wanting to risk endangering Karis. "What are we to do?" Alyssa's blonde hair showed the feverish activity of moments ago for wisps of it had escaped her hood and trailed around her face.

Unconsciously, Gwynne's fingers smoothed the straggles back into place, and suddenly she really looked at Alyssa.

She stood quickly, gave her a hug, then walked to the horses. "We ride." The words were for Alyssa, but the nod was for Malin, waiting by Karis' side. He was right. Their efforts and lives would count for nothing if she and Alyssa at least did not survive.

She assisted Alyssa to mount, then followed suit. Quietly, they led the horses out of the clearing to the road. Once she looked back; her dark eyes lingered on her son before she lifted her gaze to Malin. Perhaps there was a reason Karis had exacted the promise to watch only from his cousin. She raised her hand in salute, then she was gone.

On the road south, the hunted fled over hills and down into small valleys and up over hills again in a mad dash for safety. Neither the queen nor Alyssa saw the troop of soldiers that, hidden from view, came around the curve where the road almost touched the river. The wind had begun again, and the rush of air from wind and the speed of their own horses were so loud in their ears that both Gwynne and Alyssa heard nothing until the soldiers were riding down upon them.

The horses reared, trying to avoid colliding. For a few seconds it was a melee as horses plunged about trying to keep their footing, but the soldiers were too well trained to permit the confusion for long. An older, grizzled warrior grasped the reins of Alyssa's horse and led the little blonde girl to the captain who rode at the head of the troop. The weary queen, her hair dark against the white of her face, met a like fate, her horse being brought to the captain as well.

The captain was a young man, keen-eyed, and tall in the saddle. He turned his questioning glance from Alyssa to the queen and recognition and amazement flooded his face. In an instant his helmet was in his hand.

"Your Majesty!" The queen and her daughter! Alone? With no escort? What urgent circumstances had brought them here? He knew there was trouble, that's why they had been sent, but he had not expected to find his queen and her only daughter racing south on the forest road, alone.

The fates were kind to them today, thought Gwynne, her eyes finding the silver and blue banners of Westra at the same moment the captain spoke. She knew him. These were troops from Godsel. These were liege men to Lord Lindsey.

"Captain Forsham." Even in such circumstances a greeting was required. Gwynne inclined her head as she spoke. She tried to speak, to explain but found herself breathless

"Are you pursued?" The young man was astute, or perhaps he had been forewarned.

The queen nodded.

"Are they close?"

She tried to say yes, but relief made her breathless, and she was annoyed to have to repeat herself so the captain could hear. "Yes." Time was short, she thought, perhaps run out, for Malin and Karis. And she could not even talk.

"How can we help, Your Majesty?"

She took a deep breath and tried again, purposely stilling the beating of her heart and the quickness of her breath. "The enemy is not far behind. And Karis and Malin are also behind us, right in their path. Can you aid them?"

The captain's face was suddenly stern and purposeful. "We can." He gave commands to his troop. In no time at all the regiment was on its way again, north. Gwynne and Alyssa remained behind with a small guard. They listened for the sounds of battle, but all was quiet. They could barely hear the muffled noise of horses' hooves in the soft fresh snow. The road curved behind them so they could not see the men.

Tallon's huntsmen would find a different quarry than they intended, Gwynne thought, and smiled a little, imagining the looks on their faces. If only the troop arrived in time to help Karis and Malin.

Then distantly she heard what she had been listening for and her heart sank. The sounds of battle were so close. She knew Karis and Malin had been behind that point, behind where the guardsmen were now. They had to be dead, or captured. If only it were the latter, she thought.

She touched her heels to her horse, urging him forward, but the grizzled soldier in charge of guarding Gwynne and her daughter blocked her way.

"Please, Your Majesty. A battle is not a pretty sight, nor is it safe for you and the princess. Bide a bit here. It'll be over soon."

The queen swept back her long dark hair from her face, clearing her vision. "Of course. You're right." But she bit her lip at the delay.

Soon the battle sounds ceased, and silence fell about them. The queen could wait no longer, and once more urged her horse forward, trying to move past those who were blocking her way.

"It will be ugly, Your Majesty." Once more the old soldier angled his horse to obstruct her path. "You should wait a little longer."

"My son was back there." Her voice came out higher and more shrill than usual.

The soldier's face softened. "Let me ride around this bend and see, and do you stay here until the battle signs are cleared away. They are not pretty."

Gwynne was grateful for his concern, but could not bear to wait. She felt as if she had to know the worst. "I'll ride partway with you and wait."

The curve came before they were ready, and there in all its grim reality was the remains of the fray. The dark tunics of their pursuers were stark against the white snow, but not as stark as the crimson stains around them

She gasped and caught her throat, and closed her eyes. Then she opened them again. She had to know the worst. She dragged her eyes past the signs of battle, searching for a dark head, or a blonde one, among the fallen. They were not there. She could not see Karis or Malin among the fallen. She sighed in relief.

One large dog was crouched along the roadway, one of the hunters' killing pack, worrying a saddle bag that had been ripped loose in the fray. When he saw her and her escort, he started up toward them, snarling, his eyes red with madness. The soldier spurred his horse ahead of her, thrusting his mount between the queen and the animal.

But the animal plunged ahead. He came at Gwynne, snarling, crouching to spring. Her horse reared, almost unseating her. The soldier thrust his horse between her and the dog. But the dog moved around him to attack Gwynne once more. Her horse reared a second time. Her right foot came loose from the stirrups and she slipped down on the right side, close to the rabid animal, close enough to feel his breath on her arm as he sprang at her.

Once more the soldier guided his horse past the flailing hooves of her horse, pushing the dog away from her. Again he whirled to once more spring at her, but at the last moment he shifted and leaped for the soldier. But his leap was short and he fell under the hooves of Gwynne's horse. Again and again her horse reared, his hooves striking the dog, trampling him until he could move no more.

The snow beneath the queen was red with the dog's blood. She covered her eyes. When she opened them, the soldier had led her horse away from the encounter. But beyond where they were, on the battlefield that was the road, she could see others, their sprawled corpses not far from the hunters they had served.

From behind her, a small figure rode forward. Gwynne had not meant for Alyssa to follow her, to see this. "Alyssa!" She caught her reins and held her back.

The old bearded soldier placed his horse before Alyssa to block her view. "Is he dead, mother? Is Karis dead?"

Then the captain was by her side. "I'm sorry, Your Majesty. Your son is not here. We were unable to question any before they died, so quick and fierce was the battle. Where was it you last saw the young men?"

The queen gestured north. "Further back on the trail, just beyond that point where the trail curves well away from the river and into the forest. They were at the forest's edge." She fell silent, fear and hope warring within her. Then she lifted her head, the sunset copper on her dark hair which had freed itself from the hood of her cloak, her somber eyes meeting those of the captain. "Let's ride, captain."

The captain looked at little Alyssa, then back at the queen. "Let us clear away the signs of battle first. The enemy is bested. What has happened here will not change."

He was right, Gwynne thought, though she hated the wait. She took Alyssa back south on the road, pacing back and forth along it until finally the captain returned.

"All is ready." He turned his horse to face back where he had come. A nod and the bulk of the troop fell in behind them, Queen Gwynne by his side and Alyssa beside her.

They reached the hill where Alyssa had first sighted the enemy before the queen realized they had missed the clearing.

"Mother, they were back there."

"You're right. We've come too far." They turned back, but the clearing was no longer there. Gwynne closed her eyes. She could not see the clearing, but she could feel it, could sense the singing within her that magic always brought.

She turned to the captain. "They were there." She pointed to an area now covered with trees.

The captain took two or three men and they searched the area, carefully, thoroughly. He returned to Gwynne. "They are no longer there, Your Majesty. They must have gone further into the forest. Shall we follow them? Shall we search the forest? What is your will, my queen?"

The queen was pensive and uncertain. The forest was filled with danger, but from what source she could not say. Yet she knew Karis and Malin were beyond their help, perhaps off to some quest arising out of Karis' trip to

Fainra. Very well. She and Alyssa would ride to Godsel, this time with an armed escort.

"If the enemy missed them, so will we. We ride to Godsel, captain."

But they rested first. A small detail marched forward to bury the dead. The remaining troops stopped and lit a fire. Gwynne did not refuse the hot food prepared over the fire they built, nor did she refuse to answer all the captain's questions, and they were many.

Alyssa was busy asking her soldier friend about his beard and soldiering, and telling him about Rilse. "He is really, really a wolf, though he helps us and finds us caves to sleep in and brings us a rabbit for breakfast stew." Alyssa raced on, with hardly a pause for breath.

When the captain had heard all the queen had to say, he rose with a sigh. "Duke Blandor making an alliance with the north, Mithrond replaced, the king wounded and poisoned? Black news indeed, my queen. We ride for Godsel without delay. Lord Lindsey has need of this news."

Two hours later they were riding up the same rise Gwynne had taken a short time ago. Nothing moved, yet Gwynne's glance roved constantly, feeling a darkness or a presence heavy on the land. As the winter sun dropped over the horizon and night fell quickly upon them, the feeling grew and crawled up her back to her shoulders, where it stayed for the remaining days of their journey to Godsel. The lighting of the lanterns to guide their way did not help. Only when they were finally in Godsel, within the lighted halls of Oldsbury, did the feeling leave. She counted; they had been fourteen days, all told, on the road.

Lord Lindsey hugged her and heard her news in silence. His face, so like his brother's, grew grimmer with each piece of news. "Thank goodness you're here safe, Gwynne. We'll send relief at first light to Rast and Lon and the king. If we left now, in darkness, we might miss their trail and lose valuable time."

He beckoned the tall thin man with the sharp nose and piercing eyes that waited without the chamber. "Medric, make ready. We leave at first light."

"Yes, Sire?" It was a question. The man's eyes quickened and he suddenly shook back the brown hair from his face. Gwynne thought of the hawks she had seen once brought up from the east.

"The king is on his way here, wounded and pursued. We ride up the coast road to the rescue," Lord Lindsey told him. Gwynne caught her breath. The last weeks had taught her sad lessons in trust. Swiftly she searched the face before her. Lord Lindsey, interpreting aright her look, said gently, "If Medric cannot be trusted, I have none who can." Medric's face colored with the praise, but Gwynne knew Lindsey spoke truly.

"Forgive my caution." She, too, was gracious in her turn. "We've been in hard circumstances."

Lord Lindsey turned back to his attendants. "This is a fine to-do. Send for Basil. We could use a good head about now."

The attendant looked at him, confused. "But, sir, Basil is still missing."

"Still missing? He has not returned?"

"No, sir. He has been missing since the night of the ball."

"There has been no word from him since?"

"No, sir. Not since that night. Not since the departure of Lord Malin."

"Maybe they're together," Lord Lindsey mused. "Although the message did not say so. Well, if he shows up, have him come straight here."

"Very good, my Lord. I'll let everyone know." The servant bowed and left the room.

That night, as Queen Gwynne sat alone before her dressing table, the feeling from the forest came again. Even Alyssa, fast asleep beneath the fat white coverlet, stirred restlessly, and the queen wished she had either more of the gift or less. Anything would be better than this half awareness. She lay sleepless in her bed for long hours, feeling darkness thick about her. Finally, toward morning, it lessened and she slept.

13
Through Mountains

Malin was cold, both inside and out. He listened to the fading beat of horses' hooves on snow as the queen and Alyssa fled south. He found himself listening for a similar sound beginning from the north that would herald the approach of his enemies. Minutes crept by, seemingly slowed by the cold, each one adding to the great weight across his shoulders. The riders must be less than half an hour away by now, but he dared not leave Karis' side to find out. And if he was cold, what about Karis?

The enemy would soon be there, he thought, and if he did not come to them, no matter: they would come to him. He brooded over his grim jest, wishing he had someone to share it with. Off in the distance to the north it seemed he could hear the baying of hounds and the drumming of hooves, but he couldn't be sure whether he really heard or imagined them.

He searched Karis' face once more.

"Color in his cheeks. Let there be color in his cheeks," he mumbled. And there was. For the next few minutes he was in a frenzy of impatience. What would be the good of having Karis return safely from Fainra just to be plucked like a chicken for the pot by their pursuers? He had to do something.

He reached out about him into the forest, looking for Rilse. No Rilse. He went on, touching the minds of small creatures, passing by them, searching. Finally he found something. A herd of deer grazed in the woods across the road. Into their minds he placed the image of the clearing, with grazing rising above the snow. He had not worked a lot with deer. Would they respond?

They stirred, restive. Once more he sent the image. The deer began to move slowly toward the clearing, too slowly to help with the danger that was almost upon them. Maybe they were not hungry. Desperate, he tried another tack. He sent images to the deer of wolves around them, then images of safety in the clearing, and down the road. That was all he could do.

Anxiously, he touched Karis' hands. They had lost their icy feel and were once more like human hands. In a few moments Karis had regained his color and his breathing deepened and became faster and stronger. Then he opened his eyes and raised himself up. For a moment he had the blank stare of a sleepwalker or someone newly awakened. Then he was Karis, weary, his strength drained out of him, but Karis.

"Can you ride?" Now Malin could clearly hear, in the distance, the baying of hounds, the jingling of harness, and the thud of hooves in the winter snow.

Karis, too, heard and understood. "What choice is there? Just help me up."

Malin thought a moment, then half dragged, half carried the slighter figure of his cousin over to the horses and pushed him up and secured him in the saddle on Malin's own horse. Malin swung up behind him, trailing Karis' horse.

"Mother and Alyssa?"

"Ahead of us, going south."

They could not follow; their pursuers could be heard topping the rise. So into the forest they went. Malin said afterward that he would rather have gone to Fainra than into that forest. Within its edge, as soon as they were safely hidden, they stopped and froze. To race to safety in its depths would only attract the attention they wanted to avoid.

Their pursuers came in sight. Down the road they could see hounds and riders, in the russet and orange of Anor. They seemed to fly, so fast they went on the snow-covered road. Down the last high hill they came, disappearing from sight for a short space of time into the last valley. When they next appeared, it would be too late for any action from Malin or Karis.

Malin reached out for the deer once more and suddenly found the clearing filled with them, with more on the way. Deer rushed in from across the road, from their side of the road, from all possible directions. They milled about in the clearing for a moment, trampling any tracks the royal company may have left, then hearing the hounds and the drumming of horses' hooves, they fled, one group following the road south before they entered the woods.

One minute the road was full of the sound and motion of deer, the next it was empty. Seconds later it was filled with Tallon's hunters and their hounds and horses, layering more tracks in the small clearing and the road before it. Malin left nothing to chance, however. He thrust image after image of deer into the minds of the dogs.

It worked. The dogs were confused. They whined about, rushing here and there in the tracks of first this deer and then that, trampling snow, racing into the forest on the far side of the road, but only the far side of the road. Malin made sure of that. They had forgotten what they were about.

As the cousins watched, not a single horse or rider turned to glance where Karis and Malin sat their horses within the dark forest. Not a single dog turned a nose more than a foot or two into the clearing. It was almost as if the clearing had never existed, Malin thought, as if they had never stopped there, nor rested their horses, nor made a fire.

Malin looked over at Karis, then he knew. Malin had brought the deer, and muddied the trail and sidetracked the hounds. Karis had erased the clearing and muddied the road even more. His lips were moving, one hand slightly before him, describing symbols in the air.

Malin had seen Karis create illusions, but several piled on top of each other, with a trip to Fainra for good measure seemed beyond what was humanly possible. Malin remembered that the Fainra trip with Karis years ago had cost Karis an afternoon and a night of recovery, even though he did drag Malin with him and back. What would this cost him?

The two young men watched the hunters scatter into the forest on the opposite side of them. Karis clung tightly to Malin's saddle horn and Malin steadied him, keeping control of Karis' horse while they watched. It was at least half an hour or so until the hunters and their animals were able to gather again in some sort of order on the road.

There appeared to be an argument. One of the men seemed to be trying to persuade the others to leave the road and enter the forest on the far side. The main party waited, while several men entered the forest and returned. They shook their heads and shrugged. More discussion followed before the whole party continued down the road, well away from the clearing.

"I hope the queen and Alyssa have enough of a head start," Malin said softly, as the baying of the hounds and the noise of the horses and riders vanished down the south road.

"Me, too," Karis echoed. Malin had to lean forward to hear the answer and was just in time to catch Karis as he slumped forward over the horse's neck. He looked down at Karis and back at the road.

No matter what happened a few miles away, they could not help. The road would become a pretty unpleasant place, and Karis was in no state to navigate such a road, even if he wanted to, let alone help his mother and sister.

Furthermore, if they remained on the road and their hunters returned, they would have no chance of eluding them, not with Karis unconscious. The road was closed to them. Mind touching Karis' horse so that it would follow, Malin took them into the woods.

Karis needed food and rest, but before he could have it, safety demanded they place some distance between themselves and their pursuers. Malin reached out again for Rilse, finding only a faint presence across miles of distance. No help there. If the day had been gloomy and dark along the road, now in the late afternoon, in the brooding forest, it seemed twice as dark. The woods of Afton seemed to hold their breath and wait.

For two hours, Malin rode steadily, into the very heart of the woods, hoping the forest would hide them from possible pursuit by Tallon's men. He, too, was weary from their mad ride to Heath Halls and back. Karis was worse; he slid in and out of waking and sleeping and seemed not to know the difference.

Soon Malin's eyes also began to close, in spite of himself. The wind had risen slightly, and the murmur of pines, the wind sounds, and something else he couldn't quite name, soothed and sedated him. He would wake startled when the gait of his horse changed to clear a fallen tree or avoid a rough part of the trail, then nod off again.

The horses finally stumbled upon a faint trail and like all good horses, their instincts led them to follow it in hopes of food and rest when they reached its end. They came to a high ridge, and began to climb. Their riders made no move to change the way, for one nodded in the half-world of sleep, while the other was completely given over to it.

Suddenly the horses stopped, almost causing Karis to slide over the horse's head had it not lifted it and stood tasting the smells on the wind. The horse made as if to neigh, and Malin, suddenly awake to possible peril, stilled the sound before it was born. He, too, lifted his face to the wind, which had once more shifted to the southwest. It was a bitter wind from the sea. Listen as he might, Malin could hear nothing to have caused the horse's reaction.

The woods were thinning as they approached the backbone of high hills that formed a ridge extending the length of Westra. On the sea side of the hills, the woods were thicker and taller, evidence of the greater moisture that descended upon them as rain. In the summer, moss and ferns and wild flowers grew there in profusion. In winter, they were snow filled and difficult to traverse.

Malin reminded himself that he must stay awake. The sun was gone; the shadows were long. Soon it would be dark. Twilight was short in winter, and cold. A howl in the distance caught his attention. Dog? Wolf? Then it slid out of his sleep-dampened mind.

The pace of the horses quickened as they left the trees and the way became more open and clear. Karis was still a dead weight in front of Malin, and Malin's left arm, which held Karis from falling off, was numb. Malin meant to stay awake. He meant to stay alert and watch and listen for what had startled the horses. Heaven help them if their hunters found the trail, but even that thought could not keep him awake. Sleep was irresistible.

In spite of himself, his eyes closed and his blonde head nodded above Karis' dark one. The horses, on their own again, climbed slowly to the top of the ridge and stopped. Even the change of pace did not wake Malin this time, and he slept on.

He did not see the horses paw the snow nervously, looking down from the woods of the ridge into the west forest, nor did he see the dark figures spread out below, waiting at possible descent points. He did not even see the figure that appeared suddenly out of the swift darkness of the winter night. A hand reached and caught the bridle of Malin's horse and led it north and east, back off the ridge and down, the other horse following.

Karis, for the first time, stirred as if he would wake. He struggled to open his eyes and speak, but unconsciousness would not release him. The horses were nervous from whatever waited in the woods. They followed their guide silently, almost willingly it seemed, as if they were relieved once more to have a human to direct their way.

The wind was still in the west, and the night was dark, for clouds were thick in the winter sky. A light snow was falling, but the rising wind indicated a new storm before morning. Temperatures had dropped with the coming of night, but both Karis and Malin slept on, dreaming in the bitter night that began to feel warm and comfortable.

Their guide led them on, his hopping gait covering the rocks of the bare hills unbelievably fast. Then they were on a trail that wound down from the ridge, away to the foot of the mountain and around its base, ever northward and slightly east. The distance was not far, but they were soon back into thick forest, for the woods grew high up the base of Mount Alden.

If he had been awake, Malin would have questioned their guide, would have demanded answers before trusting him, for none lived in that part of Westra, and only a few roving hunters trod its paths. It was a little-known and seldom-sought area of the country, and it was said that strange things walked those woods. Hunters told tales of going to sleep and waking to find horses and supplies gone, but finding no tracks.

The hunted, too, seemed to vanish without a trace, and strange and fearsome animals were said to prowl the heights of the mountain itself. Yet their guide, nimble and quick, led them directly into the unsavory area, with a brightness of eye that seemed to see through the darkness to the faint trail beneath his feet.

Behind them, a southwest wind flung snow at them, almost in anger, stinging the flanks of the horses and whatever parts of the riders it could find, but the two cousins dreamed on, of warmth and food and safety in Godsel. Especially of warmth. The images of fires and blankets and hot broth surrounded them, and the winter storm driving them before it seemed remote, part of another world, another time.

By now they had circled the edge of Mount Alden so that they approached it from the spot where the mountain folded in upon itself. It looked as if they would walk straight into the wall of rock and brush before them. Then the trail shifted north around a curve and into an open space right at the base of the cliff wall of the mountain.

In the clearing was a rude hut and a slightly larger, but still small, stable. Entering the clearing, the little man walked swiftly into the stable. Within one of the two stalls on either side of the door was an old brown donkey, with one ear shorter than the other and notched on one side. He brayed mournfully as they walked past, his stamp lost in the soft dirt for the stable relied on nature's help for walls and floor.

It looked as if they were heading straight into the mountain, which formed the back wall of the stable. The horses shied a bit and snorted, but the hands holding the reins quieted them. Then their guide raised both hands to his mouth, put a small flute-like instrument that had hung about his neck to his lips, and blew. A rhythmic sound emerged, high and piercing, yet anchored by a low drone that maintained a consistent rhythm. Malin stirred and half opened his eyes at the sound, then he drowsed once more.

The small brown man blew again, then yet a third time, the sound bouncing off the stone in front of him. The sound increased, swelling like the drone of the pipes from the ancient Keeps of Westra. Malin struggled to lift his head and open his eyes, but he could manage only a moment. The horses became calm and quiet. The little donkey's face, sticking out of a crack in the stable, smoothed out and he, too, seemed to listen. In his dream, Karis heard the sound and knew an old, fine magic was at work, a magic he longed for, but he was lost in weakness and exhaustion.

Malin, on the other hand, sat loosely in the saddle, all tension gone out of him. If his eyes had been open, he would have started with surprise for before him the mountainside became translucent, light streaming through it like a curtain on a white July day. The solid stones dissolved, the rocks, the few straggly trees, and there was only light - white, iridescent light - that fractured into all the colors of the rainbow.

Still the sound grew, until Malin felt he was riding on it, riding into safety and summer and home. As they went forward, gradually the sound and light faded, and the rock behind them reformed, a solid wall once more. The old donkey brayed, a demanding sound that changed to a lost and lonely cry as the horses left him behind, back in the stable in the dark winter night.

Malin heard the sound inside his mind. He could feel with him, knew his ears would be drooping sadly about his lowered head. He had smelled fresh grass. Hard to smell spring and be shut out. The feeling brushed away sleep, and for the first time, Malin could truly see their guide.

He walked forward, and the horses followed him in. He was small and quick, brown and wrinkled, with smile lines all around his eyes. His clothing was brown, his eyes were brown, and what Malin could see of his hair was brown. Malin caught a sense of age, much greater than the man appeared, though he was old. It seemed the most natural thing in the world to be following him through a cliff and Malin dozed once more.

Before them was a passageway through a hollow space, seemingly inside the mountain itself. They could see light coming from the far end. As they rode slowly toward that light, Malin came to once or twice, grinned, and went back to sleep. Karis dreamed on of a place where the earth did not age, and no shadow could come.

They reached the opening, high up on the side of a great mountain overlooking a meadow below. The valley was oval shaped, but they could tell little else about it, for wild weather intervened.

"The mountain protests when I bring in strangers. But it'll settle down soon." The words drifted back to them, a light chirp on the wind. Their guide seemed to pay no more attention to what was going on around them, but continued to lead them down into the valley.

The going was hard. The trail was narrow and the cliffs were steep. The wind gusted about, pushing at them. Rain poured down, then cleared up, then came again as hail that pelted them fiercely. It was as if all the world's weather was in a great churn that whirled about them.

Their guide pulled them close to the mountainside, letting the wind carry the hailstones beyond them. Other than that, he paid no attention to the adverse weather conditions, nor did he seem too concerned about the sheer cliffs, the precipices and drop offs that lay to their right as they followed the switchbacks down the mountain. An occasional boulder crashed down and blocked the path. He pried at them one at a time, shifting them until they tumbled over the cliff and bounced away. Their noise was lost in the continuous rumbles of thunder overhead.

Then they were down. Malin smelled spring earth, the soil moist and rich with growing things. He caught images in the horses' minds of water and sweet grass. There were trees freshly green with sap springing through their trunks and branches. Though drowsy, Malin felt more awake than he ever had in his life. Their horses whinnied, others as yet unseen, replied.

Further into the valley, their horses stopped before a brown cottage with a roof thatched with branches still green and living. There were brown shutters, and an open door. Behind it was what looked to be a stable, its doors wide with the fragrant smell of hay riding on the breeze. Their horses were unsaddled and turned loose to eat and drink.

Malin roused enough to help carry Karis in to a soft bed, then tumbled into one himself. Once in bed, Malin half awoke, mumbled something about Basil and a steaming cup, then slept. Karis never stirred. Both slept deeply, their eyes shut, bodies still, the mountain's pique forgotten in the valley's gold light and green grass. How long they slept, they did not know for time seemed to have no meaning where they were.

When Malin awoke, through the windows of the cottage he could see blue skies and sunlight, yet the peaks of the mountains were hidden in gloomy clouds. Snow could be seen in places where the cloud cover broke before it reformed and dark firs climbed the mountainsides to vanish into the clouds.

But it seemed as if the weather and harsh conditions at the summit were forbidden to enter the valley itself. An altogether pleasant place, Malin decided, then he fell asleep again and dreamed of a strange people who could merge with things of the earth and heal them, and one who stood with rainbows of light streaming about her. There were people around him, some felt familiar but he could not be sure. It was as if he dreamed through a mist, or a veil.

Their guide left them there, and returned to the winter mountains, to the lone donkey, settling him down for the night, while the wind played with the snow, making drifts here and bare patches there. In the stable he removed any traces of the travelers' trail. The wind had already taken care of those outside. In the meager hut, he stirred a dying fire, drank a cup of thin gruel, and sat on the bed with its several thin blankets and one worn coverlet, and waited. As he waited, he, too, drowsed and nodded.

He woke to the sound of horses filling the clearing and a sharp banging at the door. He rose up to answer it, but the weak bar was snapped, the hinges jarred, and the door thrust inward before he could reach it. Filling the doorway were three men, small and lean. Their dark eyes and hair and faces, plus the strange stuff of their robes announced them as foreign before they spoke and their accents further betrayed them. Past the door, the bright eyes of the old man could see their horses as well as three other riders still mounted.

The foremost of the three strode quickly through the small hut, thrusting his hand against the faded hangings on the far wall that butted the cliff. Like the brown donkey's stable, the floors were dirt and the man stamped off the dust contemptuously as he strode back to the old man.

"You're alone here?" Although the tones were quite mellow, something in the voice grated on the ear, some hidden menace in the tone.

"Alone? As you see me, sir. As you see me. What can Lide the Hermit do for such visitors? A bit of fire? Some gruel for the frosty night? My house is poor, but it is open to you. Old donkey has room in the stable for company, too." His words tumbled over each other and as he spoke he hopped to the fire, added wood, and pulled off the kettle of thin gruel.

"Don't often get visitors, and on such a night, too."

The voice of the taller man broke in on him again, but the words were not addressed to him, they were not even in his language. The men in the courtyard dismounted and disappeared.

The man turned back to Lide. "Have there been others here tonight?"

The hermit fixed his bright eyes on the man. "None been in this hut but yourselves." He chuckled and skittered in front of his fire, his face to its flames. "Will you sit by my fire?"

The men made no response to him. By now those who were sent to check the stable had returned, shaking off snow as they did so.

"Nothing there. Just an old donkey." On his way out of the door, the leader paused. "If others do come, Coomb of the Black Horses will pay for news."

"Pay?" The old voice was almost eager. "Pay for news?"

"Aye. Two shecuts for word and if we catch up with them, ten more."

"Twelve whole shecuts? For who?"

"A traveler. A slight young man with black hair and blue eyes."

Lide's voice was high and shrill, his voice calculating. "Pay, you say?"

Mounted, the man turned in the teeth of the storm to once more face the open doorway.

"Two shecuts for word and ten more when we catch up with him. But if you do not send word, we'll drive your donkey out to the wolves and throw down your house and stable and close in the mountain about this place. Coomb of the Black Horses has spoken."

"What do ye want with such a traveler?"

"Someone wants to talk to him. Remember!"

"Where shall I send word?"

The man stared at him for a moment, then he took a small stone from his coat pocket and handed it to the old man. "If they come, put this in your fire and leave it there. We will know." Then, with a jangle of bridles and saddles they were gone, the sound of their horses lost in the wild flurries of the storm.

The old man peered after them a moment, holding the stone, shifting it from hand to hand. Then he suddenly placed the stone in a jug of water, watching it dissolve into nothingness. He closed the door. The wooden block that had held the bar had been snapped, but it was only a few minutes work to replace it and bar the door.

But even in those few minutes the storm was so wild that the floor was dusted with a layer of snow, and the fire in the hearth burned low and smoked, almost extinguished by gusts of wind. Usually the hut was quite sheltered, but tonight, a fierce wind forced itself around the cliff and into the clearing, where it lost all sense of direction, and like a summer dust devil, spiraled, sweeping the yard.

Inside, his door closed, Lide the Hermit once more sat upon his bed with the coverlet about him, staring at something no one else could see, his eyes fire bright.

"Pay, is it? So. They're coming to old Lide, now. They must want my traveler pretty badly. They've good woods skills to find their way here." He licked his lips. "Twelve shecuts, they said. Worth twelve shecuts? We should look at such treasures."

He rose up and almost scurried out the door and into the storm, where the bare cliff loomed above him. Once more the strange humming was heard, the curtain of light appeared. Then, taking his donkey, he led it through the mountain of light into summer, while the stone reformed behind him. The howling wind, shut out, tumbled a small avalanche of loose stones and snow off the mountainside to block the entrance into his small clearing. No other visitors could come. His hut would wait untouched until his return.

14
The Valley

In the valley, Karis slept in a warm cottage with a glowing fire, watched over by Malin and Lide, their guide, a little cricket of a man who chirped his way through walls. Karis slept for two days; he had only a dim memory of liquids being poured down him, of Malin and a small man coming and going. The mind had taken the body far in his workings of magic, and it was a long time returning. In the back of his head, or perhaps somewhere in the back of the world, darkness grew. In the middle of it was Lon. Somewhere, a lodge was empty, its fire burning low, its door open to the storm.

Then his dreams changed. Karis dreamed of singing that surrounded him and out of which worlds were made. It grew and so did trees and flowers, animals and insects and fish. Suddenly, he felt filled with spring and laughter and the strength of sunlight. He stirred in his sleep and smiled.

On the morning of the third day after their rescue by Lide, Karis awoke, really awoke, to see sunlight streaming into the room through an open door. On his face he felt the warm breath of early summer. Summer? How could that be? He had fallen asleep in winter. Nevertheless, it was. Six windows were scattered around the room he lay in, and through each one, morning sunlight poured. Karis relished the food and the rest and the warmth, but he drank in the clean magic as if it were water in a dry desert.

He raised himself to a sitting position, breathing deeply the air that smelled of fresh-cut grass. Then he tossed back the covers. Short pants and a shirt were on a chair by the bed. He dressed and walked through the open door out into the center of a grassy meadow. He walked for the delight of walking on a sunlit plain under a warm sun. Care and shadow fell from him; fatigue and worry slipped away. In the center of the meadow, he dropped from weak legs to lie flat on the sweet grass. He looked up at the clear sky above him and laughed, delight dancing in his dark eyes. There was no dark mage. In fact there was no darkness.

Malin, brown and loose-limbed, came and dropped beside him. "So you're finally awake. I was afraid you might sleep forever."

"Malin, where are we? Summer, sunlight, safety—all in a valley that shouldn't exist in a season that's not supposed to be here for months. I know I slept for a long time, but not that long. How did you find it?"

"I didn't." Malin was a little rueful. "You were out cold, and a heavy sleep overcame me. Lide the Hermit brought us here. The woods were full of hunters searching for us, with Tallon's dogs howling on our back trail."

"Who or what is Lide?"

Malin stretched himself out beside Karis on the grass. "The animals' protector, a guardian, I don't know. He says he doesn't usually work with people, but because we were hunted he gave us a hand. Animals are his care." Malin plucked the inner piece of a grass stalk and bit off the soft tender shoot. "A good thing, too," he continued. "Not only were Tallon's hunters behind us, but there were also servants of the dark mage west of the ridge. Six of them tracked their way over to Lide's outer cabin searching for us. They offered him money for news of us."

"Southern riders? Looking for us?"

"Lide says they came from the south. Want to know how much we are worth?" Malin's eyes were bluer than usual with mischief.

"How much?"

"Our inestimable carcasses are worth twelve shecuts."

"How much is that?"

"Lide says it would buy about two or three horses."

"Phew!" Karis whistled softly. "Well, at least if we're hunted, we're somewhat valuable. How does Lide know what a shecut is?"

"He was rather vague when I asked him. It felt like he couldn't remember how he knew." They were silent together.

Malin spoke first. "Karis, what happened in the Spirit Walks?"

Karis shivered. At first Malin thought Karis would not answer him, but with an effort, Karis began to speak. "I made my way past the shades in the lower stretches, where you and I went years ago. They don't touch me, you know. My gifts make me part of Fainra, and I attract about as much attention there as a leaf falling from a tree."

"If I have gifts as you say I do, why do they come after me?"

"You push Fainra away, rather than accepting it. If you relaxed, you, too, could feel at home there."

"Right." Malin was skeptical. "As if I would want to."

"Really," Karis insisted. "You could."

Malin changed the subject. "Go on. What happened?"

"In Fainra, there are places of light and places of shadow. There are places to see what is, and was and will be. Beyond the shades, up over the hills and into a higher valley is a pool. On one side, its edges lap the foot of a mountain; its bottom there is dark and pebbly. The other sides are lost in the long reeds and rushes that finally become meadow. If you walk around the mountain edge, you come to a small promontory made by the steeper curve of the mountain that protrudes into the pool. The waters are deeper there, just below a small ledge. If you sit there and watch, visions come. You can see what is, what moves in the world of men."

Karis fell silent. He neither stirred nor spoke. Malin wondered if he would continue. When he did, Malin had to look to be sure it was Karis. His voice had changed; it was almost harsh sounding.

"I went there. I settled myself and gazed into the pool. Soon I could see images of Lon and Rast and the king, sleeping soundly in an old hunting lodge, sheltered from the storm, the cold. Then my seeing was disturbed. I was no longer in the forest in the hunting lodge. I could see the waters of the pool were troubled. As I continued to watch, they darkened and began to roil, the depths churning, a froth forming on the top, obscuring my vision. Suddenly *he* was there."

It was anger, thought Malin, in Karis' voice. Karis was filled with rage. "Your watcher?"

Karis almost spat the words. "My watcher. Yes. I felt him moving across the ridge I had traversed, coming toward me into the valley as I sat at the mountain's foot. It felt as the forest had, that night he came." Karis was silent for a long moment.

Malin urged, softly, "And then?"

"The mists above the waters gathered into the shape of a young woman who fled the pool and ran up the mountainside past me. The pool water began to bubble and boil, as if a fire were under it. Steam began to rise; the heat scorched my face. I followed the figure, for I took it to be the spirit of the pool. I didn't know what protection she might offer, but there was none elsewhere. I left the pool's edge and ran after her, for my life, it seemed. Maybe for my soul." Karis paused.

Malin said nothing.

"I fled, and the mage pursued me. The woods rising up the slope of the mountainside beyond the pool led to a great labyrinth of caves, beginning with a large central opening filled with formations that stretched deep into the cliff." He paused, remembering.

"I had meant to explore them sometime in my life, but with the threat of the mage in Fainra I never had. Many of the caves and passageways ended in rock walls, but some of them threaded through the caves and emerged on the hill of the sacred stone. I knew if I could just make it there, I would be safe. There, only beings of light can come."

Malin looked out over the meadow, behind Karis' back, suddenly startled to see a white creature slowly emerge from the distant woods, moving with a measured gait toward them.

Karis did not notice Malin's attention was elsewhere, and continued. "He was stalking me. I could feel his presence behind me, taking his time, sure I had no escape. He was right. I didn't know my way through the caves, and I could not climb the mountain in time. He was fresh, and I was worn. Even my spirit was tired."

Malin's creature emerged fully into the sunlight, one bright ray glinting off the sheen of a single horn on its forehead. Malin caught his breath. A unicorn. He had not ever thought to see such a thing in his world. They were only stories, right? But there it was, walking toward them.

He interrupted Karis, leaning forward to touch his shoulder. "Look!"

Karis stopped his narrative and turned. "A unicorn?" Amazement filled his voice. For a long moment the unicorn surveyed them. Karis' tension dissolved and his anger dropped away.

Malin heard a new voice in his head, quiet, solemn, yet piercing. *Thou of earth magic, keep safe this bearer of light.* The unicorn's gaze rested upon Malin, and inexplicably, in that moment, Malin bowed his head in acceptance of the charge, realizing he had already shouldered that responsibility. Then the unicorn vanished back into the trees.

"What did he say to you?" Karis knew the unicorn had spoken, and Malin had heard it.

"To keep you safe."

"Why?"

"Who knows what's in a unicorn's head? But if you're going to rush madly into storms in the dead of winter unprepared, someone has to keep you safe." Malin had one eyebrow raised, a glint in his eye.

"I see. That's all he said?"

"That's all. A unicorn comes to visit and all he has to say is take care of you. What about my issues?"

Karis laughed with Malin. "Apparently, you have none. Did he mention me by name?"

"No."

"Then how did you know it was me?"

Malin repeated the words of the unicorn.

The two cousins were silent for a long time, before Karis once more picked up his story. His voice was lighter now, his tale less troubling to him. "I followed the water spirit to the cave entrance, not knowing what else to do. She fled inside, and I followed, fingers of dark already crawling up my spine. I stumbled and fell, for my eyes were unaccustomed to the black. I regained my footing, looking for the water spirit, but I could no longer see her. I was blind in that cave, but something drew my heart to the left, into one of the passages there. I hugged the left wall, trying to get as far as I could from the mage." He fell silent, remembering.

Malin waited, unmoving, not wanting to break the vision that held Karis, but glad he already knew the ending of the story.

Karis' voice softened, as if he spoke to himself. "Then there was light. Just a brief moment, but the pool spirit shone, luminous, before me. Then she vanished, like our unicorn, except for one hand, visible and extended. I reached and caught it before I thought, and was surprised to find it tangible. It pulled me into one of the side caves, tugging me now here, now there.

"I ran, out of breath, seeing nothing but the faint light from the hand. Time did not exist. I gasped for air, and felt like I had run forever, that I had to continue to run forever. Behind me came the mage.

"But I held a pool spirit's hand, and it led me on. When I would have fallen, it lifted me up, when I had run my last and could run no more, it pulled me forward and I could continue.

"Around a curve we came, and the walls converged, the ceiling descended, until I could hardly go forward. We curved again to the opposite side. I hoped that the mage was too big, that the cave would stop him before he could reach me. I was down on my knees, scrabbling toward the faint light that spilled through a small opening in front of me. Behind me, I felt the mage, still coming. He had slowed, sure of his quarry. He could just reach out and snag me.

"The spirit hand pulled on mine, and I threw myself flat, sliding on my belly after it, using my limbs to propel myself forward, and then I was suddenly through, as if spat out of the mountain's side. I rolled onto my back, pulling my legs through, tumbling away and down. I was in full daylight, on a hillside. The brightness stung my eyes after the blind black of the cave. I turned back to the small opening I had just squirmed through, wondering if the mage could follow, but there was no opening, only earth and rock."

"How did that happen?" Malin discovered a growing curiosity about magic, in spite of himself.

"I'm not sure. It was as if the light had hedged out the dark. Anyway, I was left facing another meadow that rolled forward to a great, steep hill. On the top were stones rising straight up into the sky."

"There's sky in Fainra? When I was there, everything seemed gray and cold, mist covered."

"In that place there was sky, clear and cloudless, and a blue so deep you couldn't see its end, like here. I don't remember moving. Perhaps I just thought about it, but the next thing I knew I was there, on top of that hillside, sitting on a flat stone inside a circle of standing stones. Before me was the largest; it drew my gaze. The sides of the other stones were roughhewn, as were the other three sides of this one, but the side facing me was smooth and dark. As I watched, images appeared across its face, images that finally assembled into a map of Fainra. It showed me the presence of the dark mage as a black figure, and his path as a red line.

"I sat there for a long time, watching him try to reach me. But no matter what trail he took, the way was hedged. He finally retraced his steps out of the cave, past the pool and down to the gray mists, and out of Fainra. I had eluded him; in that place, he could not find me. But I was pushed to return. Back in Westra the hunters were still pursuing us, and we had little time."

"When you went to leave, was the mage waiting? Was it a trap?"

"I wondered that, too. When I entered the valley and saw the standing stones on the hilltop and thought about being there, suddenly I was there. That was not true for the other places in Fainra, just for this inner place. When I went to leave, I tried it again. I thought of the place of entrance, by the gray shapes, and suddenly I was there, but I was in a cocoon of gold light that surrounded me until I left Fainra. I think it protected me from the mage's awareness, or perhaps his power, or both." Karis lay back full length on the grass, and was silent.

Once more Malin could hear the chatter of insects and birds, the shiver of leaves on the trees when a sudden breeze shook them. He could hear the brook falling lightly, insistently on pebbles in its path. Give me the earth, he thought. No spirit place. Give me the earth.

"This isn't our world," Karis said. Malin knew it was a statement, not a question.

"I think—," Malin hesitated. He was out of his element in such things. "I think this is a fold of our world, a pocket where time isn't. From what he says, Lide must be at least three hundred years old, but in this valley he doesn't age, and neither do his animals."

"I see. That would make sense. And us? Do we age?"

"No." It was Lide; unheard by either, he had joined them.

"While we are here, does time continue in our world?"

"Yes. Two days have come and gone while you've slept. But it's food time for you and then more sleep."

"Right." Malin rose to his feet. "We haven't bent our backs and worked our fingers to the bone to throw our efforts away on a malcontent who will not stay abed," he joked, reaching a hand down to Karis.

"Two days." Karis stood and ran his fingers through his dark hair, his voice thoughtful. "It seems longer than that. Much longer." After his walk down into the valley, Karis found his legs weak and shaky. Malin had to support him on one side and Lide on the other to return him to the cottage.

The sunlight was warm on the back of his neck and legs, for the pants he had put on were short. He felt the sunlight pouring into him, healing him, strengthening him. Back under the fat coverlet and the thick down bolster, Karis devoured a bowl of stew and some fresh-baked bread. Then sleep claimed him and he gave in with a smile, tasting the sun-fresh breeze once more. Over this valley not even the shadow of the black mage could come.

In the next days his strength returned in a rush, but Karis found himself more and more reluctant to leave the valley.

Malin fretted and waited and wondered if a spell was upon Karis.

On the sixth day, at sunset, Karis saw the unicorn once more as he walked alone, following the stream, and knew it was time to go. He could delay no longer. He sought out Lide, whom he found in the barns, tending a young doe with a fawn.

"Just newly come. Chased by wolves and the bitter weather," he told Karis, wiping the blood from a cut on the fawn's leg.

"Can things come here over the mountains?" Karis stood watching the old man, until shrewd eyes were turned upon him.

"No. Only through the mountain passage, and then only with my help."

"In the morning we must go." Karis sighed. He said the words, almost wishing to have them returned as unacceptable.

"Aye. You've a work to do. The hunters have returned to the southlands, I think, and your road is now open." Lide released the little fawn and watched her spurt away from him. "The dark one's servants have left the woods."

"And the lodge lies empty." Karis' voice was suddenly hollow, his eyes black and flat. He met Lide's gaze. "At least I dreamed so, when we first came."

"True dreams come to those who rest here. False ones fall away."

Karis nodded. "I know."

"Your horses are healed and will bear you now." Lide's eyes were full of compassion. "I will prepare them for the morrow." Hopping out the door after the fawn, he added, "For such as ye, the cliff door is always open." Then he was off, across the meadow, where he disappeared into the woods.

"The morrow." Karis sighed bitterly, almost wishing that it would not come.

15
Potters Woods

The next morning, their horses, saddled and bridled and packed with provisions, were before the door of the cottage when they arose at sunrise. They dressed and ate the berries and cream and bread and cheese laid out for them on the table, but there was no sign of their odd host. They gathered their few things, stowed their coats behind their saddles since it was too warm to wear them, and then stood waiting.

"We can't leave without thanking him, right?" asked Karis.

"Right," Malin replied.

They delayed a little longer, tightening a strap here, shifting a bag there. But no Lide. Finally, not knowing what else to do, and catching the restlessness of their horses, they mounted and rode slowly away from the cottage. On the edge of the meadow, they turned for one last look at Lide's haven before they started on the trail up the mountain side.

When they turned back toward the mountain, they could see Lide waiting for them at its foot, sitting on his drooping donkey.

Malin looked at the poor donkey. "Can't really blame him," he said to Karis. "No one wants to leave summer for a winter storm."

Karis' smile was grim. "No one, indeed."

They followed Lide, climbing the mountain, circling through the switchbacks, waiting for the wild weather to descend upon them, but the weather held fine. "Guess the mountain is willing to let us out, just not too willing to let us in," Malin pointed out.

They climbed single file through the mountain passage until they were face to face with the stone wall on the inside of the cave. Karis watched in delight as Lide lifted his small instrument and played and the mountain once more became transparent and let them through to the other side.

Then his delight faded as he saw the cold and snow, and once more remembered his dream. Outside the stable, a bitter wind was waiting, but not as bitter as the thoughts that flooded Karis' mind, and the feelings that rushed into his heart. Somehow he knew the enemy had Lon. Whether the knowledge came from Fainra or from his dreams in the valley, he could not be sure. But he knew it was so.

"I'll take ye as far as the ridge trail," Lide said, guiding them out of the clearing. "Back to where I found ye."

They followed him silently, Malin first, then Karis, down the narrow twists and turns, then up to the ridge, winding south along it. Bits and pieces of the trail touched a memory or two in Malin's mind, but as a whole, he was astounded at how little he recognized from the way they had come. He had really been asleep. He shuddered when he thought about what might have happened to them if Lide had not come.

Lide stayed with them until they were on the ridge overlooking the west woods where he had first found them. They turned to thank him, but he was already disappearing back into the storm.

They took the trail down through the woods, toward the sea, where they found Rilse waiting.

You are slow.

Karis has been resting.

The others took shelter over here. Come. Rilse led the way to the lodge.

"Where is he taking us?" Karis tried to squash his feelings of dread.

"Down to a lodge in the woods."

"But they're not there."

Rilse, is anyone still there?

No.

"He says the lodge is empty now," Malin informed Karis. "How did you know?"

"Dreams, I think."

But his twin and the king and the hunter were here.

"Rast and Lon and my father were here." Karis was not asking, Malin realized, he was just confirming what he already knew.

Days earlier Lon and Rast and the king had outwitted Tallon's men and found refuge in that lodge, thought Karis. But they were not there now. "What happened?"

I came too late. Rilse paused on the trail before them.

"He says he came too late."

So his dark dreams were confirmed. But Karis could not yet bear to share his fears with Malin.

Too late for what?

The enemy was already gone.

Malin pulled up his horse and stopped in surprise. *The enemy? What enemy?*

"What is it? What is Rilse saying?"

"He says the enemy was here." Malin was astounded.

The enemy found them in the lodge.

The enemy from the north?

No. The south. They took Karis' brother.

Took Lon? Malin was aghast. Rast and Lon and the king had outwitted Tallon and his hunters, only to be snapped up by southern riders? He turned and looked searchingly at Karis. Suddenly he understood. Karis knew. Something in Fainra or Lide's valley had let him know.

At the lodge Karis dismounted in silence.

Still in silence they tethered their horses in the stable.

Only Rast could have known the lodge was even there, thought Malin. It was off the road itself, down a thin trail that was hardly even visible to the untrained eye. So how could the enemy have found him?

So the enemy has Lon.

Yes.

But not the king or Rast?

No. Not them.

Where are they?

Gone on to Godsel, I think.

And Lon?

They take him south.

Who are they?

Riders and something else from the south. Something not quite like men, servants of the dark mage. They do not ride horses; I don't think horses would bear them. They are foul.

They walk? In this snow and cold?

Not exactly. Rilse was hesitant.

What?

I don't know.

Karis was standing at the threshold of the lodge, staring inside at the room. Behind him, Malin's glance took in the logs of the cabin, the large hearth with the rough oak mantel over it, the pile of wood stacked beside it. In front was a bearskin, to the side a cot. A table and a couple of wooden chairs completed the room. There were no secret corners, no closed spaces. What was taking Karis so long?

"Dark magic." Karis' tone was flat. He walked several steps into the room and froze. Then he tried to move and stumbled about until Malin led him to the cot. Karis sat there, unmoving, his eyes glazed.

Fainra? Malin asked Rilse.

No. A seeing of some sort.

In his mind's eye Karis, in the forest lodge, could see the king's party sleeping, as if he were there. He could see both Lon and Rast try to rouse themselves without success. He watched, helpless, while fragments teased their minds, little things not in place, but as in nightmares where all action is slowed or stopped, they slept on. In their room a heady scent grew, sickly sweet, coming from the fireplace. A black vapor arose, flowing across the floor.

Once, with a mighty effort, Karis saw Rast half rise, his weight resting on an elbow, his eyes gazing at the fire. But his eyes soon closed, and against his volition, he slumped over, asleep once more.

He slept on as dark figures gathered outside the lodge. Karis could sense their presence beyond the door. They grew, shadows out of shadows. There were six of them in a semi-circle about the entrance, silent as stone, shrouded in dark robes. The door they were facing suddenly swung inward.

They entered the lodge and, in total silence, bound Lon, paying no attention to the sick king on his cot by the fire, nor to Rast, where he lay awake now, eyes open, but helpless to move. Four of them lifted Lon up and carried him away as if he weighed nothing, their movements synchronized, working together effortlessly.

Just before the last two left, one went to the fire, reached in and plucked up something, a coal, a rock, something. Karis couldn't see what it was, but it emitted a black light and darkness filled the room, in spite of the white snow that now blew back into the room from the door that stood partly open.

In the present, Rilse went to Karis, putting his paws on his knees, his tongue licking his face. Slowly Karis came back to them, suddenly burying his face in the coat of the white wolf before him, his arms about Rilse's shoulders.

Then he raised his head and looked at them. "They have taken Lon. The mage has sent foul servants and they have taken him." Karis' voice was harsh, his eyes burning. "Just as I saw it or dreamed it. The servants of the dark mage have my brother."

Malin sank into one of the wooden chairs opposite Karis, not knowing what to say.

"I think Rast has taken the king on to Godsel." Karis' voice faltered. "But they've got Lon. I think his servants think he's me. The mage was far away, and we were in Lide's valley. He couldn't find me there. And Lon was asleep. He doesn't know he's got Lon. He thinks he has me."

"And when he finds out?"

"I don't know. Lon will be of no use to him."

Malin understood his fear, that if Lon was of no use to him, the mage would kill him, or absorb him. "Not so. He'll not harm Lon. He will become the bait he uses to catch you."

"Then Lon has a chance?"

"He does. We'll find him."

They both became aware of their surroundings about the same time. They discovered there was a stench in the room that even the wood smoke and fire, and a good airing out, could not remove, no matter what they did. The floor also had a foul blackness neither Karis nor Malin could wipe away.

Rilse would not stay there. *I'll come in the morning,* he said and was gone into the night.

Malin wished he could go with him. The winter woods were cleaner, but he stayed. Karis seemed fixed to the cabin, and he might need Malin.

Neither slept well that night; whenever Malin awoke he found Karis staring into the fire. The capture of his twin was a great blow to Karis, especially since the mage, or the watcher, was really after him. Finally he fell asleep only to cry out strange words, "The stones, the stones! The black sleep——." But he didn't wake. When Malin asked Karis later about his words, Karis had no memory of them, nor of his dreams.

When the first light of morning touched them, they were up and off, as if they couldn't leave fast enough. They did not even pause to eat. Rilse joined them outside. They discovered, as Rilse had said, there was no trail to follow, but they had to try. At least Karis had to and Malin was his tracker.

But their efforts availed them nothing. Even Rilse's nose couldn't ferret out any real information. The storm had wiped out all traces of those who had been before them. The wind had broken many branches, so they couldn't use those to track with. There was no scent of those who had come and gone, except the vile smell they had found tied to the black marks on the floor. Outside, the storm had removed any smells, even those of Lon. It had also filled in all tracks with snow, blowing some into drifts that changed the shape of the land. They found no trace of the enemy, or of Lon. They had both vanished into the storm.

But Lon had been that way. Days earlier, Karis' brother had felt himself bound hand and foot, and still paralyzed, carried out of the hunter's cabin into the storm. He had felt the bite of wind, the cold of snow like someone in a dream, someone remote and detached from the world about him.

He could not have said how long they carried him before they stopped, those black servants of the watcher. Somehow he knew they had come from the watcher. They had felt that way. It could have been minutes they carried him, it could have been hours or perhaps even days. He had no way of knowing. He was in and out of consciousness and his sense of time was totally disrupted.

They had wrapped him in a robe of the same fabric they wore, bundling it about him so that he could not see. He tried to fight them, but the paralysis he had experienced wore off very slowly. One of them, perhaps the one carrying him, finally loosened the robe and sat him up, forcing a drink down his throat that burned as it went. But even that did not chase away the cold that filled him at the creature's touch. Something more than the storm, he thought, a bitter cold that was part of the creature, a cold that he could taste.

He moved in and out of consciousness, possessed by a terrible weakness that left him truly helpless, too weak to even find his way out of the net that was the robe. The drink, he thought. It had to be the drink. But even that thought faded out of his mind.

Eventually they stopped. Somewhere out of the wind, Lon noted, as he came to for a few minutes, for the sound of it subsided and the force of it on his body lessened. They sat him down against a stone wall and left him there for what seemed a long while. In addition to the wind, he could hear the roar of the sea on the rocks of a shore, and he struggled to free his face and eyes from the black fabric.

He could hear the shouts of men, more distant, but the servants of the enemy, like the one who carried him, made no sound. Not from the north, he thought. Not Turgor's men. Who then? But it was too much for his dazed state and he gave up the puzzle and went under again.

When he next awoke, he could hear not only the shouts of men, in a language he did not know, but the grating of wood on rock, and the splashing of water. Like small boats being launched, he thought. Yet they were sheltered, Lon sensed. The full force of the storm still did not reach them.

A cave near the sea? But his thoughts were small bits floating around in his head. They seemed to mean nothing to him, to have nothing to do with his life. He was lost in strange dreams, in nightmare images that rose up, swelled, then died away, lost in masses of gray interspersed with sharp, horizontal black lines. And through it all he was drowning in a gray numbness interspersed with nausea.

Somewhere beneath it all, he kept trying to catch something, a thought that would come close, then recede, an important thought, something about a drink. But he never could quite remember it. Once he remembered the king was ill. But his own nausea swallowed that, too.

Then he was picked up and put in a boat, the cloth dropping from around his face, his arms free for a moment. And the motion outside and the motion inside combined together against him. He leaned weakly against the side of the boat, then the inner convulsion rocked him and what was inside was now outside and, hopefully, outside the boat. No one seemed to pay him any attention. They were busy launching the boat and rowing it—where? That small thought came and went quickly.

After that, his mind cleared. He had thrown up the potion before it spread throughout his system. He could see they were on the water heading to a small ship not far from the coast. Why? He thought. What had that to do with Godsel and rescuing his father? How had he gotten there?

He looked around him. Who were these men? He looked ahead in the moonlight to the misshapen lumpy shadows in the front of the boat. Who were those silent creatures whose touch froze the very blood in his body? Those creatures had now left him to the care of the men, and he was glad for that.

Then they reached the ship, and the movement as the men lifted him on board was too much. Once more he was unconscious, arousing only now and then to reach the borders between sleeping and waking, but not sure which was which. Once he stirred, seeing Karis' face, his hand reaching out to touch him, but then Karis vanished and only a dark shadow was there.

Lon found he had no memories of actually boarding the boat, but he came to briefly in a bunk below deck, with one of the black garbed silent ones beside him that froze his blood. The creature raised Lon's head, pried his mouth open, and once more forced a drink down his throat. It burned all the way down, taking away his breath and his mind, while his body froze. Weakly, he raised a hand to push the drink away, but he was feeble and strangely reluctant to touch the being beside him.

The drink went down. For long minutes after, the burning consumed him and derailed his mind. Then he found himself shaking with cold, his lungs gasping for breath, breathing in air that was so cold it burned.

Yet in that moment, though he was too weak to push the draught away, he had been aware enough to recognize his danger. That gave him hope, before he was back in drug induced confusion. If he could elude the drink, he could recover.

Time passed. How much, he could not measure. He thought briefly of Karis, wondering if this was how he had felt. He was conscious of only two things: the bitter cold of the touch of black robed things—he could not bear to call them men—and the burning of the drink they forced down him.

In between was only vague madness, the confusion of half dreams, of nightmares.

16
A New Music

Back in Godsel, Myrrha was caught up in the regular routine of her life there. She continued to play each week at the church, and by invitation in the wealthier folk's homes.

She found, as her playing increased, so did her sensitivity to sound. Noise became unbearable. The clatter of carriages on cobbled streets, the shrill voices of children, their shouts and yells, drained her energy.

As a defense, she sought the solitude of the woods, spending less and less time in town around people. Whenever her playing evoked glowing symbols in the frame of her harp, she would reap a wild whirlwind of dark emotions that buffeted her for hours afterward, leaving her exhausted and numb. She began to take great care to avoid those glowing symbols, but despite her efforts, noise was like an irritant to her mind.

She discovered that if the church were empty, she could find peace there, her attention caught by the murals on the walls. There was one that drew her, a man and a woman in a garden, the woman offering fruit to the man. She thought she would like to learn more about them, and the one god.

She was also troubled by the presence of the king's son at her concert on the ship. She had not been able to deal with the welter of emotions that assailed her then, so she had wrapped herself in sound and retreated. But when she went up on deck, what was that great darkness she had felt surrounding him at the ship's rail?

Afterwards, she had felt he and his cousin were waiting for her, watching for her after they had docked in the harbor. What had they wanted? They came to no more of her concerts, but when they didn't, that disturbed her, too. They had looked for her, but no longer.

She was restless. She tried to bury herself in her music, but she felt she needed to find and learn more of the music of the area. When she asked for sources, everyone said, "Talk to Basil, the scholar." She remembered Rose's words about the city of light, about seeking out the scholars in Godsel for information and counsel. Thoughts of Rose took her back to the inn in Mythro, and the meeting with the king's son. It was complicated.

She had no hesitation about meeting Basil, but meeting the king's son, whom she knew lived there as Komran, was uncomfortable for her. Meeting him had destroyed a beautiful memory she had carefully locked away, a rare moment of understanding and kindness that had sunk into her heart and remained there. Looking at him now, it was as if that moment had never happened, yet still he drew her.

She had wandered several times to the small manor, set back under tall trees, with the woods just behind. Each time she approached carefully, wishing to see Basil, both hoping and fearing Lon would be there. Each time she was disappointed. Neither Basil nor Lon was there. In fact, no one but the cook ever was, and after a few days, the cook came no more. Myrrha asked about town, but they didn't know about Komran, nor did they care. Malin, their Lord's son, was off on business it was said, but no one said where.

"Basil?" someone else had said. "He has relatives in the country. Probably he has gone there."

Even the guards at Oldsbury Hall knew nothing. "Probably off with family, or Malin. You can be sure he'll be back when it suits him."

Myrrha fretted and became tense. What if Basil never returned? What then? Would someone else be able to give her the information and the songs she desired?

Days passed, and no one seemed to live at Tegyn anymore. She began to toy with the idea of entering the house in secret, walking where they had walked, looking through the music on her own, letting the silence of the house wash over her. By the beginning of the second week, she had made up her mind. Gathering a cloak of soft night sounds about her, she found herself standing outside Tegyn House late one evening. There were no lights. Briefly she wondered if it were locked and bolted, but she did not worry about that. She knew she could enter, unseen even, but should she?

She hesitated, undecided. She moved noiselessly around the edge of the house to the back. There she also saw no lights, no evidence that anyone lived there. Why had they left so suddenly? On an impulse, she tried the main door at the back. It was locked, but a hum or two of sound and the knob turned gently in her hand. Instinctively, she headed toward the front of the house, past the kitchen area, past the study and a small sitting room. She hesitated at the bottom of the stairs, glanced up, but lingered instead on the main floor, finding her way to the library.

Moonlight streamed into the dark house wherever there was a window, and the library was no exception. Windows made of stained glass cast faint reflections of color and patterns on the walls of the room. She stood in the center of the mists of color, soaking up the patterns, twirling so they shifted on the skin of her arms, her face. When she was done, she shut fast the drapes and sank into a chair by the table before she fished a small candle out of a pocket beneath her cloak. She fumbled for a match and lit it, realizing that she really had made up her mind what she was going to do long before she stood outside the back door.

Around her, on all four sides except for the space taken by the window, were floor to ceiling books. A sudden longing to read them all, to know the information they contained, struck her. She had really had no access to books, but she knew a few basics about how to read from before Jandillo, though she had rarely done it. And writing was very awkward for her.

Across the table were papers, a few books, and a couple of old scrolls. Idly, she picked up a book, then sat down to read the title. At first it was difficult. Every creak and sound in the house sent her heart racing, as she stiffened in the plush chair she had claimed. Then, too, there was so much she could not remember. She discovered that if she said the words aloud, her hearing of the sounds would allow her to make sense of them.

Then she tasted some short writings about a fire gate scattered on the table, including a map, with a gate marked between the mountains of Tor and Antor. Absently, she wondered what a fire gate was. Even Myrrha, who had seen few maps in the course of her life, could tell that the map was very sketchy. There was a river, a coastline that curved inward, narrowed, and finally became just a line inland. There were a few ridges which she judged to be mountains, but nothing else. No cities marked, no villages. Surely there had to be more than that.

Then she took down several volumes from the nearest shelf and really began to read. Several hours passed, but she was oblivious to everything until her candle guttered and went out. Startled, she gathered up its remains and let herself out the back door. Sound whirled around her, and the lock clicked back into place. Invisible once more, she returned to the front of the house, wound her way down the empty lane, then into the town proper, past the church and back to the house of Rilda, who asked no questions and gave her the space she needed.

After that, she could not resist. She came the next night, and the next, even after her concerts. She lost herself in the old scrolls, in the books. She learned more about the city of light, about fire gates and light bearers. Words and meanings flooded her mind as if they belonged there. It seemed that this room and those shelves filled with books were there just at this time for her. Tegyn House was empty just to give her access. She grew bolder. She came on the third day in the daytime, for she discovered the only person about was a caretaker who came in the early morning and again just before sunset, to check the outer doors and see that they were still locked. He never went in.

She passed the rest of that week, her life a rush of delight in the music she made in all the right manors and households, and the music of the words she found in books. She drank them in, as if she had thirsted all her days. She even forgot that she waited for Basil for songs, but though she found none of those, she had her music. Days flew by and the library became her refuge and her joy.

Dale, Rilda's son, grew concerned. "We never see the minstrel anymore. He never plays just for us. Does he think he's better than we are?"

Rilda, who somehow knew Myrrha's heart, answered him. "Not our Rolan. He treats us just the same."

"Have we hurt his feelings?"

"Not him. But he has a lot to think about and learn about. He's studying somewhere."

"Where?"

"At one of the manor houses." She might have added which one, but she did not know for sure. She also might have said that girls did not need to hide. They were as good as their male counterparts. But she did not. "Rolan" must have "his" reasons, she decided.

Though for the life of her she did not know how the rest of Godsel could not see what stared them in the face, that Rolan was female. The bones of her face and hands were fine, the features delicately sculpted. And any emotion behind the eyes was clearly reflected in the face.

So she did her best to protect Rolan's secret and give "him" space.

But Dale watched. He was gone working with his father during the day, but one night, after a concert Myrrha had given in the church, he lingered outside the church door, waiting in the shadows until she emerged. He watched outside the door as she visited with a man and his wife. They were looking at her favorite mural on the wall. Dale couldn't hear what they said, but he knew it was the one of Adam and Eve in the garden. Dale slipped off to the side into the trees and waited.

The couple finally emerged, still talking to Myrrha.

"So after they ate the fruit," she asked, "death came into the world? Death and change?"

"Yes. But also life. For they could then have children and the whole human family began," the man answered.

"But what good was that, when their future held only death?" Myrrha was upset, Dale could tell.

"That's why God's son is to come. To create a path for all the human family to escape death. And if they choose, to return to God."

"And how does he make that path?"

The woman spoke, softly, surely. "He offered his life as a sacrifice for us, and died."

Myrrha shuddered, remembering Samlt. She had seen death.

"And then death died," the man added.

"He undid death?" Myrrha was silent, thinking. Maybe there was hope for her, and a good life if death could be undone.

"We'll see you at next week's concert," the woman said, and they left the church.

Myrrha closed and locked the door, watching, thinking, as the couple walked out of sight.

She collected her thoughts, wrapped her velvet cloak tightly around her and started off. Her mind was on their conversation and she forgot all about her sound cloak. The fear she had known with the Jandos and even in Esfalia had faded somehow, with the love and approval of those around her.

It was a cold night, a somewhat dark night. But Myrrha was warm with the lingering excitement of her concert, with the couple's words, and for what awaited her at Tegyn. It never occurred to her to look behind her. She had forgotten all about being an intruder in someone else's house.

Dale followed. He kept his distance and moved quickly past brighter spots into the shadows. Myrrha, lost in her inner worlds, didn't hear or see him. She came to herself several streets away, well on the edge of the center part of town when a coach rattled by.

"Good evening, sir," the coachman called out, as he passed. Myrrha was a well-known figure to the common folk.

Startled, she looked around her. There was no one else there, for Dale was well hidden, crouching in the shadow of a hedge.

She had forgotten her sound cloak. As the coach rattled off into the distance, she quickly gathered the night sounds to her, sounds sharper in the cold air, created her cloak, and vanished within it.

Dale stared. People did not just vanish. But the minstrel had. He stared at the spot where she had been standing. He looked around, then he stared again at the spot. He could see nothing. Then he widened his gaze, covering a large circle around the spot. His eye caught movement. A leaf was kicked up. About a step further, a spray of grass moved in a wind of its own, for there was not even a breeze that night.

Slowly he walked toward the spot, fearing to lift his eyes from it because he might lose track of where it had been. If that happened, he felt he would have no hope of finding the minstrel.

Unaware, Myrrha walked swiftly, eager now to reach her goal, more aware of her surroundings. But Tegyn was still some distance away.

Dale listened, but Myrrha's cloak also muffled sound. The only thing he could hear was a coach in the distance and the cry of a night bird settling down for the night. He saw nothing more, though he tried his best. The minstrel had disappeared.

Finally he gave up and returned home. But he tried the next night and the next. However, Myrrha had learned from the incident with the coachman. She waited until the church was empty. Then she closed it up, wrapped her sound cloak about her before she left the building, being sure to check for anyone watching. She laughed to herself, imagining the look on someone's face who observed the door closing on its own. She would have been surprised to see that look on Dale's face, night after night, as he watched for her. But he never saw Myrrha herself. After her concerts in the church she just vanished.

Then one night Myrrha had a concert at one of the manors. Dale walked her there, as he usually did, though by now Myrrha knew the location of quite a few of the manors about town. Often now, a carriage would come for her and take her back home. But tonight they were walking, the manor was fairly close and the weather had warmed a bit.

After the concert was over and they were on their way home, Dale decided to take the bull by the horns.

"How do you do that?"

Myrrha, her mind still on her performance, answered absently. "Do what?"

"That thing that you do."

"What thing?"

Dale hesitated, wondering if he really wanted to know. Then, finding no way to subtly ask his question, put it in one word, "Vanish."

Myrrha found herself at a loss. She had thought she had been so careful.

"What do you mean?" she asked softly.

"The other night at the church. You came out and started off for the south edge of town. You reached Fernden Manor, then you just vanished."

"You were following? Why?"

"You had been so different lately, staying away, coming home very late. I just wondered what was happening, and if you were all right. Then I saw you vanish. Are you all right?" He paused, waiting for her. When she remained silent, he pushed on. "Does some dark power have control over you? Snatching you away to do fell deeds in the middle of the night for it?"

The words gushed out from somewhere, and he stopped surprised. "Well," he fumbled for words, hearing how ridiculous it all sounded. "I just wondered."

Myrrha, for her part, stared at him, speechless. "A dark power? Controlling me? What are you talking about?" Then she fell silent. For what could she say? What should she say?

Rilda and her family, especially Dale, had been very good to her. Should she tell them the truth? Would they even understand let alone continue to accept her? Yet Dale's imaginings were far worse than the truth. And he truly cared about her, was worried on her behalf.

Would he think her a witch? Would she then be hunted as she had been by the Jandos?

She looked at Dale, at his kind open face, his obvious concern for her. And suddenly her heart opened. Better to slow some of his imaginings, she told herself. But it was more than that. She wanted someone who knew her, not just how she seemed, but truly knew her.

So she blurted out the truth. "I use sound and make a cloak and wrap it around me just like you put on your coat. And when I do that, you can't see me. I'm still there, but it appears I have vanished. You can't hear me either," she added.

"Why? Why do you do it?"

"Oh, to be alone, or when I don't feel safe."

"Or when you don't want people to know where you are. Or where you're going."

"Exactly."

Dale digested the information. "Where were you going the other night when you didn't want people to know?"

Myrrha was caught. Dale had dived right into the heart of the matter and wasn't going to let her off the hook easily.

She looked up at his face, the clear eyes. And she told him. "I was going to Tegyn. No one is there and there is a whole library of books. They sing to me, just like my music sings to you. I have been and been and can never find anyone home, so one day I just went in."

"You went into the house of Master Basil when he wasn't home?"

"Yes. To read and learn things I need to learn from him."

"So you're not enchanted."

"No."

"Not forced to do evil."

"No."

"You just choose to."

"What?" Myrrha was appalled at his take on her actions. "I don't do evil, I just read there."

"Then why do you hide?"

She fell silent. He was right.

"You could just wait for Basil to come home, or for Lord Lindsey's son Malin or that student to be there."

"I could. But I've waited through these last weeks, almost four of them, and no one is ever there."

"No one?"

"A caretaker still checks the grounds every evening, but the cook stopped coming. There was no need of her."

Dale was troubled. "That's not usual for Master Basil. Maybe we should let Lord Lindsey know." He thought a while then spoke up again. "Like as not he's off with Lord Lindsey's son. You just need to wait."

"Wait. Such a distasteful word. But I guess you're right, I should wait. However, I keep dreaming of a city full of light. Even the cobblestones of the streets are filled with light. Does such a place exist? I don't know, but I want to know. And if it does, I want to know all about it. Everyone said ask Basil. And it seems urgent, somehow."

"The city of light? You've dreamed of that?"

"Yes. Often."

"I thought only those with magic gifts dreamed such dreams." He caught Myrrha by the arm and stopped her, then turned her to face him. "Do you have magic?"

Cornered, Myrrha said nothing.

"Do you?" Dale insisted. Then he answered his own question. "Of course you do. Your music is magic. Isn't it?"

"Maybe," Myrrha equivocated. Then she hastily continued. "And I found some writings about the city on the library table. I just had to know more," she insisted.

"Still. It's not your house and they didn't invite you there."

Dale was stubborn, but right was right, Myrrha thought. She had just overridden all her similar thoughts in the urgency of her need. She spoke slowly, reluctantly. "All right. I'll go tomorrow to make sure everything is back in place, but after, I'll wait until they return."

Dale knew Myrrha well enough to know that though she wasn't happy, she would keep her word. He grinned, and clapped her on the shoulder and turned her back toward Rilda's. When they were nearly there, he stopped and held out his hand. "Then I'll say nothing. I'll have no need and it will be nobody's business but our own. Agreed?"

Myrrha reached out and took his hand. "Agreed." She also knew him well enough to know he would say nothing to anyone.

"You can keep your studying, just no more secret studying," he cautioned.

"No more," Myrrha agreed, reluctantly. "I'll wait until they return. If they ever do," she mumbled disconsolately.

"They will," Dale assured her. "They will. Besides, they're too important to be out of sight with no one aware of where they are. Why, Malin is Lord Lindsey's only son. If something had happened to him, we would know. And Basil, too. He's the town's scholar. Everyone knows him. You just wait and see. They will come."

"They'd better," Myrrha mumbled. "They'd better. And soon."

17
Tegyn's Secrets

Back at the hunter's cabin in Potters Woods, Rilse and Malin scoured the area, searching all trails leading south, trying to guess which one the enemy might have used to spirit Lon away. For two days, they searched the coast, looking for any small cove where a ship could have been hidden and launched again. Malin touched the minds of all the nearby woodland creatures as they went, looking for any vestiges of agitation due to the presence of strangers. But they turned up nothing. The small creatures forgot so quickly, and the storm had erased all evidence.

Karis accompanied them, growing more and more intense and worried. The passing of time decreased their chances of finding Lon and increased Lon's danger. While Malin searched the trails for signs, Karis mind-searched for his twin. He tried first their twin bonds, but turned up nothing. Then he light-sensed. Again nothing. Try as he might, Karis could not reach his twin. He even braved another trip to the Spirit Walks to look in the pool of the present, but found nothing. There was no trace of Lon. Yet he knew Lon was not dead.

"If Lon were dead," he said to Malin, "I would know. But though I can't find him, I know he still lives."

"So what would cause you not to sense him, not even in Fainra, if he still lives?"

Karis ran both hands through his hair in a gesture of despair. "I don't know. I can only think the black sorcerer has encased him in magic."

"Well, even then wouldn't your twin-ties lead you to Lon, even though the mage's magic shut yours out?"

"I would think so, but I can't find him. Not anywhere."

"What if you just looked for black magic, for what we sensed in the hunter's cottage?"

"I tried that. Nothing close enough to really examine."

"Well, they can't have traveled far down the coast by ship in this weather. And we found no trace of them in the woods."

It was a mystery. And neither Malin nor Karis liked mysteries of that sort.

But they and their horses were exhausted. Finally Karis consented to leave off searching for his twin's trail, and head to Godsel.

"It may be that Rast knows something we don't," Malin suggested. "After all, he was with Lon and the king."

Karis' voice was bitter. "Right. His minions think they have captured me, so the mage no longer looks for me. But why hasn't he discovered he has Lon? And why can't I reach Lon?"

"I don't know why you can't reach your twin. I don't know how that works. But the mage still thinks he has you, because he does not yet have Lon. He's still on the way to him."

"Let's hope he never finds out."

The next day found two weary, travel-stained young men riding south. Karis was particularly low in spirit. His twin, Lon, had been taken by his old nemesis, the dark mage, or at least by foul servants of the mage, because they thought he was Karis. The stench of the hunter's cabin was still in Karis' nostrils, the black stains before his eyes. The servants were foul indeed. What did that say about the master? And yet, how could anything be worse?

Days later they rode out of the forest. The sharp smell of the sea and the wind finally blew the stench from their nostrils and the darkness from their minds. Godsel town rose up solidly against the skies, and both Karis and Malin felt the tightness around their hearts relax a little. Here was safety and family, maybe even news of Lon.

They found they had no need to urge their horses onward, for though the horses were weary, too, they sensed that needed rest and food were just up ahead. They kept a steady pace on down the road.

On the outskirts of Godsel they met up with Rast, who was returning from his second foray out to search for Lon.

"Did you find anything?" Karis could not stop himself from asking.

Rast slowly shook his head. "Not really. There were no tracks. Wind and snow have erased most everything. Outside the cabin at first there was a faint sign, a strange trail as if something had been dragged. Maybe they were dragging Lon, but someone had to be doing it. Someone human. But we found no other prints."

"We found no trail to follow, either," Malin volunteered. "By the time we found the cabin, the storm had erased everything."

"Did the enemy say anything that would give us a clue where to look for Lon?" Karis could wait no longer for his questions.

"Nothin'. They said nothin'. Six goblin figures in black robes burst in the door. Four of 'em picked up Lon, t'other two followed and they all left. And they never said nothin'. It was as if the king and me didn't even exist."

"Did they do anything else? Anything else strange?"

"The whole thing was strange. But as the last one passed by the fire, he stooped and pulled something out, a coal, a black rock, something. Then they left. They vanished into the night."

"How did they get in? If I know you, Rast, you would have latched it tight behind you."

"He did," Malin agreed. "They broke in. When they left, they also left the door ajar."

Rast continued, as if he had to talk, as if he had to share his thoughts with someone, and someone who might understand the magic involved. "We couldn't move, you know. We could only lie there and watch. It was several hours before we could even lift a finger. And it was morning before I could lift myself off of the floor where I was asleepin'.

"And it was cold. A lot of snow had blown in and the fire was almost out. I had to wicker the door shut. You're right, Malin. They broke the latch. Then I had to build up the fire and take care of the king. He was right chilled. Hours later when he was some better and the room warm, I left and went looking."

"And what did you find?" Karis held his breath.

"Nothing, really. There had been wind and snow in the night. I tried to follow the dragging marks, but they faded out almost immediately; it looked like they was headin' for the coast. But that was no help. The winds were the most fierce there."

"They disappeared?"

"They seemed to. I continued in the same direction. But when I reached the sea, there was nothing. No boats, no people, no tracks. The weather was bad, so bad I would have sworn no one could have left by boat."

Malin reached over and clapped Rast on the shoulder. "No one could have done any more, Rast. You did all you could. The king had to be cared for, and the storm was unstoppable."

Rast looked up at Malin. "Mebbe if your white wolf had been there—."

Malin's voice was low when he answered. "Like you, Karis and Rilse and I were too late. There was nothing left to see when we arrived, just some foul blackness and a stench about the place."

"Aye. You've been to the place, then."

"Yes. We found no answers there. Maybe we can figure things out in Godsel." Malin tried to cheer him up, to leave him and them with some hope.

"We have no answers and no Lon," Karis said flatly. The party continued onward to Godsel, Karis even more glum than before.

Surely, thought Karis, if Lon were taken, he would have cast away something belonging to him so they would know. He would have left some clue, something, knowing we would search, would follow.

But they found nothing. It was as if Lon had been sliced out of their world and it had closed behind him.

At the gate, they were recognized, and word sent ahead, so when they rode into the circle before Oldsbury Hall, Lord Lindsey and the queen were waiting for them. Karis watched the queen's eyes move from one to the other of the figures in front of her, scanning each face. She paused a moment when she came at last to Karis. He watched her hope die quickly. She had not expected to find Lon with them, but she had hoped against hope that he might be, that she was wrong. Karis understood. His mother would have known something had happened to Lon, long before news could come. And if Lon were rescued, she would know that, too.

Karis dismounted to greet her. "Mother."

Malin also left his horse. Little Alyssa tugged at his coat and gave him a quick hug. "Where is your white wolf? He's all right, isn't he?"

"He's just fine. Off in the trees over there," Malin waved his arm in the direction of the nearest cluster of trees.

"Will he come to see me?"

Malin looked down at the small girl. "He'll come. He's our friend, but kind of a secret friend. He doesn't like lots of people around."

"Oh. A secret friend." Her eyes grew big, and a smile appeared.

"Father?" Karis questioned his mother.

"He grows stronger every day."

So, thought Malin. They had all made it but Lon. Fortune had surely smiled on them to have accomplished so much, but the loss of Lon was keenly felt.

Lord Lindsey enfolded Karis in a stout hug, then stood away and looked down at him. "We have men still searching. We'll keep searching." Karis understood that his words were a promise.

"Malin, Malin my son." Malin found his father blinking his eyes furiously and smiling broadly at the same time. "Welcome home." He was enfolded in the tightest hug he had ever experienced. "Troops would have headed north sooner, but your message was delayed. The groom was kidnapped by southern riders as he came upon them trying to steal some of our horses. He was hustled south on horseback for miles before he was turned loose to make the long walk back. Without any wood's lore, he became confused and lost precious time."

Malin looked at him, astonished. "Kidnapped? From Oldsbury Stables themselves?"

Lord Lindsey was terse. "Yes. Several horses were taken, the rest turned loose and scattered. We're not sure how many. A few trackers from the garrison are still working on it."

Their horses were led away by grooms, and Lord Lindsey ushered them into the Halls, past the great rooms and council chambers to a small salon, where they were soon seated in comfortable chairs. Food and drink were brought for the two cousins.

Malin looked around questioningly. "Where's Basil? Didn't he share the message we left for him?"

"No. We've not seen Basil since you left."

Malin stopped. "We didn't see him after the ball. He never returned. So before we started for Godsel, we left him a note on the library table."

"Another note?" Lord Lindsey's eyebrows lifted almost high enough to touch his hairline.

"Another note," Malin confessed. "We were in a hurry," he explained apologetically, noting Karis' grateful half smile that he stopped there, not explaining it was Karis' decision.

"Well, we haven't seen nor heard from Basil," his father worried. "Not a word. And it's been four weeks."

Whatever could go wrong had, thought Malin.

"As soon as we heard from the groom, we sent a company up the inner road. Thank goodness it reached the queen in time."

The queen smiled gently and added, "Thank goodness, indeed. And thank goodness for Rast. He kept the king safe." Queen Gwynne spoke softly. She said no more, but they could all hear the rest of that sentence in the silence. Only Lon is missing.

Malin said it aloud, thinking it was better so. "Only Lon, and Basil." Malin felt the sting of the latter, because he had left knowing Basil was missing, leaving only a note which had gone astray as he had predicted. True, Karis' need was dire, and he could not have accomplished the rescue without Malin, but Basil was his friend and had claim upon him also. Why was life like that? he mused. Always several things thrown at you at once, all needing doing right now.

He sighed. "We'll check Tegyn first, then try to pick up Basil's trail at the docks. It'll be cold, but Rilse is clever."

The queen looked at the travel worn, weary young men and signaled Lord Lindsey, her hand on his arm. "Let them bathe and rest now, then return. Over dinner we can hear their story."

"Basil is both mentor and friend," Malin said. "We'll look a bit before we return."

The queen nodded.

Word had reached the stables, and a carriage came to take the young men home. Their weary horses were led away, and they seated themselves in the carriage. Rilse, who had waited a short distance away, followed behind.

Karis' brother is not close by.

As I feared, Basil too is gone. He has not been seen since we left.

I'll go ahead to Tegyn. Maybe enemies came there, Rilse suggested.

Maybe, thought Malin. *Maybe. Maybe even Basil is there, but no one's seen him. After Tegyn, we'll check down by the docks.*

Both Karis and Malin had been riding too long. Even Malin found himself stiff from his days in the saddle. At the beginning of the driveway to Tegyn, they stopped the carriage and asked the driver to let them out. "A short walk will be just the thing to stretch our legs," Malin suggested. Karis was too worn out to protest.

As they watched the carriage drive on, Malin spoke up. "A quiet approach is important if any enemies are about, or there is a trail to follow that we don't want ruined."

Just as they reached the front of Tegyn House, Rilse appeared beside them. *Someone is inside,* he said.

Basil? Malin caught Karis' arm, and they stopped.

No. Magic circles this one.

The black mage? Malin found his muscles tight, his throat constricted.

The minstrel. In the library.

In the library, Myrrha lingered as she made sure all was in order. Today was her last day. True to her promise to Dale, she planned to return no more until Tegyn's occupants had returned home.

She moved slowly, dreaming a little, wondering what her life might be like if she were not Rolan but Myrrha, and had met the king's son and he had remembered her, and had been as she remembered him.

She readjusted her favorite chair, collected her spare candles, the bread and cheese she had stored there, her water. She had needed nothing else. The place had been solely hers. The watchman who made his rounds never entered. He did not worry her, for if she did not wish to be discovered, he would never see her.

Nor had she been anxious about the candle's light. The curtains were heavy, and she had drawn them so tightly no light could be seen. She had stood outside herself one night and looked, just to make certain.

She had read and dreamed and caught up on the world she had missed as a child. Now she had to leave it. Goodbyes were always hard, she thought.

Carefully she replaced all the books she had used on the shelves they had come from. Then she moved the writings and scrolls so they were where she had found them, at least as best she could remember. She sat down, just for a moment and closed her eyes. It was hard to leave. Before she knew it, she was asleep. The concert had been late the night before.

A quick hand on Karis' arm warned him to silence. The two young men tried the front door. When it resisted, Malin left Karis and went around the back. That door, too, was locked, but one window was slightly ajar. He and Rilse slid through it and crept slowly and inexorably toward the library.

If Myrrha had been awake, she might have heard them. Or if they had made more noise, but Malin knew which boards creaked and which part of the floor did not. They made little sound. Malin let Karis in the front door, and together they approached the library. Myrrha was miles away in sleep, dreaming of the exotic peoples and their customs she had read about, curled up in the chair she had claimed as hers, wrapped in her sound cloak.

But something bumped her sound cloak. She was instantly awake, listening, knowing someone was in the house. Her heart jumped within her. Why had she stayed? She should have left as soon as she was done replacing books and gathering her things. How could she explain what she was doing there if Malin and Basil and especially Lon, were back? How could she explain or even defend her actions?

When they reached the door, Malin stretched and put out his hand for the knob but found something in the way. Some barrier was between himself and the door knob and he couldn't reach it. Magic. Used against him in his own home. He tried again, to no avail.

Karis touched him on the shoulder, and they changed places. Watching, Malin thought wryly, magic against magic, but he watched closely, nevertheless.

The magic is there. Rilse pointed with his nose.

How do you know?

How do you know when it is going to rain?

I just do.

Exactly.

Malin did not know, but he sensed magic encircled the room. He had opened that door a thousand times, with no barrier between himself and the knob. Now he could not reach it. Only magic made things run amok like that.

Karis closed his eyes, drawing light with his hands, weaving an opening into the barrier before him. Malin saw the shimmer, the thinning of air before them, saw a light-etched door appeared around the real one. Before they could use it, however, it vanished.

On her side of the door, Myrrha sensed magic and sprang to her feet in a panic. Her cloak spun about her, whirling her so that she was unbalanced and stumbled against the door. If they hadn't known before she was there, they would now, she thought to herself grimly.

On his side, Karis was hurled back, his outstretched arm knocking Malin aside as well. Then the library door was flung open.

Out from the room burst a figure of power in a cloud of sound. It touched not only their ears but surrounded them, cut them off from each other, and slammed them into the wall.

Karis, when he had first sensed the magic, started to shield himself, but he was too late. Before they knew it, both young men were pinned to the wall by an invisible force. And there they remained. They could not even move, except for their eyes, fixed and watching. A figure rushed out from the library, stumbled over a white wolf, angled strategically across the doorway, and fell.

You should stay, Rilse told Myrrha. He yawned in her face and grinned at her. *You really should stay,* he repeated.

18
Library Magic

Watching, still pinned to the wall, Karis and Malin felt the initial force of Myrrha's exit, and heard the sound of her fall over Rilse. They heard her cry out as she became visible. At the same moment the two young men slid down the wall, freed from what had held them there. The minstrel lay beside Rilse, sprawled, his harp fallen from his grasp. Rilse sat up on his haunches, laughing, wolf style and very pleased with himself.

You should stay and talk. Rilse grinned up at Myrrha.

She had been right, that last time they met. He had spoken directly to her mind. She rubbed a bruised elbow and looked at the two young men across from her. Malin and Lon.

Then she understood. This wasn't Lon. The sound around him was somber and discordant, and Lon was harmony. He looked like Lon, but wasn't.

"You're not Lon." Amazement and joy filled Myrrha's voice, and the words burst from her before she could control them. Then other thoughts pushed up behind. So who are you? And where is Lon?

He's Karis, Lon's brother.

Not Lon. She had known that, but had not known she knew it. She wondered if she could talk underneath back to the wolf.

Yes. Rilse was enjoying the situation.

Just get your muzzle out of my face. You've wolf breath.

You smell like sound. He understood. It was wonderful. She forgot Karis and Malin, who though still weak, were no longer helpless and pinned.

Karis snapped out. "What do you know of Lon?"

Malin, too, was disturbed. Being whacked about and flung to the ground was not his idea of fun. Even worse, someone else was talking to his wolf, underneath. Even though he himself had insisted Rilse wasn't his wolf.

Sure, Rilse. Sit there talking with the intruder, the enemy that struck us down. What kind of friend are you? Malin struggled to gain his feet, still fighting the residue of the force that had pushed him against the wall.

Rilse turned his head to gaze at the minstrel. *He thinks you're the enemy.*

"Enemy? Enemy?" Myrrha was incensed. She would have nothing more to do with Malin, or Karis for that matter. She had pushed the enemy away from Karis, but apparently he had forgotten. She reached for her harp, but Karis beat her to it.

"That's how you do it, isn't it? You use sound." Then he grabbed for her harp. "Oh, no, you don't. Next time you'll slam us through the wall and into the next room." The minstrel struggled for the harp, then suddenly became aware that her hood's cloak was down and her features open to scrutiny. She ducked her head and drew her hood up around her face, her fears forcing her to relinquish her hold on the harp.

Rilse pawed her harp aside from both of them, and held it down.

"What are you doing here?" Malin's voice of reason broke in. Uninvited strangers were in his house, using magic and talking to Rilse. If they were not the enemy, they had to have a good reason. If any reason was good enough for that.

"I was waiting for Basil. Everyone said talk to Basil, but he was never home. You were never home, so I sat down in the library to wait. No one came, so I started to read." Myrrha was defensive. She was no enemy, but who would believe her now? She had been foolish.

I would believe you're not the enemy. Rilse dropped his muzzle on his paws and grinned at her.

Myrrha looked over at the wolf and laughed in spite of herself. *Yes, you would. And you would be right. But who would believe you?*

"You were waiting for Basil? He has not been here?"

"None of you were here. Not you two, nor Basil. Not since the night of the ball."

Lord Lindsey was right. No one had seen Basil since the night of the ball, nor had he been home. What had happened to Basil? Malin wondered.

Then a thought struck him. Malin scrambled to his feet and made for the front door. And there it was, the note he had left for Basil, still on the table beside it. The note looked as if it had not even been unfolded. "The minstrel is right. Basil has not been here since the night of the ball."

Karis had followed Malin to the door. "What could have happened to him?"

Malin thought back. "He left before the ship drifted from its anchor and you had the problems with the dark mage. He was ashore by then."

"Could he have seen something? Could he have had a brush with the riders ashore? Tegyn isn't too far from the south wilderness trail they use."

"I don't know. But Rilse and I must go see." Then he looked back at the minstrel standing by Rilse down the hall near the library door. What should they do with him? Was he in league with the dark mage?

No. The minstrel is alone, and no friend to the mage.

You're sure?

Yes. I was there, you know. I could see things other than Millicent.

Malin turned red, but said nothing.

"What is it? What is wrong?" Myrrha had caught their consternation.

"You were right," Karis told her. "Basil has not been here since the ball and he should have been. We don't know where he is."

Myrrha caught their real anxiety underneath their annoyance with her.

"What was it you said?" Karis focused back on the minstrel. "So you started to read and—?"

Karis is too friendly by far, Malin thought, to an intruder in his house, even if he was looking for Basil. He pushed away the fact that Rilse seemed to trust the minstrel. Malin was still disgruntled.

The two cousins stared in silence at the minstrel, standing beside the wolf, his midnight blue cloak flowing about him, the hood over his dark hair, his blue eyes almost black.

Karis studied Rolan. Something teased at him. Almost he had it. He closed his eyes and light sensed, then it fled. The minstrel's sound defense, though it could no longer be heard, still rang through his mind and legs, leaving them floating and not completely under his control.

Malin, still angry and truly worried about Basil, snapped out, "If you're not an enemy, what are you doing here?"

Myrrha flushed, red flowing into her face and out again, leaving it pale. She was an intruder, but she had never felt so intensely as if she belonged somewhere as she had in the library. This was her place, if she had one, her secret place.

But her daydreams wavered before their sharp eyes and accusing stares and she dropped her eyes, unwilling to meet theirs. Her gaze fell on Rilse. For a moment she gazed miserably at the silver-tipped white wolf beside her, her delight dimmed. How could she ever explain?

Malin spoke abruptly to Karis. "He knows you're the king's son."

"I thought at first you were Lon. But you're not." Myrrha wanted to add, I've been waiting for you, king's son, but you're the wrong son, but she didn't dare. Then she blushed, realizing Rilse might be able to pick up her thoughts, even when she was not trying to send them.

Karis took a quick step toward her. "Lon? What do you know of Lon?"

"Nothing really. I met him once before I came here; he was with some troops that were going north to the war."

"How long ago?"

"In the summer. At an inn in Mythro."

"In Mythro? Then why are you here, in Godsel?" They were giving her no help. Well, she was Rolan the minstrel. She needed no help. She had rescued Karis from the evil force on the ship and the wolf liked her. She had survived the Jandos and their hunt and made her way through Mougos territory. Her chin took on a stubborn tilt, her eyes clearly angry in their turn.

"I've been waiting for Basil."

"Why?"

"I—." she paused. Could she tell them? Would they believe her? And would it matter to them? She temporized. "I wanted music and I was told to talk to him."

Karis and Malin were silent, unbelieving.

Well, then, she would tell them. She had reasons for her actions, good reasons. Myrrha went on. "In Mythro, I lived and played at the inn where I met Lon. But I dreamed often of a city with light streaming up from its streets, from the faces of its people. They told me to go to Godsel and find the scholar, Basil.

"So I came here for Basil, but he was never here. And no one knew where he was. And you were gone, too. The dream seemed so important I felt I should wait here. Besides, you were asking about me. So I've spent my spare time here, waiting and reading, when I wasn't playing." Her voice had the ring of truth in it. She had chosen an indiscrete place to wait, but she intended no harm.

"In the library of someone's house when they are away?" Malin was not placated.

"Well, yes. He didn't come and he didn't come, and no one knew where he had gone. And you both were gone, very suddenly." She stopped then, trying to be as honest as she could under the circumstances. "After the night on the ship, I was worried. Here seemed the best place."

Karis spoke slowly. "Why here?"

"It was the books." Myrrha's voice petered out. Then she tried again. "Once I picked up the books and began to read, there was nowhere else I could wait. I had not known books such as these before."

"The books?" Malin struggled with such thinking. "You came and stayed for the books?"

"Yes, the books. When I came here and saw the books, well, I had to stay. The words sang to me." As she spoke, the joy of her reading returned to her, all those words, pouring up out of the books, raining down upon her mind. She forgot her circumstances, their suspicion and remembered only her joy.

Karis caught her joy, so intense was it in her mind. He sighed and let his anger pass through him and away.

But Malin was still cross at the intruder. "Why did you avoid us on the ship, after the mage was gone?"

Myrrha struggled for words, she who was usually so fluent with both words and music.

So she simply told them the truth. "I thought you were Lon," she said to Karis, "but things didn't feel right, and I didn't want to talk with you until I sorted it out. I'm sorry. It was not the best thing to do, but events seemed so strange."

The minstrel speaks truly, Rilse brushed his nose against her hand.

"Then you're disappointed as well that Basil has disappeared. We don't even know where to look." Malin was curt.

Myrrha was dismayed. "Disappeared? What could have happened?" She walked swiftly to stand beside them at the door; Rilse followed close beside her.

Malin noticed her hand fall to rest on Rilse's head, and tried to shake off his annoyance. "We had to make a quick journey north and expected to find Basil here when we returned, but even my father has not seen him, no one has seen him since the night of the ball."

"Where might he go?" Myrrha realized that somehow Basil was an important piece of the future. "Where have you looked for him?"

Once again Malin, who was almost always on an even keel, felt himself flood with annoyance. He was short with the minstrel. "We haven't. We had to go north on an urgent errand. We've only just returned." Malin felt so guilty he had to defend himself, even though Myrrha had not really attacked. He was testy and disgruntled.

Karis seemed suddenly to have decided the minstrel was all right. It was the mention of Lon, Malin thought. Or the memory of the night of the ball and the minstrel's protection. "Lon is also gone. We went north for him and the rest of my family, to bring them south. On the way, Lon was kidnapped, perhaps by the dark mage, the one you felt the night of the ball."

Myrrha was dismayed. A king's son kidnapped and taken was bad enough. But Lon? Her Lon? She digested this news in silence. Karis didn't take time to explain the whole situation to Rolan and his explanation, too, sounded strange.

Malin thrust his hands deep in his pockets. Basil gone. The minstrel in his library. The world was not a comfortable place. He wanted to search for Basil. He needed peace and quiet and a bath, he thought, as he dropped his gaze to his stained shirt front.

But Karis was not about to let the minstrel escape from them again. If there was even the slightest chance that Rolan had gifts that would work against the black mage, Karis wanted him not just around, but close by. He wanted him in the same room, or at the farthest, the next room.

"When you played, that night of the ball, it seemed to limit the influence of the black mage." Karis couldn't bring himself to say "on me." He paused, wondering how much he should tell the minstrel. But they would need all the help they could get if they were to find and rescue Lon from the black mage himself. That seemed a huge task, in the face of lots of opposition.

He didn't have to like Rolan, Malin thought, as he listened, just work with him.

Karis plunged recklessly onward. He spoke of the dark mage being pushed away from him, of Lon, of their wild ride north and now Basil's disappearance.

The news was all bad, Myrrha thought, yet Lon was a magic word. Her mentioning him assuaged Karis' anger and spilled out all the rest of the information. Here was a chance for her to help Lon, who had given her so much. She wasn't sure she even liked Karis, but Lon, she would do much for him. Besides, a black mage should be stopped. If her music could do it—.

"Will you help us?"

Find Lon, thought Myrrha. "Yes."

Karis continued blithefully on, seemingly unaware of what he was doing to Malin. "We dine at Oldsbury Hall tonight," he said quickly. "At eight. You should join us there."

That did it. Malin was really out of sorts. Here was Karis, inviting someone to dine at his father's manor, Oldsbury Hall. This wasn't Karis' territory. Malin felt a sudden stubborn resistance take hold of him, erasing the feelings of camaraderie the ride north had created with Karis.

"I may still be looking for Basil," Malin said pointedly. He could leave Karis and his family to their own devices. In the meantime, he would search for Basil, alone. He wanted to forget Karis ever existed, let alone the minstrel. He found himself glaring at them both.

Myrrha caught Malin's flush of anger, the annoyance in his mind. She had no need to be where she was not wanted. Then she realized that his anger was not directed at her, but at Karis, and she understood. Things were going too fast for her, too.

"Dine at the Hall?" She stalled.

"Yes." Karis was both eager and determined. "We'll take counsel tonight and make plans for finding Lon and

Basil. I would like you there." Lon's brother wanted her help, wanted her there. She hesitated. "We need you there, as well, Malin. Rilse, too, if he can come."

Karis was right. Malin knew it, but he didn't have to like it. "Rilse and I have some important scouting to do first. If we can we'll meet you there later."

Karis heard the unvoiced "maybe," and hesitated. But he had a plan, a plan that might save Lon and that was worth a great deal of risk. He turned his attention back to Myrrha. "It would be nice to have your music as well."

Myrrha relaxed. Her music. She could take her harp. She would have power and meet the royal family, and still be safe. They wanted her. Well, Karis did.

"So. Will you come to dinner?" Karis was insistent.

Myrrha ran over things in her mind, undecided.

Quickly, Karis added, "I can tell you about the city of light."

That tipped the scales. "I'll come," Myrrha promised, finding herself a little breathless. Some Lonish trick of the voice had won her over, plus the promise. She could not have said exactly why. "I have to play for Lady Whetton at five this afternoon. She wants a programme, as she calls it, for her husband's birthday, but I should be done by seven." She had given her word. She would come. She would come to dinner and play, at the court, no less. She, Myrrha. Well, Rolan, or whoever she was.

Elated, Karis rushed on. "Perhaps you should move into one of the rooms down the hall, so you're close by, in case the dark magician shows up again."

A quick intake of breath behind him warned Karis that he was moving too fast and making invitations to commit space that was not his. Tegyn was not his home, even if Lon was his brother. He turned red and stumbled around for words. "That is, if Malin agrees. Malin?"

Malin had been wool gathering and did not realize where Karis was heading until he was there. He found himself not only annoyed but also very edgy and angry.

Nice of him to ask, he snapped to Rilse.

His thinking is not clear.

That's an understatement. Malin realized that at some level he also was annoyed at the minstrel for talking to Rilse, though he felt foolish about it. He sighed. He needed food and rest, and Basil.

Come live at Tegyn. Myrrha turned the idea over in her mind. With Basil and all those books. She remembered how she had felt, reading in the library at Tegyn. Like she was where she should be, needed to be. And then there was Lon. If she could help find him—.

Let the minstrel come.

Even Rilse was messing up Malin's life. Both Karis and Myrrha were waiting for his answer. Malin found himself unable to do much except mumble reluctantly. "There is room at Tegyn. Upstairs, just down from Karis' room." What he wanted to say was, Certainly not. You don't have the right to invite people to my home, and especially not a house-breaking minstrel who is also a dabbler in magic, who pins me to the wall and talks to my wolf.

"You're sure."

Malin found the minstrel looking at him strangely and wondered if he was accessing his thoughts. Caught, he stammered a short, "Yes."

"Then I'll come." She reached over and touched Karis on the arm. "We'll find your brother. We'll find him in spite of the mage and bring him home." Home. The word had a cascade of sound that almost undid her. Would Lon even remember her, let alone be glad to see her? And what did she know of home?

"As long as Basil is gone, we will keep the place locked. Do you need—?" Malin stopped himself. It was obvious that the minstrel did not need a key to enter Tegyn. Though how he had come there Malin was not sure. Sound, perhaps. But a key granted the bearer the right to be on the premises.

"Do you want a key?" Perhaps it was not good to point out the minstrel's powers to all and sundry. He, too, should use a key.

I'll look for Basil. Rilse padded past the others and to the front door. It was still ajar from Malin's trying to sneak Karis silently inside to surprise the intruder. A push from a paw and it swung wide, and Rilse was out. It would be good for these young people to sort things out without him. He had work to do.

Suddenly, everything fell into perspective for Malin. He mentally shook himself. He was tired and edgy, but he couldn't allow trivialities to get in the way of what really had to be done.

Me, too, he said to Rilse. *Wait for me.*

"I'll see you later, Karis. Now, I need to look for Basil." A little cooling off time never hurt. And Basil, if he were found, would put everything to rights. That is, if he were all right. If he could, he would have been at Tegyn. That meant he had to be a prisoner somewhere, either by accident or design. Malin tried not to think of other, less pleasant, alternatives.

Without even stopping to change his clothes, Malin pushed through the front door after Rilse. He would need his horse and he was already worn from his journey to the north. Walking to the stables seemed exhausting and futile. It would waste valuable time and they had already lost a month in their search for Basil.

Frustrated, he reached out, trying to touch Lanier, his own horse. But he was out of range. Then he searched randomly, almost idly through the nearby woods, not really expecting any results.

Rilse had stopped and was watching him.

You hope for a horse?

I do. I sure do.

Rilse grinned. *You steal one?*

Malin was chagrined. *No. I borrow one. Unless I can ride you?*

Not a chance.

Malin went to work. To his amazement he found one. It felt like one of the restive, smaller southern horses that the enemy rode. He had no qualms about helping himself to one of their horses. It would serve them right.

Soon the horse showed through on the fringe of trees fronting Tegyn's lane. It moved almost reluctantly, or fearfully, Malin thought. If it was a stray from the foray on the night of the ball, no wonder. Its caretakers were gone and dogs would harry it.

It came slowly, Malin soothing its mind. As he did so, Malin felt his own mind set aside the anger and frustration and guilt that was weighing on him. The important thing now was to secure that horse and look for Basil.

The horse had lost its saddle, but the bridle was still on it. Malin caught the reins carefully. The poor horse would likely have sores in its mouth. He removed the bridle, slid up on the horse and he was off after Rilse. He needed neither saddle nor bridle to manage the horse. Off he went without even a backward wave.

Left alone at the door with the minstrel, Karis stewed. Finally he fished in his pocket, produced his key and held it out to the minstrel. "Here. I can get a spare later."

Myrrha stood looking down at the key Karis had handed her, saying nothing. Then another thought struck her. How long could she live around Karis and Malin and Basil, assuming Basil was all right when they found him, and not be discovered? From a distance she could successfully masquerade as a boy. How about in the same house? In the next room? She would have to be careful.

And what about Rilda and her family? When she thought about leaving them, she found herself saddened. In the short time she had been with them, Rilda had mothered her and Myrrha had soaked up her care like a sponge. Yet she knew they would soon need their work space back. She could not stay there forever. And Lon—the thought of Lon steadied her. If she could help find Lon, she would, even if it meant moving to Tegyn and working with Malin and Karis. At Tegyn, they could work together, find Basil, and rescue Lon. She would find out more about her city of light. It was what she wanted, wasn't it? All threads led to Tegyn.

She hardly heard Karis as she walked out the door and down the curving driveway. As she walked, she felt doubt creep in. What rash decisions had she made? Decisions that would change her life. After tonight, she thought, it would never be the same. Was it really what she wanted? She didn't have to go to Oldsbury Hall, or move into Tegyn. As Rolan, she could make her own choices, king's son or no king's son. She could send a message, make an excuse.

But she knew Karis would not accept an excuse. Not when his brother's life was on the line. Nor, she realized, could she. She had the chance of her life before her, and she would take it. She would follow where it led.

Karis found himself staring miserably after the figure of the minstrel as he strode away down the tree-lined lane in front of Tegyn. He had done things all wrong. He'd upset Malin and rushed too fast with the minstrel. What if the minstrel was in the service of the black mage? How could he be sure he wasn't? Rilse had vouched for him, but what did Rilse know about minstrels? What did a wolf know about music and magic?

Then he thought of Lon, in the fell clutches of the terrible power that had haunted his life. To free Lon even scant moments earlier than otherwise possible, he would risk offending more than a cousin or a minstrel. Lon was taken because the mage thought he was Karis. It was his fault Lon was gone. He should have sensed a trap. Would the mage realize it was Lon before he merged with him, or would Lon go mad and die? Or, as Malin thought, would Lon become the bait for Karis?

There were no answers so Karis went to work. Soon he was bathing and dressing for dinner. He would go early and meet with his family. They would sort things out. It would have to be all right. Malin would forgive him, and the minstrel, untainted by the dark mage, would have the power they needed to defeat him. Lon would be freed. They would rescue him. They had to.

19
Wine and Roses

Once more to the window. Basil sighed, and gathered his severely weakened energies. He climbed carefully, making sure of his footing. A tumble now would not be helpful. He lifted the window and tried his girth. He sighed dismally, wriggled a bit, then prepared to descend his makeshift tower of barrels. On a hunch or an impulse born of desperation, he tried again, this time shifting his girth diagonally to the window. Could it be? After all this time, could it really be?

It was. He was through, a soft plop on the small roof beneath, a squawk of victory or surprise, he wasn't sure which, and Basil, Lore Master and Scholar, was out of his prison. In his great glee, or his weakness, or his strange angle, he wasn't sure which, he lost his balance on the small roof, falling through the shrubs and bushes to the hard ground below.

Astoundingly, he landed on his feet, but one ankle gave way, and he dropped to the ground. It wasn't broken, he decided, after feeling it gingerly. It was probably just a sprain, but dashed inconvenient whatever it was. In that state, it would take considerable time to get help, isolated and disabled as he was.

He crawled over to the trees and found a branch to turn into a makeshift cane. Hobbling along with it, he returned to the doors, which were unlocked. He entered and made his way back until he reached the larder.

He selected a cheese, some bread, and several apples, and stowed them about his person until he looked like a larder himself. Food was first. Then he grasped a bottle with a little wine still remaining in it and filled it to the top with water.

Supplied, his next thoughts were on travel. He had not expected to have to deal with a badly sprained ankle. He had planned to walk to the nearest inhabited manor, which was Lady Whetton's down the road several miles, and ask for a ride to Oldsbury Hall. He sensed there was no time to be lost. Lord Lindsey needed the information Basil had as quickly as possible, and it was now four weeks later.

While he contemplated his best course of action, he limped back to the front door, and seated himself on the steps to rest, eat, and restore his strength. Food was now his friend. In fact he had eaten a little even before he walked out of the larder. Just a careful bite or two of cheese, a hard, crusty morsel of bread, for it was no longer fresh. In fact some of it was moldy. And of course, wine to wash it down. Marvelous the restorative power of food and drink, he thought.

Even so, the prospect of walking several miles on his injury to the nearest manor was not appealing. Yet if he lingered about Thornton, there was the possibility that Gray might return to finish him off. The obvious solution to his problem was to make his way to the road, flag down the first transportation possible, and he would be on his way, unless that first passing carriage happened to be Gray or Lord Norton. He wondered why Gray had not been by to finish Millicent's work and get him permanently out of the way. Maybe they didn't know what he knew, or where Millicent had left him.

He would have to find someplace secluded where he could watch and make the decision whether to flag down whatever horse or carriage he encountered. He needed someplace where he could see the drivers, yet not be seen. Immediately across from Thornton Manor, the fields had all been harvested. In addition, the woods were too far back from the road to provide any cover. However a little farther down the road toward Lady Whetton's, the road passed over a wooden bridge that spanned a small stream. The water levels in the streams and rivers were very low that season, and Basil was sure there would be enough room to hide in the weeds and bushes under the bridge. That would have to do.

He patted the provisions on his person, grasped his cane and stood on his good leg. Awkwardly and slowly he ventured down the stairs, almost losing his balance. By the time he had finished the stairs, his brow was wet with sweat. He looked grimly down the length of the lane. It had never looked quite so long before. At the rate he was going help was a long way away.

Then out by the road, on the lane to Thornton Manor, he heard a horse and rider. Had he been that preoccupied that he had not heard it earlier? A flash of hope crossed his mind. Lady Whetton, returning? He made himself a mental note to thank her for her hospitality. The provisions of her larder, in the end, had been quite sufficient.

The rider was close, too close for any real action on his part. With his disabled foot he was stuck where he was. He peered intently. Friend or foe? Help or danger?

It was Gray, Lord Norton's henchman and "hobnobber" with southern riders. He had not returned earlier. Why now? Had he hoped Basil had been wiped out by Millicent? What did he know? What did he suspect Basil might know? Basil carefully arranged his sleeves, and prepared a semi smile of greeting.

Gray reined up his horse directly in front of Basil, its hoofs hollow on the cobblestones beneath it. Gray looked a little the worse for wear, Basil thought, noting evidence of a fading bruise on the side of his face. Millicent had been none too gentle.

"Master Basil." Gray was in control of himself. There was the proper note of surprise in that voice.

"Gray. Pleased to see you survived the rough handling of the southern riders." Good to get in the first words. Let the fellow know he had seen the attack and sympathized.

"Glad to see you alive, Basil."

Glancing at his face, Basil noted no signs of gladness. The man seemed surprised and chagrined, if Basil was any judge. Gray continued, somewhat hastily. "We searched the woods for you, especially around where the thugs left me for dead, but we found no trace."

Basil's glance was keen. Maybe the man didn't know what had happened to him, and Millicent was more clever than he had expected. Still he couldn't push away the thought that his being alive was an unhappy surprise to Lord Norton's henchman.

"I am, Gray, alive and fairly well. Fortunately for me, they left me locked in the larder. I have just emerged from my prison a few minutes ago. Your timing is great."

"In the larder?" Gray was astonished, or one of the best actors Basil had met. "Lady Thornton's larder?"

"The same. The larder of good provisions, a thick oak door, and only one high and narrow window."

Gray's mouth was ajar, more than was really polite. "How did you get out?"

"Through the window, causing me a small problem with my ankle. Could you loan me your horse to get to Tegyn?" Basil cast his small pebble and waited for the result. If Gray loaned him his horse, maybe he was an innocent bystander after all. But if he devised excuses and went for Lord Norton and a carriage, then Basil knew he would intend him no good. Having Basil return hale and hearty would not be in their best interests. Basil could see Gray adding up the situation in his head and coming to a conclusion. "You got through the window, and fell and hurt your ankle."

Slow, Basil thought, but Gray was getting the picture. "Exactly."

"I can't loan you my horse, I'm on an errand for Lord Norton."

I just bet you are. And if you weren't before, you are now, was Basil's unvoiced thought.

"But I can detour and let Lord Norton know so he can send a carriage back for you."

So it was to be the carriage. "Wonderful. I'll make my way back to the porch and await him here. Can't get far with this ankle."

Gray hesitated.

Basil turned himself about and started to hobble toward the front stairs he had just left. Then he looked back over his shoulder. He could just see thoughts chasing themselves around in Gray's head. "I would appreciate your haste, my good man. It's beginning to swell."

The last suspicions left Gray's face, and he turned his horse and headed back down the driveway. "Lord Norton should be here shortly," he promised, and he was gone.

Basil watched him go the length of the driveway and onto the main road beyond the trees. By the time he was that far, Gray's horse was running. "So, Lord Norton wants me, does he," Basil mused. "He's likely the last person I'll see if I'm still here waiting."

As soon as the horse was out of sight, he stood, reaching for the rude stick he had impressed into service as a cane. He took a quick step or two, and his ankle collapsed under his weight.

"Can't go far on this," he muttered to himself. "Nor very fast." He returned to the steps and went to work to create a makeshift splint and bandage to support his foot. His fingers flew through their task, for he knew he would not have much time, an hour or so at the most. A stout straight stick was easy, but he grimaced severely as he shredded the end of his shirt for a bandage. When he was finished, he stood weighing his options: afoot through the woods, bolted in the house behind a stout door, or hidden under the bridge.

None of his choices sounded all that great. If he chose the woods, though it would take a while to find him, dogs would take care of that problem. No locked or bolted door in the manor would offer enough protection against Gray and Lord Norton. They had too much to lose.

As for the bridge, maybe if he could lose his trail for a while in the water, he could escape pursuit. He looked down at his dress pants, now anything but fit for a formal occasion. If it must be done, it must be done, but the streams were especially low that season. Would the little water in them hide his trail? Besides, how would he manage a walk through the pebbles of the stream bed? And could he even get there before the carriage returned for him? One thing he knew: he wasn't about to remain where he was and just wait.

What did he know about Thornton Manor and Lady Thornton? What information did he have that would help him in this situation? Lady Thornton had employed only a small staff and spent her time between her town and country home. Jinks was her butler, a decent sort as Basil remembered him. She liked to garden—roses wasn't it? He looked around. Roses were blooming everywhere.

Jinks had complained of their wine cellar. What was it he had said? Just a crude entrance into a small dirt cellar beneath the house. Lady Thornton didn't believe in wine. She had even joined the temperance league.

Lady Thornton's late husband had added the small cellar without her knowledge and kept the bushes close to hide the fact. Jinks had discovered it one day. Said the wine there was pretty good, if you could get to it, but you couldn't reach the cellar without getting dirty and scratched to pieces by thorns from the bushes unless they were well pruned and trimmed. Since Lady Thornton had been gone the last couple of months, the latter wasn't likely. With a little luck, the place might be overgrown enough with rambling roses to provide him a temporary hiding place.

He rounded the corner of the house with his lopsided gait and peered hopefully around. There were roses everywhere, long sprays reaching up and out, climbing every available surface or falling to the ground. Grimly, he hobbled through them to the edge of the house. The cellar would be connected so that would be the easiest, surest way of finding it. He stumbled once, grasping a stem to catch his balance, impaling his hand upon its thorns. He took to running his stick along the manor at what he thought was the right level, looking for anything that protruded.

Painfully and doggedly he poked and stumbled through the bushes, tripping and falling to his knees at one point. He finally reached the back of the house without finding what he sought, only to find another wild wall of rambling roses. At the rate he was going, Gray and Lord Norton would be back before he found the cellar.

He stepped back and surveyed the house. Where was the kitchen? Surely the wine cellar would be near the kitchen, which would be near the larder he had just escaped. There was the larder roof he had fallen from. Bit by bit his eyes searched through the roses, looking for any changes in the shape of the walls, making his way across the back of the manor. There, perhaps. Or there? He sighed and walked close to the manor and its roses once more, thrusting with his makeshift cane at the walls, listening anxiously for the sound of carriage wheels on the road. He found nothing.

Well, if he couldn't find it standing, maybe he could see the spot at ground level. The roses were tall; perhaps their foliage was less dense at the bottom. At least they would have fewer thorns, he reasoned. He knelt and looked long and hard at the roses before him. They were a little less thorny but just as thick with leaves and blossoms as they were higher up. He lay flat, pushing his body forward until his head was in their roots. There, to his right, there was something.

He squirmed back out and attempted to stand, his injured ankle giving way on him. He struggled to his feet once more, the perspiration dripping from his brow. He seized his handkerchief and mopped his face with it.

Four feet to his right, a greater distance from the larder than he would have expected, the roses jutted out. Once more he jabbed with his cane, striking it soundly against the wall, listening for any change in tone, feeling for any change in structure. Nothing. In frustration he gave one powerful thrust and found himself falling forward into the roses. His cane had not found a solid wall, but something flimsy that moved forward at his pressure. Several boughs parted, but others caught and held him fast. He had found the cellar, but the thorns had found him.

Long minutes later, finally freed from the thorns, Basil crawled into the roots and wriggled painfully past them to the spot where his cane had found nothing. There was the cellar. A small door was partly open revealing two sunken steps that led down into the earth. The door was flat and into the main wall of the house itself. There was nothing that announced its presence; roses climbed the wall, higher than the door, as if it were not there. If he had not pushed in the right place, he would not have found it.

Finding, however, was not the same as entering. Quarter-inch thorns protruded from branches and stems. No one in his right mind would try to enter without first chopping away the thorns, unless he had an urgent need. He unbuttoned his jacket and lifted it to cover his head, thrusting an arm upward and around it for additional protection. He sensed he was out of time.

Half-formed thoughts about how he was going to get out teased through his mind. He could get in and hide. But could he get out? If, as Jinks said, there was no connection to the house, and if Lord Norton and his servants discovered his "hidey hole," he would have no possible escape, even if he were fully functional.

Well, Basil thought wryly, the cellar was by no means a perfect solution, but it might buy him some time. When they did not find him waiting on the front steps, they would search the house, the woods. And just maybe they would overlook this little spot, at least temporarily. He had encountered a great deal of trouble finding it. Hopefully, they would too. If they did not bring dogs with them, he might yet have a chance to escape.

He dropped down and burrowed beneath the roses, keeping close to their roots. Thorns snagged his clothing, scratching the hands that held the jacket, but by keeping low he missed most of them. Basil thought of Malin. His protégé would have a good laugh if he could see him now.

And where was Malin? He had expected Malin and Rilse to find him in just a few days, but more than four weeks had gone by. He calculated it out. No, it had been four, with no sign of them.

He slid down the two stairs on his belly, head still wrapped in his jacket, wincing as thorns pierced the fabric.

His sprained ankle banged once on each step, before he came to a stop at the bottom. He shuddered when he sat up and removed his jacket from his eyes and viewed the dark smears across the white of his shirt. He was not sure which hurt more, the thorns and bruises, the sprain, or the disgrace of the dirt on his white shirt.

He looked up at the door. It was a simple latched affair. If he was lucky, he could jar it shut with the rude cane he carried and not have to stand. On his third try the door closed back outward an inch or two, and he hastened to push on it, suddenly finding himself sliding down three more stairs, before he jolted to a stop at the bottom. He lay there, checking his body parts. He sighed. They hurt enough that he knew they were still all there. He turned and pushed again with his stick, closing the door. Luckily, unlike the larder, this was a two-way latch. He seated himself on a step and gazed around him distastefully.

This part of the manor was obviously an afterthought. There was only enough earth moved to provide space for the wine barrels and bottles. Over by the nearest wine barrel was a large chair, probably originally brown, though it was now hard to tell. The floor was earth, like the walls, with a bit of straw strewn here and there. Basil, stooping because the roof was low, found the armchair and settled himself to wait, propping his now swollen and tender ankle on the foot stool before him. He thought about reciting, briefly, wistfully, then leaned back, cloaking himself with silence.

He dozed, fitfully, not sure if it was for a brief time or a longer time. He was finally awakened by the noise of horses and a carriage clattering across cobblestones. He heard the shouts of men, faint through the ill-fitting door. Someone, it sounded like Gray, called his name.

Outside the house, Lord Norton emerged from the carriage to confer with Gray, who had followed the carriage on horseback. Lord Norton went up the steps and tried the door, which Basil had left unlocked. It yielded easily to his touch. Gray went around to the back of the house.

"Master Basil? Master Basil?" There was no answer to either Lord Norton's call from within or Gray's shout from without. The calls came again, this time louder and more irate. Gray continued to make a full circle around the house. Lord Norton searched the house itself. They met again in the front.

"He's not around back. He said he'd hurt his ankle and would have to wait here."

"And you believed him? You dolt. The ankle was probably faked, and he's halfway to Lindsey with his information. Take the east road and go as fast as you can. If you find him, you know what to do. I'll take the carriage and follow the road west. Meet back at the hall. If we haven't found him, we'll get the dogs and start over. And Gray, we'd better find him." The rest of the threat was unvoiced, hanging in the air between them.

Gray set off at a furious pace, looking across empty fields and down roads. Lord Norton entered his carriage and rode recklessly west, without seeing anyone. By sundown both he and Gray were back at his holdings. They had spent the afternoon looking to no avail. Perhaps Basil had proceeded afoot through the woods. They would need the dogs.

After they left, Basil emerged from the cellar, fought his way through the brambles, to rest a moment beyond them. Scratched and bleeding, he found his ankle so swollen he had been forced to unlace his shoe before he started off. He tried the bridge with the stream, but it was dry and would not conceal his trail. Still he waited for long minutes, close to the road, listening for any travelers besides Lord Norton and Gray. No one had passed that way, save for Lord Norton's carriage earlier.

Grimly, he had listened to it, rattling on the bumpy road, knowing it would return, with dogs this time. He reviewed his options. They were far fewer than he would have liked. He could continue on toward Lord and Lady Whetton's manor, down the road past the bridge. But it was farther than he really could go on his swollen foot, certainly farther than he had time to go.

Perhaps someone from the manor would come along and give him a lift, if he stayed close to the road, but also perhaps not. And brush for concealment was more sparse than he would have liked. In fact his real and only option was to crawl away from the bridge and hide himself. And he couldn't crawl far. He looked upwards at the trees themselves, thinking to climb above the dogs and perhaps lose them that way. But there were no trees strong enough or tall enough to do the job. The growth about him was low and thick.

Of course, he consoled himself, those hunting him did not know if his ankle was a real problem or not. And they might focus on a wide circle about Lady Thornton's manor, and then work their way inward. In the meantime, close to the road as he was, he could make it out for help if anyone did come by.

He puzzled over how the dogs would find his trail. How would they know which scent was his? Many feet had passed over the grounds and porches of the manor. And they would not have anything belonging to him. Then it hit him. He himself had helped his enemies. He had told them about the larder. They would take the dogs there, where his scent was fresh.

"Well, Basil, you've done it this time. You told Gray where you were imprisoned. He'll start there, find your trail and soon enough, you." He began to walk, as best he could, with a limp and a shuffle and many pauses for breath. He crossed the road to be on the manor side. His only real hope was to make it to Whetton Manor as fast as he could and hope it would be before Gray and the dogs. Rescue by road seemed a lovely but lost hope.

His hunters arrived just after sundown. The sun set early that time of year and darkness followed quickly on its heels. Gray came on horseback, with a group of Lord Norton's men, while two servants brought the carriage. Just in case he had told the truth about his ankle, Basil thought. And as Basil feared, they had brought the dogs.

He imagined Gray finding the larder, then with the dogs' help, the cellar. Basil smiled a little at the thought. He could imagine Gray cursing rose bushes in general and Basil in particular, before setting out on the real trail with the dogs and men, while the two servants waited with the carriage.

Maybe if he had waited back by the manor, he could have taken the carriage and escaped. But he would have needed to be more agile to accomplish that. He looked regretfully at his tender, swollen foot.

Lord Norton himself would not come, Basil mused. He wouldn't want to call too much attention to the hunt. He would likely be back home, alternately pacing and furiously stirring up the fire, or just sitting back in a fat chair, plotting Basil's demise.

Meanwhile, Basil sat waiting in the woods between Thornton Manor and the Whettons. Dirty and bleeding and exhausted, he had stopped to rest. He could no longer run, in fact he could no longer walk. Besides, he had nowhere safe to run to.

In late afternoon he could hear the occasional baying of the dogs. They had found his trail and were having no trouble following it. Though still in the distance, he could hear them close to where he had crouched in the stream bed. They would reach him a lot sooner than it had taken him to reach where he was, Basil thought.

And though the manor was not far, it was too far. His rush of energy in the role of the hunted had long since subsided. He had been four weeks on little or no food, and the day had been long. He found he could no longer navigate straight but wobbled around in circles, on an ankle that would not work and a foot too swollen to touch the ground. Though not inclined to quit on a reasonable course of action, he did feel he should pause and rest a bit.

He looked longingly over at the roadway, just a few paces away, but it looked back at him empty of life. He sighed and half closed his eyes. He would rest just for a moment he told himself. Just for a moment. Then his eyes closed the rest of the way.

20
On Basil's Trail

Leaving Tegyn, Karis, and the minstrel behind, Malin breathed a sigh of relief. Here was something he understood: a trail to follow, a friend to track and find, and a horse and a wolf for company. He set off after Rilse on the southern pony, keeping his distance, for the southern horse was skittish. He was happy as he could be under the current circumstances. Everything can't be rotten, he told himself. Not everything.

Where do we start, Rilse? The docks?

Why not? Everything else started there.

That's also where we last saw Basil, the night of the ball. He was getting out of the dinghy onto the docks with my father. Seems no one has seen him since.

Then to the docks. I'll see you there, and Rilse headed straight across country.

As the crow flies, thought Malin, though Rilse certainly was no crow. Malin took a more circuitous route, suitable for a horse and rider. By early afternoon he was at the docks. He searched for any sign of Basil, though he didn't really expect to find anything. A month was a long time. And true to his expectations he found nothing.

He reached out for Rilse. There was no answer, but in the sand beside the docks, he found the wolf's fresh prints, which continued along the edge of the shore for a short distance before heading in a more direct route for the sandbar. He hadn't heard any commotion that Rilse would create if he were seen, so as usual at that time of day, the docks had to be almost deserted.

As they would also have been the night of the ball, he realized. The grooms were waiting in town, not at the docks, for their patrons. Visualizing that night, he could see the carriages hitched to the posts. A few single horses as well. His eyes swept the shore line. He couldn't see the sandbar from that point, but if the ship had been drifting, Basil would have guessed where it was heading.

He could not have traveled by carriage, it would have been too cumbersome and the roadway too long. It would also have announced his presence to any watching enemies. A single horse would have carried him quietly, but Malin could not remember ever seeing Basil ride a horse. Still, that was the only reasonable option. He hadn't walked, that would have taken too long and he would never have been close enough to the action to be involved.

But looking at the tracks, there was no sign a horse had ever gone that way. Whatever had happened the night of the ball had been swept away by the tides. Though they were sheltered in the bay from the worst of the winter seas along the coast, Godsel still had high tides. And a month had passed.

He had found exactly what he expected—nothing. But in spite of that, Malin was disappointed. He had hoped for something more. He considered the facts. The most glaring was that Basil had disappeared. Back in Malin's mind was the specter of the others who had disappeared, and found their way south by boat. It could be Basil was beyond their help, that he had already been taken south. But if the black sorcerer was after Karis, and had Lon, thinking he was Karis, would he still have attempted to kidnap others? Likely not.

But what if Basil had been close enough to pick up information about Godsel people who were helping the southern riders? And what if he were seen? The obvious answer made him shudder, so Malin skipped past it. Besides, if Basil were no longer alive, they could do nothing for him. And Malin felt driven to search. He felt Basil was still alive, though he also wondered if that was a forlorn hope.

Malin mentally chided himself. If he and Karis had checked the docks that night immediately after the ball, perhaps they would have found Basil. At least they would have known if someone had taken a horse.

Malin tried again. *Rilse?*

He was rewarded with a faint *Here.*

He followed Rilse's tracks along the shore for a ways, then followed them inland until they disappeared. He stopped, calculated the direction he had sensed Rilse, and cut inland. After some time and trouble he finally ended up at the thicket where Basil had hidden to spy on the southern riders. There he found old footprints that might have been Basil's, but he certainly found Rilse's. However, the wolf was long gone into the woods, as Malin read the tracks.

Rilse?

Here. Where are you? Are you coming?

Of course I'm coming. Some of us are more thorough than others of us.

Or just slower.

Malin ignored that. *I'm in the thicket close to the sandbar. There's a handkerchief here. Is it Basil's?*

It is.

So he was watching them.

Yes.

Did he follow them to where the trail split that night? To where we followed the main group?

Yes.

And he went after the small party.

That's another yes. You've got it.

Where does it go?

It cuts south before Roswood.

Malin hazarded a guess, though it was more than a guess. *To Thornton Manor?*

Looks like it.

Once again, Malin could see those brown eyes fixed on his, that small waist lost in the filmy white of a dress. Millicent. He sighed. Surely not her. But who was she? He thought she had been staying at Lady Thornton's. At least that's what Millicent had said. She had claimed to be Lady Thornton's niece. And Deirdre had introduced her to him. Why was it that Deirdre was always trouble?

And then it clicked. Lady Thornton was a widow and spent most of her time out of town. Did she have relatives? He thought back. He could not remember ever meeting any. And her empty manor, placed close to the south wilderness would be just perfect for a southern hideout. How could he have been so blind?

He heard Rilse's laughter echoing in his head. *She was pretty.*

Malin ignored Rilse's comment, though he was right. *Where are you now?*

In the inner forests.

The woods are thick, here. I'll have to return to Tegyn and take that road to Thornton Manor. I won't be fast, but this horse will get me there.

I'll nose around the woods, and meet you there.

"Lady Thornton's," Malin muttered to his horse. "Who would have guessed? And I bet Millicent is no relative."

Finally, by early evening, Malin found himself at the crossroads to Tegyn. Longingly he thought of Lanier, stabled close now, just at Oldsbury Hall. His horse's gait was so much smoother than that of this smaller southern pony. But Malin found he was reluctant to take the extra time. Something kept pushing at him to hurry, to find Basil. They were finally, after a month away, on Basil's trail. After so long a few more minutes shouldn't make any difference, right? But what if it did? He couldn't shake off a feeling of urgency.

He sighed and turned west on the road toward Roswood and Thornton Manor. It was also the road to Lady Whetton's. Briefly he thought about the minstrel. How would that all turn out? Life was just getting more and more complicated and uncomfortable, he thought. He smiled as he remembered his early assurance that Basil would sort it all out. He might, but they had to find him first.

By sundown he was at Thornton Manor. He turned into the lane and followed it up to the manor itself. *Rilse?*

Here. At the back of the manor.

Malin rode the horse to the back and loosed it among the trees. Rilse interrupted his thoughts. *Where are you?*

At the back. Where are you?

Over here. Looks like Basil hid here for a while.

Malin followed the voice, crouching low enough to see the cellar, where the door stood open. Rilse emerged.

He's not here now. He went into the woods.

Which direction?

Toward Roswood and the Whettons. It was several long moments before Malin heard Rilse again. *Others search for him as well. Their tracks fold over his. But his trail is strange and he's moving very slowly.*

Malin joined Rilse. *He's dragging one foot. He has hurt himself. Rilse, how long ago was he here?*

A couple of hours. Maybe more.

A couple of hours, and others were also on Basil's trail. Once more Malin felt the need to hurry, a sense of urgency.

But again circumstances intervened. The horse could not go through the undergrowth that Rilse was threading. He would have to follow Rilse on foot. *I can't take my horse, can I?*

No. Besides, he's not Lanier. He won't like me.

Malin followed Rilse laboriously over the rough terrain. Basil had kept to the woods, for cover at first. Then he had stayed as close to the roadway as possible, and still remain in hiding. *He's hoping for a ride,* Malin thought to himself.

Go find him, Rilse. I'll come as fast as I can.

Rilse was off like a shot, loping through the woods, skirting thickets, his nose filled with Basil's scent, and something else he had not smelled before on Basil. *Fear,* he thought. Basil understood what was happening and knew he could not win.

Fifteen minutes later, Malin heard the sounds of horses and riders and dogs, to the east of Thornton.

They think he's trying for Oldsbury Hall, Rilse, and they're trying to cut him off.

Good thing he went the other way.

What do you think happened, Rilse? They've held him prisoner and he's escaped?

Maybe. Better move fast. They're almost to Thornton.

Malin came fast, but Rilse was right. In just a few minutes Malin was close enough to hear horses and dogs and men in the woods surrounding the manor. He tried to touch the minds of the horses, the dogs, but he was too distant. He paused and turned back to face the manor, traveling along the road several yards before he veered off into the woods, trying to get a little closer to those at the manor, while still on the trail to Basil.

Have they found his tracks? Malin asked Rilse, pausing to listen. He could hear the occasional bark of a dog, the whinny of a horse, but no real baying as they caught the scent of their quarry.

Not yet, but they won't be long. They are at the manor now.

Malin could reach the minds of the dogs. They were still unfocused, nosing about. Malin did his best to distract them, feeding them bits about other creatures, buried bones. But he could only buy them a little time. They had already smelled something of Basil's and were looking for that scent.

A few minutes more and he heard again from Rilse. *They're down by the stream.*

By the bridge?

Yes. Malin could see in his mind's eye both the stream and the bridge. *There's no water there.*

No. It's too dry.

But Basil went to see.

Yes. Then he followed along this side of the road, Rilse commented, nosing along the trail.

To find a ride if he could.

Likely. He's injured and going even slower.

That's why he tried to hide. Until he remembered the dogs. What direction is he going?

Toward Roswood.

To Aunt Aila's? Malin was incredulous. *It's too far. He won't make it. Wait, he's heading for Whetton Manor. Will he make that?*

No. It's also too far and he is too slow.

Then we'd better help.

Good idea, Rilse agreed. *But how?*

We have to reach him first. Then we can tell where to send his pursuers.

Right. But we have to reach him ahead of the dogs. And they're coming fast, Rilse warned.

Yes. And they will harm him. I feel that in their minds.

Can you change it?

Maybe, Rilse, maybe. If they come closer to us and further away from their masters. Have they found where he reached the streambed? Malin tried to gauge where he was.

Yes. They hunt between you and me. They are also much closer now, to your Basil.

Much closer. Their baying is suddenly louder. They sense he's nearby.

The men on horseback had been forced to take to the road. They could not follow the dogs through the woods. So although the men and dogs were separated, they were all nearer, Malin thought. Near enough to touch their minds? He had to try. Basil was running out of time. And if the hunters reached Basil first, Malin was quite sure they would not be solicitous of his welfare. In fact from the sound of the dogs, Basil might be killed by them before the men on horses ever reached him.

The woods dipped lower at the point where he thought Basil was. The hollow seemed to swallow all sound, even the cries of the hounds. He tried to reach the dogs' minds, and could not. They were in the hollow, locked off from his thoughts and images. Besides they were caught up in the frenzy of the hunt. He tried again, to no avail.

On the hill overlooking the hollow he could hear the horses and men. And though they were more distant, he could feel the horses' minds. He could reach them. But the more immediate threat was the dogs. In spite of all his efforts he could not pierce their focus and the hollow's insulating properties to reach their minds. In frustration he mind called to Rilse.

A wolf howl or two? The gytrash?

Rilse obliged. Malin felt the dogs hesitate, sensed a momentary uneasiness in their minds, an opening in their focus.

He added his efforts to those of Rilse. *Wolves. Many.*

Coming close. But Malin was too far, his message still too faint. He put on a burst of speed, running toward where he thought Basil was.

Have you found Basil? Malin asked Rilse.

I'm near.

Malin continued to run, yet even as he ran, he knew he would be too late. No matter what he could do, he would be too late to save Basil. Beyond him he could hear Rilse, could sense his change into the gytrash. He had to leave Basil to Rilse.

But he could work on the horses and delay the men. He went to work. He built up the images of a horse-eating monster in the woods, huge and black and menacing. Of their riders leading them directly into danger, and abandoning them there. Suddenly the riders found themselves in a full scale battle with their horses, horses that refused to leave the road and enter the woods.

A few howls, Rilse? But Rilse was the gytrash and could no longer hear him.

He left off his work with the horses and turned to the hollow. The gytrash was there, protecting Basil, Malin hoped. If only the dogs were far enough away for Rilse to reach Basil first. Down he went into the hollow, heedless of his footing, slipping and sliding on the damp ground, careless of any noise he might make. It would be swallowed up in the baying of the dogs. The time for caution, for planning was past. Basil's safety depended on speed and it would be close.

21
Hunted

Earlier that afternoon, Myrrha had walked slowly down the road to Lord and Lady Whetton's. The weather was mild for winter and she had decided to walk there from Rilda's. She had a lot on her mind and walking and thinking along unpeopled roads came naturally to her.

She did not look for others on the road, for it was a private family affair rather than a public party. Only one carriage had passed her by, no others. And it had been in a big hurry and had no time nor interest in her. Good. She was glad to walk and solitude suited her just fine.

Winter in Godsel was cool but snowless, with blue skies and a warm sun on the back. A cloak was all Myrrha needed, and her harp of course. Even evenings were not really cold.

At Rilda's, as she readied herself for the evening's concerts, she found herself reluctant to tell the others she had been invited to play at Oldsbury Hall, and for the royal family. It seemed such an amazing turn of events she didn't know quite whether to believe it herself. And what if she changed her mind?

She would leave the Whettons' at six, or six thirty, and it was a long, slow walk down the lane, past Tegyn and on to Oldsbury. The sun would set by then, but twilight would linger and the moon would be almost full. There would be quite enough light to see by.

As she had guessed, the dinner party at the Whettons was a small family affair. Their three children and spouses, and their children, seven in number, had gathered to celebrate their father's birthday. After dinner, the program was also a family affair. The three grown children participated. The eldest daughter read a tribute to their father about his life which she had written. The second daughter sang a sentimental song about fathers, in general, and the youngest, his only son, read *The Charge of the Right Brigade,* by a new poet named Tonnlyson, honoring soldiers. Their father had been a soldier for much of his life, before his older brother died and he inherited the family manor.

Then it was Myrrha's turn. She would have no need to draw upon the symbols on her harp this night, thought Myrrha. Something homespun and simple, something about family would be just right. She unwrapped her harp and placed it upon her lap. Her fingers ran through her strings, strumming them briefly, testing how the sound played out in the hall. Then she began.

At first things were as she expected. Songs of home, family and children filled the small dining room. She noticed even the servants had gathered to listen. Some stood about the edges of the room itself, some lingered in the halls leading out of the room, obviously with the master's permission.

Myrrha smiled. These were the folk she had started playing for, back in the church. She still played there at least once a week, for these people who had first accepted her and loved her when she was no one, just a stranger and a musician come to town. She played several of those first tunes, glad for the smiles upon the faces of many. Several times the family clapped along with her.

Then she suddenly found herself in the middle of a new piece, both words and music were unfamiliar to her.

She looked down. Sure enough the symbols were glowing, and some of them seemed to be whirling about.

The song was about new roads opening before you, and how you should welcome them and move forward with gladness. As she played, the father's face cleared and a heaviness seem to lift from him. His new role as heir had seemed a burden to him, something his role as a soldier had not prepared him for, and he feared to tarnish the family name.

But now he could see that he brought something fresh and personal to the title, something that included all of his household as individuals and welcomed their contributions to making the place work. He sensed the new feeling of joy that coursed through his halls and he laughed, a sparkling merry laugh that was echoed around the table.

Soon everyone sitting had risen to their feet and were clapping their hands to Myrrha's music. This was a new life, and they all had an important part to play. The standing servants joined in. Then those lingering at the doorways slid in, as if they had always been there and the clapping was doubled.

Flushed and joyful herself, Myrrha was still astounded at the course the evening had taken. Her music was only hers some of the time, she thought. The rest of the time it belonged to itself and she was only permitted to participate. As she finished, she carefully rewrapped her harp, putting it away. The family gathered around, thanking her, and the father walked her to the door.

"That's powerful music you have there, minstrel. Powerful music. And let no one tell you any different."

For a moment, Myrrha wondered if he could see into her heart, into her fears and confusion about the course her life was taking. But she forced a smile and a nod. "Thank you, sir."

He took her hand and bowed over it. Then he added softly, looking her straight in the eye, for he was a good judge of men and women. "That song was for you, too."

A new life, a new world, even if she was female. For a moment Myrrha thought she could just be Myrrha. She would no longer have to wander about as Rolan to be accepted. Could it be true? She politely refused Lord Whetton's offer of his carriage to take her where she needed to go. She had to think. She slipped out of the house and followed the lane south to the road that led both to Oldsbury Hall and to Roswood, one at either end. Lady Whetton's manor was closer to Roswood, so she would have to pass Tegyn to arrive at Oldsbury Hall.

Myrrha found she wanted to walk past Tegyn once more before things changed so drastically in her life, to remember her time there, to feel the thread of its music. Tomorrow she would move in and things would not be the same. Almost she wanted to reach out and stop the rush of events; yet at the same time she wanted to leap in the middle of them, to ride the wild tide of her fortunes to wherever it would take her.

Almost unaware, she reached the road and turned left, toward Oldsbury Hall, toward Tegyn. A little farther down the road entered the woods, threading through them like a ribbon through lace. The woods had been her refuge. In Jandillo, they were the closest thing she had to a home. Whenever strong emotions surfaced, she had sought the woods, and tonight she needed to think, to feel their peace. She found her emotions in a whirl. One moment she was ecstatic about her possibilities, the next she felt like a rat in a trap.

Just as Thornton Hall loomed in the distance, a sudden impulse took her off the road and directly into the woods opposite it. Her heart was a whirlpool of emotions spinning apart from conscious thought. The familiar crunch of leaves underfoot, the tug of branches on her clothing, brought her back to herself. She was still Myrrha. Living at Tegyn or Rilda's would not change that.

Nor would trying to rescue Lon. She talked sternly to herself, squashing the ridiculous springs of hope that kept welling up whenever she thought of Lon or heard his name. He was in the clutches of a dark mage. Who knows if they might ever even meet again?

Her feet found a faint trail and followed it, moving quickly to match her thoughts. After a few minutes both thoughts and feet slowed. She had walked out her angst. She had not been pushed into rash decisions. True, she had made them quickly, but they were her decisions. She could and would decide her own fate. She would go to Oldsbury Hall. She would listen and learn. Then she would decide what she could do to help find Lon and Basil.

She toyed once more with the idea of being just Myrrha. The song she had just sung for the Whettons kept bubbling up in her head, the refrain repeating itself over and over, "You are light, you are love, be who you are."

But she couldn't go there. It just seemed too far, so she shelved that idea. Maybe later. Much later.

She cut across a field, heading once more for the road, but the darkness of the night deceived her. She was not where she expected to be. She found not the road, but another stretch of woods. No matter. She was at home in the woods. They were known and familiar. She laughed. Maybe they were her real family. She crossed another trail and followed it, then left it for another, letting whimsy rule.

Her eyes were bright, her mind keen. Overhead the moon emerged from jagged clouds. It flooded the trees around her, kept pace with her. She was Myrrha, minstrel, wielder of power, fighter against black mages. Her stride picked up a rhythm, matching the tuneless whistle she made just under her breath. Around her she whirled the cloak of sound that had been her companion for long years whether as Myrrha or Rolan.

Because of the sound cloak, it took some time for her to hear the noises ahead of her, to pick out the rhythm of horses, the baying of hounds. When she did, she came to a complete stop, almost instinctively flattening herself against the sturdy tree behind her, pushing back into the shadows, her cloak of sound masking her presence. Then finding the disturbance well ahead of her, she dropped her cloak and began to listen. Someone was being hunted, and the dogs had found the trail.

Almost without thinking, she found herself drawn to the source of the sound, walking toward the dogs, who were followed by riders on the road. She wondered what they hunted, and why. Ahead of her, the trail opened up, the moon glinted off the path where bare branches reached upward. The cold night air tightened her lungs, the fall leaves rustled underfoot. She was in a forest far south of Jandillo, but suddenly she was back there once more, her mother gasping beside her as they fled their hunters, as they fled the specter of Samlt lying dead beside the fire, burned they knew not how.

She was running now. She was not sure whether it was from or to. Her cloak was pulled tightly around her, and she ducked and twisted, weaving on the trail, avoiding by senses other than sight the branches that snagged, the twigs that grasped. She was in full flight, forgetting to cloak her presence, thinking only of speed. She half saw the partly exposed root that tripped her and pitched her headlong on the path, but not in time to avoid it. She lay there for brief moments, trying to collect her breath and her thoughts.

The dogs were closer, the riders as well. The trail was open and exposed to a brilliant fall moon that lit up and shadowed even the twigs on the trees, let alone her fleeing figure. She sprang to her feet and off the path, into the center of a thick patch of woods.

Someone was there before her, a man. His solid form, sitting upright, blocked her way. She dodged, then once more she was full length on the earth; she had tripped over his legs. She half rose, and turned to face him, her face lit by the moonlight, his face and form shadowed.

He pivoted to face her, his hand on her arm. "Not a good night for walking in these woods," he said softly. "The enemy is close. You'd best fly back the way you came."

Myrrha started at the voice. "Master Basil?" She had heard those round full tones that night of the ball, on the ship. They were so musical, she had asked Deirdre who they belonged to. They were unmistakable. It was incredible that the man she had waited for in his library these past weeks had just tripped her in the middle of the woods, with tracking dogs and hunting riders coming ever closer.

His voice, though still soft, was more urgent now. "Yes. But you'd better be off. They'll be here soon."

"Aren't you coming?"

His smile was regretful. "Love to, but my ankle simply will not cooperate."

Myrrha understood. He was trapped with no way to escape his pursuers. She glanced around. A few more yards would see them in thicker woods, where it would be easier to shield them from being seen and run into. She wasn't sure about the dogs. She had seemed to fool one or two in Jandillo, but they were mongrels, not trained hunting dogs like these.

"Over there we'd have a better chance."

Basil looked where she pointed. He nodded. "What about the dogs?"

"Come on. They're almost upon us," Myrrha urged. She could do nothing if they didn't move quickly. Basil caught her urgency and moved as fast as he could, half hopping, trying to lift his injured foot. Then they were there.

Myrrha pulled Basil down beside her in the midst of a thick bush, and began to gather the noise of the pursuit about them, whirling the sound into a shield she tightened as the dogs came nearer. The riders were not far behind. As yet she and Basil could see nothing, and Myrrha sent half a prayer to the night gods to cover the moon before she realized it was already shrouded in clouds. The ground was cold beneath them, but not as cold as she was.

Back on the path the dogs ran with their noses close to the ground, lifting them only to bay at their quarry. Then suddenly they stopped. The stillness startled Myrrha, her shield almost falling useless about them. So it was she heard the other sound that chilled her. A wolf hunted close by. The dogs whined in a sudden excess of fear, their quarry forgotten. The wolf howl came again, closer this time. Myrrha shivered.

"Never mind the wolf. He will not harm us. But the riders come." Basil's words brought Myrrha back to their peril.

Rilse, she thought. She collected the night sounds, of dog, wolf, and rider, and once more formed a shield which whirled about them, leaving them invisible to those that sought them.

The wolf howled again. Myrrha reached out and tightened the shield. Then the wolf howls were all around the dogs, a chorus surrounding their chorus, and the dogs stopped baying and froze, not knowing where to find safety.

The horses and their riders came up the road, until they were opposite Basil's hiding place. They shouted in anger at the dogs, but the dogs paid them no attention, fleeing suddenly with small whimpers into the night.

The riders pulled up on the path the dogs had fled, milling just a few yards from Myrrha and Basil. The moon had escaped the clouds once more, and without her shield they would have been sitting ducks for the riders and the rifles she could see in their hands. This was no rescue party. She had been right. This was a hunting party.

Beyond Basil and Myrrha, the riders became aware of the wolf howls, the sounds of a pack closing in.

Then suddenly a wolf was visible, a giant black wolf with red eyes.

"A gytrash!" the foremost rider mumbled almost incoherently. "A gytrash!"

"Fool," snapped the rider directly behind him. "Superstitious fool. Gytrash indeed. They don't exist."

Then he gasped and pulled up his horse, as he, too, saw the creature before him. The horses grew frantic, fighting their riders, tearing the reins from their grasp. One horse pulled free, then another. Soon all were fighting their riders. Mindlessly, in great panic, they ripped their reins from their riders' control and raced off. Some ran headlong down the path in one direction, some the opposite. Some cut into the woods and stumbled through thick underbrush until they reached the road, where they raced off, white flecks of foam visible on their mouths in the moonlight. Some cut across the fields, but all fled, out of the control of their riders, away from Basil and Myrrha.

Myrrha heard a small chuckle beside her. "A wolf can be a great thing when he's working for you. To say nothing of his companion."

"That's not a wolf. That's a creature from a nightmare," Myrrha said. "Besides, Rilse is white."

Basil peered at her. "So, you've met Rilse."

Myrrha nodded. "At Tegyn, where I was waiting for you."

"Well, I think that's Rilse. In another form. You were waiting for me?"

"Yes. I'm Rolan, the minstrel." Basil's sharp ears caught the brief hesitation before the name, and wondered, but unlooked for aid could be allowed their secrets, he thought. He had been heading for an unpleasant confrontation which might have removed his person permanently from his surroundings. Thanks to the minstrel and gytrash Rilse, he was safe.

Moments later Rilse, the white Rilse, sifted through the moonlight, past the sound shield whirling about them, and stretched out beside Myrrha.

Like me, you do good work. They would not have found you without the dogs. Maybe not even then. We sent the dogs away, in case. And the horses.

We? Myrrha wondered.

Another figure emerged close to where they crouched.

Myrrha held her breath. The figure drew closer. A piece of cloud drifted past the moon and light caught the face.

It was Malin. Surprised, Myrrha dropped the shield she whirled about them, almost losing her balance. Her hand dropped to Rilse to steady her.

Beside her, Basil chuckled. "It's a great glad gathering of all and sundry. Malin, Rilse, delighted to see you. Where have you been for the last month or so, while I languished, locked in Lady Thornton's larder?"

Malin heard Basil's words, but they made no sense to him. "In Lady Thornton's larder?" he repeated, confused. "Locked?"

"Locked. Definitely locked," Basil assured him.

"What were you doing there?"

"Starving." Basil seemed to be enjoying himself, thought Myrrha. It was almost as if he were teasing Malin.

"Why?"

"So I could escape."

"From whom?"

"Southern riders. I just escaped this morning, but injured my ankle in the process."

"Stop." Malin had reached his limit. "Tell us what happened to you the night of the ball, and fill in the rest of the story as you go." Malin's tone was unbelieving. Basil, his mentor, locked in a larder?

"Millicent, Gray and southern riders were using Lady Thornton's home for nefarious activities. I followed them there on the night of the ball, and was discovered." At the mention of Millicent's name Malin turned red, a red that quickly faded at the rest of Basil's news.

"You've been there this whole time?"

Basil's look became quite solemn. "This whole time. And the only way I was able to escape was to leave food alone until I had shrunk to the right size for the small window in the south wall." Basil sighed plaintively. "My preferred plan was to await rescue by you and Rilse, but you were too slow. I tumbled through the window, injured my ankle, encountered Gray who went for Lord Norton, took flight to the woods, met the minstrel here who hid me, and you know the rest."

Amazed, Myrrha listened to the roll of language. Basil didn't even need to stop for breath.

Malin was still trying to put things together. What was the minstrel doing there, when he was supposed to be going for dinner at Oldsbury Hall?

He hid Basil, Rilse summarized.

Myrrha heard Rilse underneath. She was grateful, unsure what she could have said.

Malin turned to stare down at Myrrha, who found that the moon had once again emerged and was flooding her face with more light than she wanted. Confused, she found she had nothing to say in her own defense, but she had another defender nearby. Basil spoke up.

"Yes. Some sort of shield. Perhaps originating in sound?"

It was Myrrha's turn to be astounded. How had Basil known? And what else did he know?

"Is that right, Master Rolan?"

Myrrha stammered, "Yes."

Basil turned back to Malin. "So what kept you?"

It was Malin's turn now to set Basil on his heels. "We've been to Heath Halls and back, to rescue the royal family. They were being held captive there."

Basil's astonished intake of breath was quite satisfying to Malin. It wasn't every day he could surprise his mentor and friend. "Heath Halls? And back? In this time? You must have flown."

We went fast.

Malin laughed at Rilse, who was never humble. *We did go fast,* he agreed.

Myrrha found her tension suddenly being released. She was no longer hunted and helpless. She was with friends in Godsel, and they had, between them, once again rousted the enemy. She felt herself smiling.

Then Malin grew quite sober. "We were able to bring them all safely here, except Lon. You know, Karis' twin. He was taken. We think he's on his way south, to a dark mage." Basil took it all in, listening quietly. "We've only just returned. We hoped to find you at Oldsbury or Tegyn, but you were not at either place. My father mentioned you had not been seen since the night of the ball. Rilse and I went looking."

Good thing, too, Rilse happily reminded them.

Malin went on. "We're dining at Oldsbury Hall in a while to share information and make plans. Will you come?"

Basil tried to stand, forgetting his ankle, and stumbled, until Malin and Myrrha each grasped an arm, steadying him.

"You need a horse. There should be one still within calling distance. I rode one to this area, and he wasn't tethered." Malin was silent, concentrating. Soon they could hear the gait of a lone horse picking his way through the woods and underbrush.

"Wish I could do that. It would have been quite useful," Basil remarked. "Can you find another for the minstrel?"

"If you're coming to dinner with us, you'll have to hurry." Malin looked pointedly at Basil. "You would stand out in that, you know, rather than blending in." Basil glanced at his once white linen, his torn black jacket and touched his mud-streaked face. Then they all laughed together.

Malin reached out once more, trying for another straggler from the enemies' mounts, but no more came sauntering up. Rilse had already taken his leave, knowing the horses would not be thrilled with his presence. Myrrha was relieved. Horses she didn't understand. She had never ridden one and wasn't sure she wanted to change that situation.

Malin helped Basil up on the horse. "We'll help you off at Tegyn and we'll go on to Oldsbury Halls to the stable. Rolan, you can ride behind me then. The horse will carry two for a short distance."

"It doesn't matter if I'm late," Myrrha protested.

Basil turned shrewd eyes upon her, wondering at the minstrel's place in the scheme of things. "Why don't you give Rolan a ride to the stables to get a carriage, then return to Tegyn to collect me. I'll hurry."

So it was decided. Basil was helped into Tegyn, knowing Rilse would be close by if needed. Rolan rode behind Malin to Oldsbury Stables, where the grooms furnished a carriage and driver. They returned for Basil, who though more acceptably groomed, did indeed look somewhat the worse for wear, now that they could see him under the carriage lamps. He was definitely thinner, with a myriad of scratches and a large bruise on his temple. He hobbled and walked awkwardly, doing better only with help, for his ankle was badly swollen.

Myrrha found herself flushing under the gaze of Basil and Malin, the hood of her cloak falling down against her face, her harp bundled on her left shoulder. In their turn, Basil and Malin both wondered about the minstrel. Malin found himself more peaceful about his presence since Basil seemed to support him. Yet Basil, too, wondered about the minstrel. A gifted singer, he thought. He had heard the tales of the minstrel, though he had only attended part of a concert at Roswood.

But there was more to the minstrel than that. He had great gifts, perhaps even greater than those of Malin or Karis. But at the same time, there was something secretive and elusive about the minstrel, and someone far more lost and alone than either Malin or Karis, even mage-haunted as Karis had been.

As the carriage rolled on its way to Oldsbury Hall, Basil listened intently to Malin's tale of the events that had happened on the ship the night of the ball. He had been able to piece together most of the story, but Malin filled in a gap or two.

Then it was Basil's turn. "Millicent was working with the southern riders, as was Gray, Lord Norton's steward."

"You're sure?"

"Very. I watched her club Gray with her riding crop to provide him some cover when I saw them together, hoping to put me off track. Gray discovered I'd escaped from the larder and he and several of Lord Norton's men were going to collect me and take me for a chat with Lord Norton." He was silent, his thoughts full of what form that chat would take. "Those were not the actions of some sweet young thing."

Red-faced, Malin steered the conversation in a different direction. "Lord Norton, a traitor? Connected with southern enemies?" Malin shook his head. It was hard to believe.

"What was happening up north?"

"Lord Tallon from Anor contrived to have all soldiers as well as the king's guard sent north, supposedly to help Prince Areth at the front. Then he brought a company of his men from Anor to take over, making the royal family prisoners. The king had been wounded on the way to a conference in Esfalia, but was well on the road to recovery when they came." Malin paused. "They poisoned him. A slow poison, but sure."

"Has Anor fallen to traitors then?" Basil was astounded.

"We don't know. We only know Tallon is one."

Basil stared at Malin dumbfounded. "The king prisoner in his own halls?" He shook his head. "Where are the king and queen now?"

"Oldsbury Hall. They're safe." The carriage pulled up to the wide stairs in front of Oldsbury Hall and stopped to let them out.

Myrrha had listened quietly to the conversation. People gathering to plan and work together to handle problems was new to her. Was this what families did? She ached a little at the thought, feeling sad she had not known a family like that. Yet maybe she could belong; she could be included. Then she remembered. It was not she, Myrrha. It was he, Rolan the minstrel. She could not be fully included as long as she hid who she was from the rest of them.

She had to keep that secret, she insisted to herself, she had to. The opportunities before her would vanish away with the emergence of Myrrha. They would never accept a girl into their plans, their company. They wanted the minstrel. He was the one they had asked to help. Her heart hurt at the thought, yet she was convinced that maintaining Rolan was necessary.

Myrrha was not invited.

22
Dinner Tales

"I couldn't even move a finger." Rast, taller and thinner than usual, but with the same unruly red hair was standing by the fireplace, talking with Lord Lindsey.

Supper that night at Oldsbury Hall was to be a private family affair, but included a few others immediately involved in the rescue. Against the wall, reclining on a blue brocade couch, was the king, pale and thin, but alert. Nearby in a matching blue upholstered chair, the queen kept watch over both the king and Alyssa, who slumbered in a brown leather chair beside her.

Close to the fireplace, drumming his fingers nervously on the brown leather arm of the chair he sat in, was Karis, his eyes constantly shifting to the doorway from the rust-patterned rugs on the hardwood floor, then back again. Behind him, heavy drapes covered the tall windows, their mingled blues and browns and rusts securing the room against the winter cold.

It was a warm, inviting room, but Karis' mind was elsewhere. He knew he had overstepped his bounds by inviting Rolan to live at Tegyn, but he hoped Malin would forgive him and come to dinner anyway. He also knew his cousin was deeply concerned about Basil. If Malin didn't show up, it would most likely be because of Basil. Malin wasn't usually the sort to let small things become obstacles to important matters. Yet, what if this were the exception? Karis sighed. If only all you had to do was get things done. It was the people business that escaped him, the people business that Lon was so good at.

His eyes rested for a moment on the king, his father. He was still fragile, but his cheeks had caught a bit of color, and his blue eyes held some of their old brightness, unless it was the reflected glow of the fire. Much better, Karis thought, than his first view of his father in Heath Halls just a few weeks ago.

Was it only that? It seemed so much longer. His father had been unconscious, and so wasted, Karis could hardly believe it was the same man. Wounds and poison had taken a great toll, but tonight, for the first time, Karis felt his father would be all right. Now there was just a kingdom to worry about.

And his twin, Lon, abducted by foul servants of a dark wizard. It seemed to Karis that their best hope to retrieve Lon was the minstrel, Rolan. Somehow the mage had no power over the minstrel, while he could paralyze and make a puppet out of Karis. As Karis sat musing, another fact struck him. The black sorcerer had no power over Malin, either. But Malin would say it was because he had no magic. Karis sighed. It seemed that the root of all his own problems lay in his magic that someone a lot more powerful wanted.

Conversations were low and soft in the room, the only movement the flickering light from the fire that cast warm tones over even the shadows. After their frantic ride south with the enemy right on their heels, Karis and his family were glad to rest, safe for the moment in a warm room with warm food to follow.

Aunt Aila and Uncle Seth were there, subdued and quiet, in awe at the events they were hearing, wondering at the part that Malin and Karis had played. Deirdre was staring at Karis, not quite believing the poor student she had tricked was really the king's son. She had blushed a little when she finally realized it was so.

Of all the company, only Rast was obviously tense, unable to sit, as they waited. For him, dinner was an obstacle to the real purpose of the evening, the sharing of information, taking counsel, making plans.

Yet, there were other undercurrents in the room. Under the quiet stillness of the queen was a deep sorrow for the son who was missing. Karis felt the loss of his twin as a tight pain in his center. Alyssa was pale and weary, sleeping curled up in the leather chair near her mother, but her dreams were troubled and short little sighs escaped her as she slept.

Karis wondered what kind of a world it was where men made war on small children. Lide's hidden valley flashed into his mind, unbidden, the white rightness of things, the slow deliberate pace of the unicorn. Suddenly he wished he could have stayed there longer. For how could they win against the darkness? There was the warlord Turgor in the north, trouble from the south, and a black mage. Still, they had to try.

For some moments the room was quiet. Down the hall, Karis could hear the sounds of voices approaching. His eyes shifted to the doorway opposite him, his fingers once more drumming nervously on the arm of the chair. He thought he could hear Malin; he hoped he could hear Malin. The door opened and yes, it was indeed Malin.

Followed by Basil? Karis stood up in surprise. Two servants assisted Basil to a chair close to the door, for he could not put his weight on his right ankle. He walked with a marked limp, in spite of their assistance and the help of a cane, but it was indeed Basil.

And right on the heels of Basil walked Rolan, the minstrel, wrapped in a deep crimson cloak, dark and silent as always, carrying his harp case. They were all there. Karis felt his stomach contract in relief, the churning slow and subside. After all his social errors, they had come anyway. As if he could read Karis' thoughts, Malin grinned at him. Karis let out his breath, just realizing he had been holding it. The mage hadn't won everything. They had all come, except Lon of course, but maybe they could begin to fight back.

Lord Lindsey was across the room in a moment, carrying on a low conversation with Basil and Malin. Karis sat back in his chair, finally relaxed, content, feeling the flow of things about him. He caught the words "Gray" and "Lord Norton," "Lady Thornton" and "Thornton Manor." He roused enough to realize a message was sent, soldiers assembled, and to hear the tramp of their marching as they went out the door. Somehow he knew they were going for Lord Norton, but who he was and why he was being brought in Karis had no idea. And he found he didn't really care. His thoughts were all of Lon, and the servants of the dark mage.

Dinner was announced and they filed into the dining room. Even little Alyssa stirred from her sleep to munch warm pastries, eat stew. The room came alive with sound and movement. As the food diminished, the buzz of conversation died with it. For a while nothing was said, or a great deal, depending on your point of view. All present, though they carefully made no mention of Lon, reviewed the events of the past weeks to each other. Myrrha, silent beside Karis, listened in growing wonder to the tales, enough to keep a minstrel going for months.

Over dinner they heard the story of Basil's capture and imprisonment in the larder.

"You lost weight with all that food around you? How did you keep from eating it?" Little Alyssa was amazed.

Basil smiled at her. "I recited my favorite poems and thought about the important information I had for Lord Lindsey."

Alyssa shook her blonde curls. "I couldn't do it."

"Rilse and I would have come earlier, but we were busy," said Malin. Everyone laughed. By now, all knew of that rushed ride; the king and queen and little Alyssa were living proof of it.

Karis and Malin added details that were not yet known. They told of Lide, and his place of warmth and light. The queen's features grew wistful for a moment. "If only there were places like that for all of us in our time of need."

The king reached his hand to touch hers. "Someone wiser than us has decreed we must choose the world we want to live in and create it. We only cherish what we work and sacrifice for."

"Maybe so," she said. "But every so often a hand reaches in to lift us, and love us. We need that, too."

Malin spoke of the southern riders who had followed them to Lide's, and of the reward they had offered.

"A reward?" The king exclaimed. "Southern riders that far north and well organized enough to offer a reward? Our enemies' arms have grown long indeed."

The queen told of meeting with the company of soldiers from Godsel, in their hour of peril.

Aunt Aila and Deirdre were astounded. They couldn't hear enough about what had happened. Aunt Aila kept repeating, "mercy," and "save us." Deirdre just looked at Malin, trying to see the hero behind the known face of a brother.

Finally, Alyssa said, "It's hard to eat. It's too noisy underneath. I want Lon." And she burst into tears. And there it was, out at last, and everyone found it a relief that it was said. Karis tucked the moment away, vowing in future to have at least the courage and sense of a child.

It was finally time. The queen could ask the question she had been burning to ask Rast all evening. "What happened at the lodge?"

Rast told them. The words seemed dragged reluctantly out of his mouth, one by one. Rast, who normally spat words like a splash of water on a hot grill. From what was said, or perhaps even more from what was not, Lord Lindsey and the queen, and the rest of the company, finally pieced together a strange story. While Rast and Lon and the king slept before the fire, the barred door burst open and a cluster of black-robed, hooded figures were upon them, their faces in shadow.

"Never a word did they speak—all strange and silent," Rast said. "They bound the lad, but they had to carry him, for his body wouldn't obey any more than mine would. Just before they left, one went to the fire and put in his hand, his bare hand, mind you, and picked out something. A great shadow spread out from it, and covered the room." He blurted out the words, and then waited, as if expecting to be contradicted. Not one of the assembled company said a word.

He continued softly. "When the shadow was gone so were the hooded figures and there was cold wind and snow ablowin' every which way and the fire was almost out. But I could not move. Finally thet white wolf of Malin's came, growlin' and pawin' at my chest. Then I was able to move, to shut the door and build up the fire."

"Did they leave a trail?" Lord Lindsey wanted to know.

"No. None that I could see or follow. But they left a horrible smell behind, sick and putrid, and a slick blackness on the wood floor."

"No trail?" Lord Lindsey was confused.

"I know things don't just disappear, but they did. Outside in the snow there was no trail. There were some strange marks, as if something heavy had been dragged, and there was some more black stuff, then nothing."

Rast broke off. He was heartsick at Lon's kidnapping. The king had been too ill to be left alone, and Rast had been forced to make a choice. He had to save the king and abandon Lon, or abandon the king and go after Lon. Either choice seemed bad, but the king would die if he left him. Lon would have to wait.

He had tended the king for three days in that hunting lodge in Potters Woods. On the fourth day, the king seemed strong enough to travel, and Rast bundled him up and placed him in the carriage and headed back to the main road, then south. Five days later, Rast met up with the search party from Godsel. The search party split in two; half continued with the king to Godsel, the other half went back with Rast to scour the woods. They found nothing. No Lon, nothing. Recently falling snow and driving winds had obliterated all tracks, if there were any. Lon and his captors had vanished.

"They got clean away," Rast said. His hands, reddened from the winter's cold, clenched into fists. He glared.

Karis spoke into the silence. "Nothing anyone could do. Against the dark mage, you would have no power. Even I don't. But I will," he added fiercely. "I will."

"Was there anything else you saw? Anything at all?" The queen's tone was tight, like the way she was holding herself.

Rast shook his head. "Nothing more, Your Majesty. Only—." Rast reddened and dropped his eyes to the floor a moment.

"Only?"

His head shot up. "I will search 'til we find him," he added grimly.

The queen gazed into the fire as if it held secrets for her eyes alone, then she turned to Basil. "When great uncle

Zache was called to the halls of learning, was there a mage that was left behind in the south to guard the fire gate?"

"My great uncle was called to the halls?" Karis repeated. "He passed through the fire gate? Why did you never tell me?"

"It was just after you were born, and you were too young. Then later, there seemed no reason to mention it." His mother's voice as always, was smooth and liquid, and so reasonable. Karis found himself embarrassed at his outburst, but the queen understood. In a sudden insight, she understood Karis' longings and frustrations. "You wish to go there."

"To the halls of learning. To the city of light." Basil's addition caught the king's interest, as well as Lord Lindsey's. Myrrha leaned forward attentively. They turned toward Basil, a thinner, paler Basil, though self-contained and impeccably dressed.

"Yes," Karis admitted. "As a light bearer there, no dark mage could touch me."

Nor could we, thought the queen, but she understood. He would be safe.

When Basil learned the full story of the dark mage and his powers that had carried off Lon, his face grew still, his eyes deepened, but he said nothing. In fact the whole company was silent.

Finally, Karis turned to Basil, picking up the queen's question. "Was a light bearer left to guard the gate?"

Basil understood what Karis was asking. "Usually one would be left. You're thinking that to balance the black mage, there is a white one, at least someone else with the power."

The queen nodded agreement. "It was usually so."

Basil continued, his voice suddenly solemn and formal. "Where there is darkness, there is light. Light and shadow, Tor and Antor. So the old records say."

"It was Karis the mage was after, not Lon." Malin brought everything into focus.

The queen's voice was not quite steady as she asked the question in all of their minds. "When he finds out Lon is not Karis, not gifted in magic, what will he do with him?"

Basil's voice was full and round. "He will make Lon the bait, to draw Karis to him."

Malin and Karis looked at each other. They had already figured that out.

The queen sighed in relief. "Then at least Lon will be safe." She continued. "As bait, he is only good as long as he is alive and well."

"Exactly." Basil was quick to reassure her.

Lord Lindsey's words followed right behind Basil's, precise and clear. "We will have the time we need to organize ourselves and find him. And when we do, Lon will be all right."

"We just have to make sure when we find him that you, Karis, will also be all right. We will plan well and carefully," the king said slowly. "And may the stars favor us. We have already won much. The rest will come."

Under her breath the queen softly repeated, as if she needed to hear the words again, "The rest will come."

23
The Call

After the king's words, silence fell over the company, each one pondering the new information they had received. They had much to do. The fire crackled suddenly. As if in answer to its summons, Myrrha rose from the table and walked to her harp, where it leaned against the wall beside the fire. Perhaps now was a good time to play.

A soft murmur rose from the company, that died out as she began to strum her harp. It was just a light strum at first, but it seemed to those who listened that their fears lifted and their hearts beat a little stronger as the notes grew and filled the room. Perhaps they had a chance, perhaps darkness wouldn't always win and power oppress those without it.

The queen could see her son Lon, beside her once more; Karis saw light piling up, pushing back the dark. Malin was in his beloved woods, Rilse beside him, creating mayhem for the southern riders. The king sat in his kingdom, strong and invincible. Basil learned great new truths, and Rast bound a dark mage while the mage lay paralyzed. Alyssa could not have described what she saw, but the world seemed lighter and sweeter once more. Deirdre felt her heart swell with pride for Malin, and even Aunt Aila smiled and nodded to the music. Myrrha stood at the center, both binding and bound by her music and her vision.

The sound became firmer, the rhythm more pronounced, with higher tones sifting through the rest like a star's kiss. Myrrha's head was bowed over her harp, her fingers moving like quicksilver over the strings, in a song she had never heard before. On the silver frame of her harp symbols appeared, glowing. Her voice soared, then cascaded back, finally becoming a whisper once more. No one moved when she finished. Myrrha's head bowed over her instrument, the fingers slowly releasing the last notes.

She lifted her head in the silence, and suddenly she became aware that there was a spot in the room that was growing brighter in spite of the blackness of the night outside. Startled, she glanced back at the fireplace behind her, then back to the spot. It was still there, its soft glow sifting over the room like gold dust, but something was happening. She stared at the brightening spot, motionless. She realized, peripherally, that Karis was also watching.

For his part, Malin felt rather than heard Rilse stir and turn toward the light. He, too, turned toward it. "That's you, Karis. Right? You're making that light."

"Light? What light?" Alyssa was puzzled.

The light grew steadily until Malin had to close his eyes against its brightness, but he immediately opened them again, unable to look away. Gradually his eyes made out the silhouette of a golden city just beyond a fiery arch, a city made of light, where bright beings shone. Under the fiery arch stood a tall figure in a white robe.

He was chanting, Malin realized, wondering if he should plug his ears and thus avoid some dire consequence, but phrases caught him even as he tried not to hear them. Something about "floods of the dark" and "a forsaking," about "riding down the wild dark" and "light bearers come!"

So it has come at last, thought Malin. Karis has his call. He'll be going to that place where all they do is practice and learn magic. It took all kinds.

Karis was motionless. After all his hoping and dreaming, his despair over his age, it had finally come. He watched the light grow stronger, and a vision appear in its center. If only he could get to the halls of learning, to the city of light before the mage got him. He could be trained and return to destroy the great darkness that had haunted him. He could see the mage shrinking before him, his black core dissolving before the white flame that was Karis, until he was merely a voice pleading helplessly in the wind. Karis savored the sweetness of his triumph.

He wrested himself from his dream back to the vision, soaking in the brightness, the light, the beauty of the golden city where light streamed from the stones in the walls, even from the cobblestones in the streets themselves. The white mage stood in a courtyard, in the center of that city, calling to him. The voice wasn't quite what he expected. Instead of smooth and melodious, it was rather sharp and piercing. But the words were even more powerful than he had imagined.

Come Bearers of Light
this is now your hour
all with gifts of light

come to the fire gate
between Tor and Antor
to the halls, the white city

so as dark rises up to flood
our world, to wound all hearts
all peoples, to smother all light

you will flame out, spilling
out of the white city
riding down the wild dark

a white blaze in the black
healing hearts and lands
Bearers of Light, Come

The last words still rang in Karis' ears as he watched, and suddenly, an arc of white fire appeared around the mage, so vivid and bright it hurt his eyes. Of course he would go, how could he not? And rescue Lon on the way.

Myrrha was spellbound. She felt the magic and power that surrounded the vision. Who would not want to be asked to be a bearer of light? Power had called and power must answer. She gave a bitter sigh. If only such a thing would come to her, but it never could. Samlt's fire-blasted face scorched her mind's eye, and she put up her arm against the image, shielding her face in shadow. But so intense was the light that it forced its way under her eyelids. They opened in spite of her, just as the chant found her ears and echoed in the chambers of her heart.

The figure repeated his message three times, before slowly fading, as did the city under the arc, and finally, the arc itself. Myrrha, Malin and Karis watched in silence, not speaking until all the light was gone. They turned back to the room, now dark by comparison, and found everyone's eyes upon them.

"What's happening? Malin, what's going on?" Deirdre was the first to speak.

Malin was not surprised. Trust Deirdre. But he was surprised, now that Karis had received his call and would be leaving, that he would miss Karis, a little.

For his part, Karis sat like one in a daze, his eyes fixed on some far point, unaware of his surroundings.

"So was that your call?" Malin asked. Not for information, but for conversation. "It was astounding. Did you see the city? All that light?"

Karis couldn't focus enough on his real surroundings to reply to Malin's question.

Malin's words tumbled out, faster and faster. "Amazing. It seemed to pour up out of the streets themselves, light rising to converge with more light, rising up and falling down, making the air thick with light. Have you ever seen so much? The mage won't follow you there."

Karis spoke slowly, as if he hadn't heard Malin. "You know what happens to a dream when it becomes real? I'm going to find out. I'll really know."

"That man had a face you don't forget easily, his eyes stabbing through you," Malin continued.

Myrrha joined the conversation. "The singing. Did you hear the singing? I've never heard such music."

"There was singing?" Malin was surprised. "I only heard the chanting." He continued, "That mage. He had no beard. Don't all magicians have beards?" he teased.

"I don't know," Karis answered finally. "I don't care." The two cousins grinned at each other.

Myrrha leaned her harp against the wall beside the fireplace and returned to the table.

"What's going on?" Rast was bewildered.

Basil thought he knew, but wanted clarification. "You've been called?"

Malin was quick with his assurances. "Karis has finally seen the fire gate. Haven't you, Karis?"

An astounded and delighted Karis replied, "Yes. Yes, I have!"

"What does that mean?" Alyssa knew something important was happening, but wasn't quite sure what.

"Karis is called to be a bearer of light," Malin exulted. "The gods of good deeds and right ways have recognized his talent and worth. The black mage will get his comeuppance."

Karis was suddenly quiet, looking strangely at him.

Malin continued, "Where were you to find it, the fire gate?"

"Between Tor and Antor." The answering voice was Myrrha's.

"Tor and Antor. Yes, that was it."

Suddenly Karis spoke, to both Malin and Myrrha. "How did you know?"

"Well, it was happening right there." Malin pointed to the spot where the mage had stood, then looked back at those around the table. They only looked confused.

Myrrha agreed. "That's right."

"What's happening?" Lord Lindsey wanted to know. After all, it was his dining room.

"You saw the city? The fire arc? The old man?" Karis persisted, pushing his question at Malin. Basil kept silent, missing nothing.

"What have we been talking about? Of course I saw him. The minstrel did, too, didn't you?" Malin turned to face Myrrha.

Myrrha nodded. "Yes." Something was happening here that she didn't understand. Light growing in the middle of a room was a little strange, but they had all seen it. What was Karis on about now? "I even heard the magician speak. So?"

"Don't you get it? Only light bearers can see the fire gate. Only light bearers can see the city of light and hear the old man give the call. You, too, are called. You, too, are bearers of light."

"Nonsense. It was just because I was there when it happened to you." Malin brushed the idea aside.

"Not so." Karis appealed to Basil. "Remember? You told us about the young boy from Norris village. He was in a room full of people when it happened to him."

"So?" Malin was still wondering what Karis' point was.

"None of them saw anything. None of them heard anything. He was the only one." He included the whole table in his next comment. "Did any of you just see anything unusual?"

Only Myrrha responded. "Yes. We all saw the light. We——." She stopped suddenly, realizing she was the only one speaking.

Deirdre spoke up suddenly, trust her for that, Malin thought. "All we saw were you three, staring at something over there."

"And the rest of you?" Malin demanded.

"Deirdre's right. We saw only you three gazing at that corner." Rast was matter-of-fact.

Malin stared at Karis in dismay. It had been a beautiful evening and Karis was spoiling it. "You mean I'm called to be a bearer of light?"

"Yes. You. Malin of Godsel."

"And I'm to go through the fire gate to the halls of learning?"

Malin wasn't as quick on the uptake as he usually was, thought Karis. "Yes. You, too, are to study magic, enter the city of light. We'll make the journey together." Karis' voice rang with his excitement.

Malin was dismayed. Study magic? That may have been Karis' great dream, but it was certainly not his.

Karis turned to Myrrha. "You saw the mage and the gate, too, didn't you?"

She nodded slowly.

Deirdre interrupted, her mouth agape, her eyes wide with amazement. "Malin? Malin saw the fire gate?" Malin savored the moment, a small moment of triumph in his series of defeats with his younger sister. He noted gleefully the wonder in her eyes, still fixed upon him.

"You really saw the fire gate?"

Aunt Aila seemed to come to. "Mercy me. Magic all over. What's a body to do?"

"It's all a mistake. Karis has magic, not me," Malin insisted.

"But it was you who kept us alive on our journey north. Besides, the black mage has no power over you."

Malin shook his head, decidedly. "I expect he doesn't feel I'm any threat."

Malin's father was troubled. Malin was the only son of a much-loved wife who had died early. He had learned to rely on Malin and was preparing him to take his place.

"And you, minstrel?" Basil's soft question was a nail in her heart.

Myrrha looked up to find all eyes shifting to her, waiting for her response. "I don't know. I don't know who I am. I don't know who my parents were and I can't find out. They are gone now. And I don't know if I have magic, or if I can contribute to the fight against the dark mage, or to finding Lon. I don't know." Her voice fell silent.

Basil spoke into the silence, gently, carefully. "Yet you've been called, just as the others have. Someone knows who you are."

Basil's words caught Myrrha in her center, like a blow. "Someone knows who you are." Maybe they did. Maybe they also knew about Samlt. What then?

Yet the vision burned in her mind and she knew she would never be free from it. Slowly she spoke, and so softly Malin had to lean forward to hear her. "But that city—it was like going home." She finished so quietly none there heard her last words. "Wherever that is."

The king leaned forward and spoke for the first time since the vision. "We've not had any light bearers called for many years. It's a lot to think about. We've also Lon to find, a war to wage, a kingdom to reclaim." His solemn voice brought them back to the moment. Called as bearers of light, or not, there were still many problems to solve, many burdens to carry.

Lord Lindsey agreed. "We've much to think about and plan." He was not sure he wanted his son and heir going to the halls of learning and the city of light never to return. Even if they could return from there, they could not return unchanged. He sensed Malin's hesitation. It seemed however, that Karis had nothing to lose.

Both Myrrha and Karis savored the vision, tasting the wonder, their delight, seeing a future they would not have thought possible. Lon, thought Karis. If only Lon were here to share his news with. They had shared everything. But Lon was gone. Sorrow washed over him. Yet he had been called. There was a city of light.

For Malin, the vision, though wondrous, trailed behind it a cloud. The real world of Godsel, of Westra, had been his delight, especially the wilderness. He had no longing for magical worlds; Westra was magical enough for him. How could he leave the forests and streams, the creatures, and all he loved? He tried to release the unhappiness he felt, to let it go from him.

Rilse. What will it be like beyond the fire gate?

Different. No forests there.

How will we survive?

We will not. Only you can go there. The fire gate will not let me pass. I can't even go deep into the southlands with you. My wolf body would separate from the rest of me.

The light left Malin's heart. He truly did not want to go if Rilse would not, could not, go with him. Misery flooded him, clouding his eyes. Rilse had helped him heal from his grandfather's death; how could he heal from a separation from Rilse?

The king spoke up again, firmly, as if now certain of their path. "We will meet again tomorrow, after lunch to plan: Karis, Malin, the minstrel, Basil, Rast, Medric, and Lord Lindsey and myself. We'll meet in this room."

The queen leaned over and whispered to him.

He nodded back to her and continued. "The most immediate quest is the one for Lon, as the queen reminds us." The king's voice faltered.

Lord Lindsey nodded in agreement, his face, like the king's, suddenly weary in the lamplight. The king continued, his clear eyes and open face troubled. "We'll rest tonight, and plan tomorrow. Minstrel, could we have one more song to finish out the evening?"

So Myrrha began once more to play, her deep red cloak flung back over one shoulder, cascading to the floor around her, the gold of her tunic glittering from the fire's light, her fine features in the shadow of her bent head. As she played, they all saw what the light bearers had seen: the light and the mage, the gate of white fire. They saw the light ride down the darkness and sweep it away.

When she finished, there was no more talk. The company parted quietly, each one with their own thoughts, the conversation soft and sparse. A thing of magic, of unreachable wonder had touched them all.

ACKNOWLEDGEMENTS

To my faithful readers, marvelous techies, expert editors and devoted contributors. Publication is certainly a group effort and what a great group I have: Jodi, Sharon, Dan, Dawn, Darren, Christl, Anne, Mornie, Ale, Tara, Melissa, Cindy, Gerri, Celeste, David, Susan, Judy and Dave.

ABOUT THE AUTHOR

Raised in southern Alberta, along with a myriad of Sillito siblings, the author has loved reading for forever, but especially since the fourth grade. As an invalid confined to bed for nine months, books became her world. The day began with them and ended with them.

With reading came writing: stories first, originally told to younger brothers and sisters, then poetry written with a sister in a west bedroom. And to be sure there was teaching, twelve younger brothers and sisters to help through school, then classrooms of her own students, both high school and beyond, to say nothing of her own children and grandchildren.

And as you might expect, mind journeys through books led to real ones, through different countries and cultures. "Stories happen to people in specific places and circumstances," she says, "like changing paths because a puma is sleeping on the one you're on."

She has a great love of the arts, both as participant and audience. She has participated in choirs, musicals, plays, and written scripts for programs for special occasions. She currently lives with her husband in Utah.

www.ingramcontent.com/pod-product-compliance
Lightning Source LLC
Chambersburg PA
CBHW062119170626
46813CB00002B/507